THE VAMPYRE LABYRINTH
Oracle

G. P. Taylor is the author of several best-selling novels, including *Shadowmancer*, *Shadowmancer: The Curse of Salamander Street*, *Wormwood* and *Tersias*, as well as the *Mariah Mundi* trilogy. His interests include beachcombing, ghost-hunting and investigating unsolved crimes.

Praise for *Mariah Mundi*

'...hen Harry Potter hangs up his wizard's cloak, booksellers will be looking to G. P. Taylor's *Mariah Mundi: The Midas Box* to keep the cashtills ringing.' BBC News

'It really is wonderful, wonderful stuff . . . Mariah Mundi surpasses Potter on just about every level there is. Highly recommended.' *The Bookbag*

'The book that combines the big story of C. S. Lewis and the plot of an Indiana Jones movie. We could genuinely be looking at the book series that will replace Harry Potter at the top of every child's wish list.' *BuddyHollywood Review*

by the same author

SHADOWMANCER
WORMWOOD
TERSIAS
SHADOWMANCER: THE CURSE OF SALAMANDER STREET

Mariah Mundi
THE MIDAS BOX
THE GHOST DIAMONDS
THE SHIP OF FOOLS

The Vampyre Labyrinth
REDEYE
DUST BLOOD

THE VAMPYRE LABYRINTH

Oracle

G. P. Taylor

faber and faber

First published in 2011
Faber and Faber Ltd
Bloomsbury House
74–77 Great Russell Street
London WC1B 3DA

Typeset by Faber and Faber Ltd
Printed in England by CPI Bookmarque, Croydon

A CIP record for this book
is available from the British Library

ISBN 978–0–571–22698–6

2 4 6 8 10 9 7 5 3 1

To Sanya Besarovic
and all the staff on the Children's Ward
at Hull Royal Infirmary
for their great work, love and kindness

ORACLE

[1]

The Oracle of Magdalene

THE BRANCHES of the dark forest of ancient yew and wild apple trees clattered as the night fog crept closer to the twisting stone staircase. With each tread the mist rose up from the canopy of misshapen staves, hugging the side of the cliff towards the tabernacle.

The house in the shadows of Mount Lazari looked as if it had grown from the rock. The slanted stone roof was etched from the cliff that towered above; the neatly chipped stones were knitted together so that they looked like solid rock. The only signs of human habitation were the mortared walls and the carved steps, which twisted and turned from the forest to the door of the grotto as if they were the helix of life. Stretching to each side were the high cliffs; at their summit, sheer and jagged, they cut a line across the star-filled sky.

Two white robed figures emerged from the gloom of the forest, treading carefully on the path. The older man gripped an iron key in his frail hands. He tried to keep pace with his companion, but his breath failed and he stopped at the turn of the steps and looked around him.

'It grows steeper with each year,' he said as he wheezed, hoping his companion would not walk on. 'I remember the day when *it* arrived. I thought that we would all be safe now the war is over.'

'And then another war comes to the shrine,' the young man answered. He pushed back the long curls from his face and pulled the hood of his robe over his head. 'And tonight after five years we plead with it to go away?'

'What else can we do?' the old man asked. 'Should we tell the world that an angel has come to live with us?'

'It is not an angel, Father Sigari. No angel would demand of us that we feed it in such a way. This is a holy place. We should cast it out and have done with it . . .'

The younger man clutched a long iron nail in his pocket. It was an old and rusted spike snatched from the wood of a Bethel tree, a relic from years past.

'You should be careful what you say, Mandas. I am sure that it knows our thoughts and listens to all that is said,' Sigari answered as he walked slowly on, clutching the strands of his white beard. 'Now the war is over it will be hard to explain the disappearances. People will become suspicious, and –'

'You will have to explain why we bring no one with us,' Mandas answered. 'We are told by the Prior to keep the angel content, happy and well fed. Tonight it will want to know why it will go hungry.'

Father Sigari looked at Mandas and remembered when he was that age. The moonlight shone on his brown skin, and his eyes burnt white in the dark of night.

'If only I had come without you,' Sigari whispered to himself.

'What?' Mandas asked. 'I hope I never mumble when I am old.'

4

'It is a blessing that only some will enjoy,' Sigari answered as they turned on a stone landing and began to walk up the final flight of stone steps to the oak door of the sepulchre.

'And you will speak to the angel?' Mandas asked as they reached the final step. He watched Sigari place the key in the lock of the wooden door braced with metal straps and hinges.

'It is what I have to do. I will tell it the truth,' Sigari answered as his lip quivered.

'Truth – what is truth?' Mandas asked. 'I remember all those we brought here, and we told them we would hide them from the Gestapo. I saw their faces, their eyes . . .'

'It had to be done. It is what the angel wanted,' Sigari replied as he turned the lock.

'This is no angel. We feed a demon.'

'But it knows the future. It can see what is to come. It is an oracle, and surely only an oracle can come from the creator?' Sigari said.

'Nostradamus saw into the future and he died an old fool. What makes this angel any different?' Mandas asked.

'The Prior believes that he will be useful to the Order. Since the end of the war, many people would love to know what the angel speaks of. It is possible to sell that information.' Sigari licked the salt from his lips and turned the door handle. 'Feeding the creature is but a small price to pay.'

'And tonight we tell it that hunger will be the only companion we can find?' Mandas asked as the door opened.

'Arrangements have been made, my dear brother,' Sigari said softly as he allowed Mandas to step inside. 'The angel only desires to eat once in every moon.'

'That was fine when we had the war to cover what we did,

but now?' Mandas asked.

'Light the candles and then we will pray together before it is time.' Sigari opened the door wider to let in the night.

Mandas stepped inside the sepulchre and lit the crumbling taper from the candle that burnt on the low stone table. He looked around the room that had been carved from the rock to form a magnificent cavern. The light in his hand flickered on the stones. Before him was a marble altar with a flight of steps that led into the darkness. On the far side of the cave, across the intricate stone floor that stretched away like a mosaic pavement, was an iron gate. It barred the entrance to a small passage cut into the rock. Above, the vaulted stone roof reached ever higher until the pinnacle could not be seen.

As Mandas lit the candles, Sigari thought again how young he looked. He was no more than a boy. The white robe tied around the waist with a knotted brown cord dragged on the dusty floor of the cave. A draught blew through the doorway and flickered the lights. An eerie, empty silence filled the cave as if the weight of the world pressed down upon them.

'And the creature will come tonight?' Mandas asked as he bowed to the altar and kissed the stone cross.

'As it always does . . . It will come to the gate and I will give it the news. The Prior needs the answer to some questions about what is to come.' Sigari's voice was sharp. He turned to Mandas and watched him again. It was as if he wanted to utter a secret but knew he could not. 'You have always been a good friend to me. I remember the day your mother brought you to us. You were five years old.'

The man stopped speaking and knelt before the stone altar. He muttered to himself with his eyes closed. His hands

6

gripped the key tightly.

'I remember you as well, Father Sigari. That was thirteen years ago.' Mandas put a hand on his shoulder. 'You treated me like your son and welcomed me to the Order. Then the Oracle appeared and we took a vow never to speak of the angel.'

'It is proof of what we believe, Mandas. Some things the world cannot understand. If we spoke of the wonders we now know it would drive them mad. It is best we keep the secret to ourselves.'

Mandas knelt beside Father Sigari and held his hand. He could feel the rough skin and broken calluses as he gripped it tightly.

'You said we would –' Mandas began.

Sigari answered quickly. 'I have left my bag by the door. There is something I need. I will be back,' he said, and he stood and quickly walked to the door.

'And then we pray?' Mandas asked.

'Constantly, constantly,' Father Sigari replied as he stepped outside the grotto into the dark night.

It was then, as Mandas knelt at the stone altar, that he heard the door close and the lock turn. The clunk of the turning key echoed around the cavern. He looked up, expecting Sigari to return, but the room was empty.

'Father?' he asked.

'It had to be this way,' Sigari answered. His voice was muffled, coming from outside the door. 'I will not leave until it is over. I promise I will pray for your ordeal . . .'

'What have you done?' Mandas asked as the slow realisation came to him. 'Why?'

'The Oracle asked for you and you alone,' Sigari stuttered

7

nervously, his voice half-choked with tears.. 'The last time the Prior spoke to the angel it made the request. Your blood for anything the Prior asked for.'

'I am to be fed to the creature and you allowed this to happen?' Mandas shouted as he ran to the door and banged his fist against it.

'I offered myself in your place, but it wasn't to be – the Prior insisted it would be you.'

'But the Oracle is locked in the cave. It cannot get into the Sanctuary of Magdalene.'

'I came this morning and opened the gate. It was what I had been told to do. I am sorry, Mandas, I am so sorry,' Sigari pleaded. 'The Prior is coming to keep vigil for you, he will soon be here.'

Mandas slumped to the floor in his grief and sat back against the door, his eyes looking around the Sanctuary. He could see the worn stone steps that led to the spring where a million pilgrims had walked before him. The candles cast long shadows as they danced in the breeze from the caves below.

Then he heard the footsteps. They trudged wearily on the rock as the Oracle walked up the stone steps.

'Mandas? Have you been delivered to me?' a voice asked.

Soon a dark shadow crossed the barred gate and a hand pushed against the lock. The gate opened slowly and a small figure wrapped in a long black cloak stepped into the Sanctuary. 'Why don't you speak to me? You have never wanted to speak to me?'

'Because you are a liar. If you were an angel you would not demand blood,' Mandas answered as he gripped the iron nail hidden within his pocket.

'You were the only one to recognise who I really was,' the voice said. The figure's face was hidden in a swathe of red silk cloth wrapped around its head like a mask. 'You hated everything to do with me.'

Mandas looked up. The Oracle stood by the twisted iron gate. It looked feeble and frail.

'I remember the day you arrived. It was my thirteenth birthday,' Mandas said.

'And I protected this place throughout the war. I knew that which only an Oracle could know. The Prior is most grateful,' the Oracle said as it stepped closer, slowly unveiling its face.

'You are a woman?' Mandas asked, seeing the figure's face for the first time.

'Not much older than yourself, Mandas, but I have lived far longer . . .'

'And killed many more people,' he answered before she could go on.

'I have been frugal with my desires,' she whispered as she stepped into the light of the candles. 'I took only those that I needed to survive.'

'Then you are mortal?' he asked.

'More than that, but not truly eternal like the one you follow,' she answered as she slipped back the hood of her cloak to reveal a curl of long red hair. 'I do know what it is like to be human. That is something I left behind long, long ago.'

Mandas got to his feet and looked about the room for a way of escape.

'That would not be wise,' she said as she threw down her cloak so it formed a pool around her feet. She was dressed as

9

if she walked a Paris street. 'I know everything in your mind. I have listened to your thoughts so many times. In fact, I have become quite enthralled by them.'

The Oracle stepped towards him and reached out her hand, touching the side of his face.

'Then kill me now,' Mandas answered, fearing what was to come. 'Take what you want. Father Sigari prays for me and he has such frail concentration.'

'Kill you – is that what you believe?' the Oracle answered, her voice broken with laughter. 'I don't want to kill you, Mandas. I want you as a companion. Someone to live with me here in the Sanctuary.'

'And the blood – how will you be fed?' he asked.

The Oracle reached into the pocket of the long jacket and pulled out a knife.

'This is a Trajithian – a knife so sharp that some say it can even cut through time itself. I can use it to take your blood and you will not even know that it has happened.'

'And in return?' he asked quickly, trying to guard his thoughts but knowing this was impossible.

'I will let you live. Even take you with me. Now that the war is over I can return home. I know that you speak English and I will tell the world that you are my French nephew. There is a house by the beach in a village called Lyme Regis. We can live together very quietly.'

'What are you? I know you are not an angel,' he asked.

'I am a Vampyre. One of a handful that have survived the war,' she answered. 'And every Vampyre needs blood.'

Mandas saw her step towards him. He took hold of her hand.

'A Vampyre? Sigari told me many tales of such creatures when I was a child. He never said they were so beautiful. This is not the right place,' he answered. 'I don't want Sigari to hear us.'

'That old fool isn't listening. He is too busy chanting and asking for you to be delivered from me. If only he knew what I was about to do to you. He would be banging on the door to join us.'

'By the spring – where the water comes into the cave. That should be the place,' Mandas insisted. 'Grant me that request.'

The Oracle smiled. 'If it matters to you,' she said.

'What is your name, I need to know?' he asked.

'I am who I am,' she answered, as if she had not said the words for many years. 'Is this the place?' she asked as they stood by a small pool of water that trickled along a tiled channel and through the wall of the cave.

'In the shadow of Magdalene,' he answered, pointing to the statue above them. He got to his knees and scooped water from the spring and drank.

'You are a peculiar boy.' The Vampyre laughed as she held the dagger in her hand. 'I promise that you will not feel a thing.'

There was no warning, no signal, no chance of escape. Mandas lashed out suddenly and stabbed the iron nail into her thigh. Dropping the dagger into the pool, she screamed in pain. The cavern echoed with her cries as Mandas stabbed her again and again.

The Vampyre fell into the water as he ran towards the door.

'Let me out!' Mandas screamed as he rattled the handle, hoping Sigari was still there. 'It is a Vampyre!'

'Vampyre?' Sigari shouted as Mandas heard him fumble in the lock with the key. 'Where is the Oracle?'

'She *is* the Oracle,' Mandas screamed as he looked back at the still pool and wondered if the Vampyre was dead. 'Open the door, quickly!'

There was a sudden loud thud. Sigari saw the door to the sepulchre judder as if it were about to fall from its hinges. Rocks fell from the cliff above and smashed around him. The door shook again and then began to open slowly.

The man stood back, his hands clasped as he still prayed. His lips smacked open and shut as he tried to speak. Without thinking, he put his hands to his face and drew a short, sharp breath to hide his fear.

Pinned to the opening door like a puppet was Mandas. His lifeless body dangled from its oak planks as blood trickled down the stone steps. He hung limply, held fast by the iron spike, longs curls of blonde hair covering his rugged face.

'Father Sigari,' the Prior said as the torch stave in his hand lighted the path. 'What has happened – is the Oracle safe?'

'Mandas is dead. The Oracle is a Vampyre,' Sigari stuttered, too frightened to touch the body.

'Of course it is,' the Prior answered incredulously. 'How else would it know such things of our lives?'

'And you knew all these years?' Sigari asked as a figure's shadow crossed the doorway.

'That was part of the agreement. I was invited as a guest,' answered the Oracle. She stepped carefully from the sepulchre until she stood by Sigari. Her long tweed trousers were stained with blood. 'You promised me a companion, Cardinal Theodore.'

'Theodore?' asked the old monk. 'That is not your name.'

'Whatever he calls himself, he will always be known to me as my dear Theodore. I have known him for more years than you have lived, old man.'

'What?' Sigari stuttered as his breath faded.

'She is right, Sigari. I am afraid I have not been as honest as I should be for a man of my calling.' The Prior laughed, his words reaching out across the trees as if they would be carried to the coast. 'Since the time of the Prophet Nostradamus, I knew this time was coming. Sadly for you, my old friend, we cannot let you see the dawn.'

Sigari gasped for breath and slumped to the ground.

The Oracle held the knife in her hand, wiping the blade across her sleeve. 'I trust you will find an explanation for all this?' she asked.

'We should send a message to Brother Notarius, tell him that he is needed here. Meanwhile,' Cardinal Theodore replied as he kicked the clinging hand of Father Sigari away from him, 'there has often been talk of a wolf in these hills. It will not be hard to explain these deaths to the faithful.'

[2]

Reverie

THE VILE SMELL of carbolic under the door of the sleeping compartment of the midnight train from Edinburgh heralded the morning. The train guard washed the corridor with his bedraggled mop, sloshing the bubbling liquid across the linoleum floor and whistling to himself as he worked. Every now and then he would flick ash from the tip of his cigarette into the bucket. Then he would scratch his bald head beneath the brim of his hat and complain bitterly.

Stopping briefly, he took a handkerchief from his pocket and wiped the brass door handle of sleeping compartment number 6. He had seen the two young occupants the night before. Only the girl had smiled when the boy had asked for their First Class tickets. He thought there was something about them that was different from all the other people who had travelled that night. Neither of them carried any luggage. They hadn't asked to eat and as soon as they had entered the compartment, he had heard them lock the door and pull down the window blind. They looked to him as if they were brother and sister. The girl had a scar upon her lip and a port-wine stain on her face. He presumed they were students from the university travelling home mid-term. As

14

the guard picked up his mop, he briefly listened at the door. Then, when he could hear nothing, he worked on.

Wrapped in itchy blankets and wedged into the juddering bunk bed of the small compartment, Jago Harker slept fitfully. Strands of long dark hair trailed across his thin face. The long, slender fingers of his elegant hands held the blankets to his face as the train rocked from side to side. It clattered over the rails and smoke billowed like thunderclouds from the engine. Every mile it screeched and whistled, and with every tunnel or bridge the engine roared furiously as it steamed through.

Yet, despite all of this, Jago Harker remained asleep. It was as if he could not open his eyes. The bed was warm and his clothes were crumpled around him as he clung to the last remnants of the fading dream. Always the same, as if it were a warning from the future or a hidden glimpse of the past, it plagued him. There was smoke and fire. A woman walked through the flames, her clothes burning. It was as if she wasn't aware or didn't care. She walked on, coming closer and closer to him, and then a man would run from the darkness and just before the woman could speak he cut her down to the ground. The sword in his hand would turn into a snake. It lunged at Jago, drawing in all the night until he was surrounded by darkness.

'Biatra!' Jago Harker shouted as he woke suddenly and threw back the blankets.

'It's a dream, Jago,' she answered, already awake. She was sitting on the bunk opposite and wrapped in a blanket shawl. 'Just a dream.'

Jago tried to wipe the sleep from his eyes as the window

15

blind rattled against the glass and kept out the cold grey dawn.

'It was the man. I saw him again,' Jago answered in a whisper. 'And the snake . . .' As he said the word, the air in front of him began to shimmer. Then, as if he was viewing through a kinetoscope, a hologram appeared. Just as in the dream, the shining black head of a cobra danced in the air. It moved from side to side, its tongue flickering as it spat silver droplets of venom that exploded in sparkles of light.

'Can you –?' Jago asked.

'Don't move, Jago. Don't move,' Biatra answered, her eyes transfixed at the ghostly image that hovered over the bed.

Jago stared into the eyes of the snake. They glowed hypnotically, blood-red.

'What is it?' he asked, staying as still as he could.

Biatra jumped from the bed, reached out and grabbed at the snake. It exploded in her fingers as Bible-black scales vaporised in her hand.

'It was nothing . . . our imagination,' she said, not knowing what it could be.

'But the dream,' Jago insisted as he looked about the compartment to see where the snake had gone. 'It can't just disappear . . .'

Biatra held his hand. She could see the look of fear on his face. It had become something she had grown used to. They had been in hiding for most of the war. Home had been an old castle on the banks of a turgid loch in a Highland valley. Five long years had passed wearily until they had received the telegram that it was safe to return to Whitby and the house overlooking the sea at Hawks Moor. Neither of them had changed, the years had not aged or wearied them, but the days and weeks had dragged slowly by. At each turning of the year they had looked down the valley and wondered when they could return. For those who lived nearby, they were the family from the south who had fled the war. A tall, thin man and his two teenage children who spent their days walking the hills.

Rumour had spread amongst those who lived in the mountains that they had tuberculosis. That was why they were never seen in the town. What food they ate was brought to the castle every week. Mrs McClure, the housekeeper, had taken it in and paid in full. The only other visitor to the house was the black van that always arrived just before the new moon. On the side were painted the words: *Medical Supplies Forthness Road Glasgow.*

Not even Mrs McClure knew what was in the box delivered by the van. She had told the post mistress in Badenscallie that it was icy cold and sealed with duct tape.

'For the sickness,' she had said whenever someone asked. 'They are always much better after they have taken delivery.'

That was all that was said of the family by the Loch and no one really cared, such were their own woes. On the day that the war ended the postman had cycled along the rough track and delivered the telegram. He knew the words off by heart, having read the message several times and told every one he met the contents of the correspondence: WAR ENDED – SAFE TO RETURN – NO SIGN OF VQ – JACK HENSON.

As Mrs McClure had opened the door he had handed her the telegram and whispered the words in her ear. Biatra had seen the man in the porch drinking his cup of tea, his cycle clips tight around his ankles. She had smiled at him and in return he had stared vacantly at her as if to take in as much as he could so he could tell all those who he met about the family no one ever saw.

Later, a car had arrived and driven them to Inverness. From there they had taken the train to Edinburgh and caught the sleeper train south. Now, as the train slowed, the guard shouted the destination and the connections for each traveller.

'Darlington . . . all stations to the east . . . Danby, Castleton, Whitby . . .'

'We have to change trains,' Biatra said as she held his hand. 'An hour to Whitby.'

Jago didn't know if he wanted to return. Even though five years had gone by since the night they had fled the town, he still felt as if it was waiting to destroy him. As he left the compartment, he looked back and wondered if the serpent was hiding somewhere. It had been in his dreams night after night and now, by some power beyond his imagination, it had appeared before them both like a ghost.

Crossing the platform to the waiting train, Jago eyed the other passengers warily. It was something he always did. Biatra held his hand as they walked. By the entrance to the station, a group of soldiers took down the sand-bag barricades and wound coils of barbed wire onto the back of a truck. Jago squeezed her fingers. It was the first sign of the end of the war that they had seen.

The journey to Whitby was slower than Jago could ever imagine. The shabby train stopped at every village that had a station, winding its way along the valley and cutting back

18

and forth across the widening river. On the side of the track, he could see the wreck of a train hit by bombers during the war. It lay in the grass, charred and broken like the bone ribs of a dead animal. And then he could smell the sea. It ebbed its way up the estuary and reminded him of the night he had arrived when he had been evacuated from London.

That seemed so long ago. It had changed his life for ever and he was no longer the same boy. He looked at Biatra. She seemed to be much older. Her lips were painted in red lipstick, her eyes gilded with make-up. Throughout their time in Scotland they had talked to one another, and Jago thought they had talked so much that they had used all the words they would ever speak to each other. Now, as he sat next to her in the empty carriage, he asked expectantly, 'Do you think Jack Henson will look any different?' He wondered if he would recognise the man who had once been such a close companion.

'He'll be covered in mud from digging graves and complaining that his cottage leaks.' Biatra tried to laugh. She remembered it was something she had not done for so long. 'Do you think it will be safe?'

'The war is over. It has been five years and nothing has happened. Jack wouldn't have told us to come back unless it was safe,' Jago said as the train rattled towards the town.

It was Biatra who was the first to see the ruins of the old Abbey on the cliff top. The high stone towers stuck up from the ground like dragon's teeth. They were swirled in mist that washed in and out of the stones.

'It hasn't changed,' she said as she pointed to the white house on the far bank of the estuary. 'Do you remember the boat on that first night?'

'Crispin Draigorian . . . Clinas Macarty . . . do you think he is still there?' Jago asked as he thought of the night they had crossed the river.

'Still talking to his parrot and cleaning the house,' she answered downheartedly. 'He was always very kind.'

Her voice trailed away as the town came into view. The pinnacles of Streonshalgh Manor towered over the red-topped cottages that clung to the steep sides of the valley. Jago traced the route of the donkey path on the glass of the train window as if to remind himself of where he once walked.

'It looks the same – just as we left it,' he said as the steam engine's wheels skidded on the steel tracks. 'What will be his first words?' Jago asked.

'I want to wait until I see him before I answer,' Biatra replied.

'So you can read his mind?' he asked.

'I can't help it. I am just very inquisitive,' she said.

'Mrs McClure thought you were mad. You always finished every sentence she tried to speak and Hugh was always livid,' Jago said, thinking of the times that Biatra would speak out of turn.

'I always convinced her she was repeating herself. It was just a game. What else was I supposed to do, hidden away in a castle in Scotland for five years?' she asked. Jago did not have time to answer. The train slowed and was consumed by the steel girders and glass roof of the station. The engine steamed as it came to a halt, gently touching the buffers with a shudder and then rolling back half a turn of the wheels.

'Whitby!' shouted the guard.

'Where else could it be?' Biatra asked sarcastically. 'This is the end of the line. Another three hundred yards and we'd be in the sea.'

She opened the door of the compartment and was the first to step onto the platform. Around them people walked quickly to the exit. It was brighter than they could remember. Large electric bulbs like gigantic mushrooms illuminated the roof and the small kiosk at the end of the platform was filled with the light from a neon sign above the door.

'The black-out,' Jago said as he smiled. 'It's finished.'

'Jago Harker! Biatra!' Jack Henson shouted as he ran towards them, arms outstretched.

'He's going to cry and say he loves us,' Biatra said as she steeled herself to be consumed in his muscular hands.

Jack Henson scooped them both into his arms and held them close.

'I never thought I could miss people so much . . . I love you,' he whispered, holding them for a moment as he looked them in the face. 'Just as I remember, just as I remember . . .'

'You haven't changed at all. Still covered in mud.' Biatra laughed as she squeezed his arm and kissed him on the cheek.

'I have brought the car from Hawks Moor. We are all to stay there together. And we have a housekeeper all ready. Mrs Jarvis came highly recommended. She makes tea, cooks, cleans and lives in the village.' His voice was excited. Henson took them by the hand and pulled them along 'I can't wait for you to see the house. You're expecting Hugh to come back tomorrow?'

'He thought it would be best if we travelled separately,' Jago said as they got into the black sedan parked outside the station. Jago waited until the door was closed and Henson was in the driving seat. 'Are you sure it is safe for us to come back?'

'It's been a long time. Much has changed. On the night you left Whitby I could never have imagined a time such as this.' Biatra sensed something in his voice. She tried to listen to the thoughts in his mind. 'I took the liberty of changing your room, I thought you would prefer –'

'That will be fine,' Jago interrupted. 'We are just glad to be back.'

The journey to Hawks Moor went quickly. The car turned onto the gravel drive and Jago looked out to sea. The high waves broke under the cloudy sky and the wind rattled the gnarled trees that covered the cliff.

Jack Henson stopped the car at the door to the house. It was freshly painted and the brass hinges were polished. The arched doorway was covered with the climbing wisteria that held fast against the sea gales. It was just how Jago had remembered.

'There is one thing that is different,' Henson said. He opened the car door and pointed to the side of the house. 'The labyrinth is gone. I chopped it down. It was just a reminder of all that had gone on before.'

Biatra looked to the clearing by the side of the house. All that was left were the intricate stone pathways that spiralled and turned over the acre of lawn. She could see where the high hedges had once stood. Where the centre had once been were the burnt remains of the bonfire.

'Does Hugh know?' she asked. 'It had been there for a long time.'

'He wasn't here to ask. Told me to renovate the house and that I did,' Henson answered gruffly.

'It looks much better. I always thought the labyrinth was a sinister place,' Jago said, hoping to reassure Biatra.

Henson ignored them both as he strode towards the house. His long black coat trailed behind him, its hem covered in grave-mud.

'I have something to tell you – now that we are at the house,' he said urgently as he opened the door. 'Mrs Jarvis will be back soon and she cannot hear what I have to say.'

Biatra looked at Jago as they followed Henson into the house. The door closed behind them without a sound. Jago looked around the hallway. The floor had been freshly polished and the walls painted. Above the fireplace was the portrait of Ezra Morgan.

'You moved the picture from the landing,' Jago said as Henson opened the door to the drawing room.

'I thought the old scoundrel looked better above the flames,' Henson smirked at his own joke.

'What is it you have to tell us?' Biatra asked, sensing his anxiety.

Henson crossed the room and pulled the drapes across the window. Taking a match, he lit the candles on the mantelpiece before sitting in the chair beside the fire.

'I haven't been totally honest with you,' Henson stuttered as if he were about to deliver terrible news. 'Hugh Morgan will not be coming to Hawks Moor. He has been called away.'

'But how? We never had any letters at the castle,' Biatra asked.

'I have been communicating with Hugh via your housekeeper. She would pick up the letters from the post office. It was the only way to keep them secret.'

'Where has he gone?' Jago asked.

'He is in hiding. No one must know where he is.'

'Why?' Biatra asked. 'You said it was safe for us to return, that the threat to our lives had gone.'

'As far as I know it is safe for you both, but not for Hugh.' Henson stared at them both, his eyes dark eyes glinting in the firelight. 'A man called Heston Walpurgis was taken prisoner by the Germans just before the war started. He was kept in a camp in southern Poland. Before the Army found him he escaped. Last week a letter arrived here addressed to Hugh. It was from Walpurgis. The letter spoke of unfinished business and asked for the return of a certain artifact. Ezra Morgan had discovered a diamond the size of a fist and perfectly round. It is flawless in every way. The letter said that within the diamond you could see the future.'

'The future?' Biatra asked, not sure what Henson meant.

'Imagine holding such a thing as that,' Henson said. 'It is no wonder the diamond is so highly prized.'

'So where is the diamond now?' Jago asked.

'No one knows. All we can be sure is that Ezra Morgan has taken the secret of it to his death. He never paid Walpurgis and now Walpurgis wants the diamond or the life of Hugh Morgan, as the contract states.' Henson reached into his coat pocket and unwrapped a folded parchment. Upon it was a scrawl of handwritten sentences. 'It is quite clear, Ezra Morgan promised to pay Walpurgis one million pounds and if he failed to do so, Walpurgis could have the life of his son.'

'Then we will find the money,' Biatra said.

'Even if we sold everything there would still not be enough,' Henson answered as he folded the contract and put it back in his coat with a sigh.

'Then we don't pay and we tell Walpurgis that he can go to hell,' Jago argued. He walked to the window and pulled back the drapes to let in the gloomy grey light of the afternoon.

'The consequence for not paying would be death. Heston Walpurgis will make sure that the debt is paid.'

'And are we to fear such a man?' Jago asked. 'Ezra Morgan should settle his own debts.'

'Ezra hasn't been seen since the night Ozymandias was killed in the explosion. You were both there that night. You saw the devastation. They were all killed. In the law of the Maleficarum the debt of the father is given to the son. That is the way of a Vampyre.'

'Then we find the diamond or just pay what is owed,' Biatra answered.

'Ezra Morgan wagered the life of his son and that is what has to be paid,' Henson answered. 'That is why Hugh is in hiding and you are here. Walpurgis was last seen in Paris boarding a train to London.'

45 Dean Street

A BATTERED BLACK CAB pulled up outside the door of the small hotel and bar. Pulling a leather strap, the driver let the solitary passenger onto the pavement. The man handed him a crumpled one-pound note and didn't wait for the change. The driver doffed his cap and held the note to the light before he swiftly slipped it into the pocket of his torn shirt. Without even looking back, the passenger crossed the litter-strewn sidewalk of the busy street and pulled on the long brass handle of the door. As it opened a flake of old paint fell to the tiled floor. He looked at it for a moment, reached down and carefully picked it up and put it in his pocket.

Stepping inside, he smiled at the redhead behind the counter. She nodded, looked down and then rustled like a hen in her tight-fitting black suit.

'It's been such a long time,' she said as she pushed down the fabric of her skirt and tried to smile.

The man raised an eyebrow suspiciously and looked around him.

'Did everything arrive for me?' he asked in harsh, deep voice.

'Everything, Mr Walpurgis. Everything, just as you asked.' She reached into a box and pulled out a thick stuffed envelope the size of a small painting. 'The man said there would be another delivery tomorrow.'

He grunted in appreciation. He took the package, broke the seal with his finger and peered inside.

'I need a barber and my tailor, Mayer and Mortimer, Sackville Street, if you could ring them for me?' Walpurgis wasn't asking. He brushed the flecks of lint from the ragged sleeve of his shabby overcoat as if to show her what he needed. The woman looked at the back of her notepad and reached for the Bakelite black telephone.

'It's your usual room, overlooking the street, just as you asked,' she said before she made the call.

'Did you get the flowers?' he asked as he picked up the keys already labelled with his name from the counter.

'Holly and yew branches with white roses?' her words ended with a question.

'And some scissors and candles?'

'Just as ordered, they are all in your room.' The woman smiled and dialled the operator as Walpurgis opened the door to the staircase and then stopped.

'And I am not here if anyone asks,' he said as he looked back.

'You don't exist,' she answered lightly. 'Many of our guests like not to be noticed.'

Walpurgis climbed the narrow staircase and turned right, taking the long landing at the front of the hotel. He counted the steps and checked each door he passed. Taking the key, he turned the lock and looked back down the corridor. He stood and listened, as if concerned with what could not be seen and only perceived through a sixth sense. When Walpurgis was satisfied that he was alone he pushed on the door.

The room was just as he remembered. A large double bed was pushed against one wall; a desk was by the window and a wireless gramophone to one side. The only thing that had changed since his last stay was the picture on the wall above the bed. He had been sure that it had been a scene of the Thames. Now it was just a swathe of colours with a human eye staring from the centre of a vivid rainbow.

Walpurgis crossed the room and pulled the bed from the wall. He traced the line of the floorboards with his fingers until a short plank gave way. Lifting it from the floor, he reached inside and pulled out a bundle of cloth. Slowly he unwrapped the parcel. Inside was a pistol. He took hold of the cork grip and pulled back the hammer.

'Nice to see you,' he whispered, as if welcoming an old friend. He lay the gun on the bed and got to his feet.

Walpurgis stopped suddenly. He was held fast by his reflection in the long mirror by the door. It was the first time he had seen himself for seven years. He stared closely at his equine face, the thin lines around his eyes and the sallow cheeks. He rubbed the short growth of beard on his chin and tried to smoothe the thatch of hair that hung down in long blond ringlets. Everything about him had changed. He was thinner, his shirt baggy around the neck. The collar was black with the dirt of several trains and three nights waiting for a boat at Calais. Walpurgis laughed at his reflection, a shrill and harsh sound.

He had not seen himself since the day he had been captured by the Gestapo and driven through the forest in the Kubbelwagen. Walpurgis had stared at his reflection in the rear-view mirror and wondered if he would ever escape.

Now, in the corner of the room the telephone rang. He waited for a moment, hoping it would stop.

'203,' he said slowly as the first drops of rain beat against the glass. 'Yes . . . in the hour . . . that will be fine . . . a little thinner . . .'

Later, as darkness fell, Walpurgis stepped from the hotel and walked through the busy Soho streets. He admired the creases of his new suit and looked at himself in the reflection of every shop window. His long blond hair was now cut short at the sides and a dark trilby was slanted on his head. On every corner he stopped and looked back through the crowds of people. It was something he always did, a habit from before the war, and part of his craft.

Walpurgis emerged from the dark, fog-filled streets into a small park, where under a string of coloured lanterns was a café. A white canvas awning covered a cart selling what they said was coffee. Walpurgis thought it smelt of straw. At one of the tables sat an old man in round spectacles; at the next table a woman scribbled notes and turned the pages of a tattered notepad.

'I thought you would never come,' the old man said as he sat with him.

'I am only seven years late,' Walpurgis answered. 'You have lived long enough for that not to matter.'

'Even so, Heston, I would have hoped we could have resolved this matter sooner. The Oracle diamond is not a crystal ball owned by a fairground gypsy.' The old man tapped the table and rattled the cup that sat on an oversized saucer. Walpurgis saw that the man's hand was covered by a burn scar.

'My dear Ozymandias, it will be yours as soon as I have it back from Ezra Morgan,' he answered as he drank from the old man's cup.

'Morgan is dead and so are many of my kind.'

'That is old news and why I seek the diamond from his son.'

'The assassination killed more than Ezra Morgan, Noel Kinross saw to that. I myself just survived. The explosion has taken most of my sight.'

'Is that why you have a companion?' Walpurgis asked as he looked at the young woman on the next table.

'If it was not for her I would never have escaped. When Kinross kindly blew up my country house and most of my friends, she saved my life. For that I will always be grateful.'

'But she is human,' Walpurgis said, 'and you are an old Vampyre.'

'Have you never been tempted to join us?' Ozymandias asked. 'How old are you now – thirty, forty?'

'I am old enough to know that I could never live your life and would never want to,' he answered.

'That's right,' Ozymandias said mockingly. 'You are an archaeologist, a finder of relics and a man who sells them to the highest bidder. Didn't you work for the Gestapo?'

'They were searching for things that interested me. When I was no longer of use they locked me away in a wooden hut in the middle of a forest. Carpathia is not a place to be alone.' Walpurgis slurped the last of the coffee and smiled at the

30

woman. She ignored him and kept on writing.

'Perhaps that is why the authorities want to speak to you.' Ozymandias spoke eagerly, as if he could help. 'We are not without influence. The few of my kind that survived still hold sway in the world of men.'

'And what do you want of me?' he asked.

'The diamond, of course. For which you would be well paid . . . And a promise that you will kill Hugh Morgan and all his family.'

'All his family? I planned to kill only Hugh Morgan,' Walpurgis answered.

'There are two others, a boy and a girl. It would be good if they could meet a similar fate to Hugh Morgan.' Ozymandias scratched the mottled scar on his hand, then pushed an envelope across the table. 'Everything you need to know is within. Madame Arantez has seen to that.'

The woman at the other table stopped writing and looked up and smiled.

'So why did Kinross want to kill you?' Walpurgis asked.

'I forget you have been away for so long. Carpathia must be a quiet place.'

'Ezra Morgan told the Gestapo where I was hiding. I wasn't hard to find.' Walpurgis laughed. 'I had found the Spear of Longinus and the price they wanted to pay wasn't enough. In the end, they just took it from me.'

'In a way we have all been cheated. Kinross tried to kill all of us who stood against the Lodge Maleficarum,' Ozymandias said. 'He even managed to coerce me into inviting all my friends to a Vampyre Ball. Without my knowing he had planted a bomb under the house, and at midnight the bomb exploded.'

'Didn't he die in a train crash that night?' Walpurgis asked.

'Many died . . . many old friends and a few enemies,' he answered as he remembered the faces consumed by the fireball. 'Now that Ezra is dead, it is the end of the Vampyre Quartet and no one will know where the Oracle diamond is hidden.'

'I am an archaeologist and can find that which is lost.' Walpurgis rubbed the smooth skin on his face and pushed back the brim of his hat. 'I am a detective of time.'

'I heard that you were a cold-blooded killer who hated Vampyres,' Ozymandias answered as he looked at him suspiciously. 'Tell me, Heston. Why is it you want to kill so many of us?'

Walpurgis looked at the waiter behind the counter and pointed at the cup. The man nodded, poured two cups of coffee and brought them over. Walpurgis slowly stirred the cup and looked at Ozymandias.

'You are an aberration and should not be allowed to live. It is as simple as that,' he said.

'So it is not that a Vampyre killed your little sister?' Ozymandias asked.

'I suppose that could be taken into consideration,' he answered coldly. 'That, and the fact that I find you all so easy to kill.'

Ozymandias shivered as he sipped the coffee from his cup and watched the shadows under the trees of the park.

'I am surprised that no one has come to kill you,' he rasped angrily. 'It is quite a threat to feel there is someone so hateful in the world.'

'Isn't that why you want me to do the job?' he asked.

'You have your uses,' Ozymandias answered.

'Make sure you kill the boy,' Madame Arantez muttered from her seat next to him.

'She has a vested interest. It was Jago Harker who took away her humanity,' Ozymandias said. 'She is now as much a night-creature as I am.'

'She still looks human,' Walpurgis said.

'She tries very hard. Madame Arantez writes books for children. It passes the time for her,' he said, and he reached across the table and stroked her hand as if she was an ailing cat.

'I could always put her out of her misery,' Walpurgis said.

'It is a shame that I know that isn't meant to be a joke,' Ozymandias answered. 'You do realise that you are quite mad – even in human terms you are deranged. I should know – for many years I worked as a doctor in Leipzig.'

'I would prefer my madness to yours.' Walpurgis held the gun in his pocket, smoothing his fingers over the cold metal. 'I find the voices in my head amusing.'

Walpurgis drank the last of his coffee and sat back in the chair. He looked at Arantez and smiled at her. She looked human; her blond hair was neat and pulled back from her face. The lights from the coffee stall glinted on her red lipstick.

'One thing intrigues me. Why did you turn against the Lodge Maleficarum?' he asked.

'It is quite simple. For many years we had been under their control. They told us how to live our lives, what to say, what to eat. They even advocated that we only drank that which had been freely given by companions or bought from

33

unscrupulous blood-dealers,' Ozymandias laughed. 'Some of us wanted more than this. There was no thrill in the pursuit, no chase. We wanted to be more *natural*.'

'A return to the old ways?' he asked. 'Hunting for your blood?'

'They argued that it would attract too much attention.'

'So he had you culled?' Walpurgis asked.

'It was quite fitting that his train exploded. He was escaping from the bomb when a car crashed into the steam engine. There were only two survivors. Jago Harker and a girl named Biatra.'

'Are you sure that Ezra Morgan was killed?'

'Completely. The bodies were taken from the train and buried. Ezra Morgan was amongst the dead,' Ozymandias replied as he rubbed the back of his hand.

'And Strackan? Is he alive?' Walpurgis asked, keeping a close eye on Madame Arantez, who by now had given up writing in her notebook and was staring at him warily.

'Not even I know where he is. There has been no sign of him since that time. Vampyres are now a scattered and fearful people. The war has cost us greatly. I hear that the Gestapo did much evil towards us.'

'They took your kind to Murano. General Missendorf was most intrigued by them. I thought I could have been of use – but sadly they didn't need my advice.'

'And now there are only five hundred Vampyres left in the whole world,' Ozymandias said sadly as the night edged in and wisps of fog swirled around them.

Walpurgis smiled, knowing that Ozymandias would know his thoughts instantly.

'A deal is a deal, Walpurgis. I will pay you well for the Oracle diamond.'

'Then there will be only four hundred and ninety seven of you left.' Walpurgis laughed as he got to his feet. 'Tell your friends to get the authorities off my back. I don't want to be answering questions about what I did in the war. They can also get me my job back at Cambridge.'

'Would that be all?' Ozymandias asked sarcastically.

'For the time being,' Walpurgis answered as he began to walk away, leaving the envelope on the table.

Ozymandias watched him disappear into the thickening fog.

'He has not taken the envelope,' Madame Arantez said.

Ozymandias got to his feet, clutching the envelope.

'Go after him, he is at Hotel Julius. Make sure he reads every word. This cannot go wrong. I will see you at Curzon Street.' Ozymandias barked the orders as he tapped the table with his fist.

Arantez vanished into the mist. As she ran along Dean Street she kept to the gutter, staying off the crowded pavement. The lights of the shops flickered in the thickening fog. Suddenly a taxicab lurched towards her and she stepped onto the pavement, pushed close to the wall by the mass of people walking back and forth. Arantez looked up, trying to see the sign for the hotel.

A hand grabbed her from the blackness of an alleyway. She was pulled back, vanishing from the street without being seen.

'I don't like to be followed,' Walpurgis said as he covered her mouth so she could not scream.

'I wouldn't,' she answered, twisting her fingers in the lapel of his coat.

'When did you become a Vampyre?' he asked, pressing his face closer to her.

'It was Jago Harker. Ozzy had asked me to search for the boy. I crashed the truck and Harker took my blood.'

'Then that gives me a better excuse to kill him,' he answered.

'I didn't think you would ever come back,' she said as she brushed his face with her hand.

'It was hard not to think of you. I had to guard my thoughts so he wouldn't see that we knew each other,' Walpurgis answered.

'I told him everything. That is why he sent for you. I have nothing to hide.'

'That I loved you?' he asked.

'Even that.'

'I left the envelope hoping you would follow,' he replied as he held her close, the fur of her coat pressed against him.

'Is that all you wanted?' she asked.

[4]

Hegira

THE WIND RUSHED IN from the cold North Sea and battered the windows of the turret room. The small glass panes were held in place with strips of lead that shuddered as the gale beat against them. Jago tried to look out into the darkness, but all he could see were the faint lights of two ships sailing south through the heavy sea. They crossed the bay slowly as the waves pushed them back. He shuddered, the thought of the water swirling around him making him feel quite sick.

'We can't just wait here,' Biatra said as she walked into the room. 'I just can't stop thinking about Hugh. He's hiding somewhere from a man we don't even know. We have to help him.'

'Where would we start?' Jago asked as he tried to count the fresh raindrops that ran down the glass. 'Does Henson know?'

'If he does, he won't tell us. Do you think he has changed?' she asked bitterly.

'We have all changed, Biatra,' Jago answered. 'We have been hidden away for too long. We don't know the real world any longer.'

37

'I asked him if he'd made any *arrangements* for us. He said that we would be getting a visit from a butcher in Dewsbury and that is all he could get. I would prefer . . .'

'Once a moon. That is all we have to have. It is no hardship,' Jago answered quickly, not wanting to speak of blood.

'At least in Scotland we had the real thing. In Scotland.'

'In Scotland we kept ourselves hidden away and pretended we were dying of tuberculosis. I hated it, hated every minute. It was Hugh who wanted to hide, Hugh who wouldn't fight. He came to an arrangement with the remnant of the Lodge Maleficarum. If we went away and lived in exile then they would leave us be.'

'We were together,' she argued as several doors slammed in the house.

'Spied on by Mrs McClure – she was there to make sure Hugh did as he was told. I heard her on the phone to someone from London. She was our guardian,' Jago answered.

'But you never said,' Biatra shouted. 'Why didn't I know?'

'What would you have done – what would any of us have done? We were prisoners until a time came that it would be safe for us to leave.' Jago looked at the open door. He realised his words had gone beyond the room. 'I don't even trust Henson,' he whispered.

'What do you mean?' Biatra asked.

'Haven't you noticed something about the house? Everything is different. The panel and the secret door in the hall are sealed. All the pictures have been moved, the Labyrinth has gone and Mrs Jarvis didn't come back to the house.'

'Henson told me she had trouble at home and we would meet her in the morning,' she answered.

'How do we know? She could be here to spy on us.'

'Why would they do that?'

'Because they know that I am the child of Strackan. That is why I haven't been killed. Somehow they have found out,' he said quietly, reluctant to speak the words. 'Or they have known all along.'

Jago looked about the room and felt he was being watched. The candle flickered on the table by the window. The house creaked and groaned as if it were taking a long and laboured breath.

'It isn't possible. You only found out before Ezra Morgan was killed, so who else could know?' she asked.

'But is he dead? That is the face in my dream. You saw the serpent. Is he dead?'

'We were there. The train exploded – Kinross, Blaine, Vibica, Ezra Morgan – all dead . . .' Biatra answered.

'There is only one way to be sure,' Jago protested. 'If Morgan is dead, then his face will be in the painting of the Vampyre Quartet. That is the law, when they die, their faces appear in the painting. If we can see it, then we will know for sure.'

'But the door is sealed,' she answered as she stood by him at the window.

'Convenient . . . Henson wouldn't answer when I asked him why,' Jago said urgently, his mind racing to find an answer.

'I know a way to the secret room. We could go there and see for ourselves.'

'Where?' he asked.

'There is a door behind the fire. An entrance cut in the stone. It leads to the cave. I found it when you had gone with Toran Blaine. We could go to the room and look at the painting. Henson isn't working for the Maleficarum,' she protested.

'How do you know? We have been away for years, anything could have happened,' Jago said hoping no one else was listening.

'He hates Vampyres. He would never work for them and . . . he's our friend,' she said.

'We have no friends – we are Vampyres, and there is a curse on us all.'

Jago's words were bitter and final. They had fermented in his heart for many years. He stared at Biatra. She looked the same as she always had. Her face was smooth, her skin soft. The moon-shaped birthmark had never faded.

'I'll always be with you,' she said softly, her voice broken.

Jago looked away at the rain dripping down the window glass, beaten into small tears by the wind. He drew breath and sighed. All she could see in his mind was a swirl of thoughts.

'This isn't the place for us,' he said softly. 'We should get away from here. There has to be somewhere we can be free.'

Biatra took hold of his hand and entwined her fingers in his. She smiled as she kissed him on the cheek.

'Wherever you go, I will be with you,' she said. 'You are all I have left.'

'Hugh mentioned a bank in London that had the money belonging to the family. He said that if we ever were in trouble we could go there. Hugh gave me a key to a deposit box. He told me not to tell you unless I had to. Now is the time.'

'How would we get there?' she asked.

'The night train from York.'

'How would we find Hugh?' Biatra asked.

'The Sinan – the Vampyre compass. Henson kept it when we went to Scotland. He would never give it away,' Jago said.

'But if he is in league with the Maleficarum – they could have taken it.'

'It's a chance we shall have to take. You could ask him sweetly as you always do,' Jago laughed.

Biatra waited at the top of the stairs as Jago crept down to the hallway. He trod lightly on the final tread, knowing the board was loose. It held his weight without making a sound. He beckoned for Biatra to follow. She made slow progress through the darkness as she listened to every sigh of Hawks Moor.

As she passed by, she listened to the door of Henson's room. She could tell he was sleeping deeply as he rolled and snored on the four-poster bed and dreamt of the sea. It took all her strength not to open the door and look inside. In the corner of her eye, she could see Jago far below. He stood by the large stone fireplace where the floor was still stained with the burn mark of Julius Cresco. It was sealed within the freshly polished floor like a memory that could never be forgotten.

The memory of the betrayal was still bitter. It cut his heart to think of it. He remembered the night when Cresco had tried to kill him. Jago had taken the whale-oil lamp and thrown it across the room. He had watched helplessly as Cresco was overwhelmed in scorching flames like a tinder-dry human candle. He looked on, not moving, as the Vampyre burnt like a corn-doll. Cresco had staggered towards Jago and held out his burning fingers as he got closer and closer. 'I loved you,' he had said, before everything Cresco had been was subdued by the flames.

The blackened carcass had slumped to the floor like a falling tree. Ash splintered over the flagstones as his body fragmented. All that was left of his former companion were broken bones, dry and charred.

'It's behind the fire,' Biatra said, breaking the memory as she held the candle she had taken from the hall table. 'You were thinking of Julius Cresco.'

'It was like a ghost. I could see it in my mind.'

'They would have killed you. It was the only way,' she replied as she put a hand on his shoulder.

Jago hesitated for a moment, listening to the sounds of the house and the wind whistling down the chimney.

'How do we find the entrance?' he whispered.

'Behind the fire cradle – on the left.'

Jago stared at the burning embers of the fire. They were held in place by the long iron grate that stood proudly in the centre of the inglenook. There was just enough room to slip by. He moved quickly; the stones were hot from the fire. Biatra followed and, turning to the left, they were both soon in a narrow passageway stained with a hundred years of black soot.

Biatra walked on. The stones were soon cooler as the passage widened. Jago held tightly to the back of her jacket as they took the hand-cut steps.

'How do we get out of here?' he whispered as the roof to the tunnel got lower and lower.

There was a sharp turn. Biatra climbed three steps to a

small wooden door. She pushed against it and the panel opened as a secret mechanism spun the floor beneath their feet and they were suddenly in the room.

Jago took the candle from Biatra and held it high above his head. He remembered the room well from the first day he had seen it all those years ago. Nothing had changed. The large gilded frame hung on the wall where it had done for centuries. Jago stepped closer and then stopped.

'Where is the painting?' Biatra asked before he could speak.

Jago stared at the empty frame that hung on the wall. The ornate painting of the four Vampyres – Draigorian, Cresco, Morgan and Trevellas – had gone. Fragments of old canvas stuck to the frame where a knife had cut it away from the wood. The painting had been roughly and hurriedly taken.

'Do you think Henson knows it has gone?' Jago asked.

'He said he did the restoration of the house. He must have known,' she answered.

'Why didn't he tell us?' Jago asked.

'Because they forbade me to,' Henson answered as he stepped from the shadows.

'You were asleep. I could see your dreams,' Biatra said, alarmed by his presence.

'I was asleep until I heard you speaking,' Henson answered. 'I knew you would come to this place. I tried to tell them but they wouldn't listen.'

'Tell who?' she asked.

'Who do you think?' he asked. 'The Lodge Maleficarum has ways of making people do what they want.' Biatra looked at Jago and wondered how he already knew. 'I thought you

43

would soon understand.'

'Mrs Jarvis?' Jago asked.

Henson laughed.

'You are a wily boy, Jago Harker. She is a guardian of the Lodge. Not that you would think it to look at her.' Henson took the candle from Jago and pulled at a piece of wood in the wall panel. 'I have something that I managed to keep hidden from them. When they came to the house they took everything that would incriminate them. I managed to hide a box of papers in the library and this,' he said as a small drawer in the wall snapped open.

'The Sinan – the Vampyre compass,' Biatra said. She watched him slide the neatly rolled parchment from the drawer.

'I knew they should never find it. I told them that it had been lost in the fire when the steam engine exploded.'

'And they believed you?' Biatra asked, knowing that they would have searched his mind to see if he told the truth.

'I was married for so many years that I know how to confuse my thoughts so they can't be pried upon,' Henson laughed.

'How can we trust you? You work for the Lodge,' Jago snapped before Henson could hand him the Sinan.

'I never thought those words would drop from your lips, Jago Harker. I have watched over you from the day you arrived in Whitby and went to Streonshalgh Manor. Wasn't it I who protected you?' he asked.

Jago stood back and looked at the shadows around him. 'Why are you helping them?' he asked, his voice still sharp.

'I have no choice. They know things – said they would tell

people in Whitby. I would lose my job and everything,' he replied sullenly. 'They have ways of making you do what they want. Sometimes they are hard to resist. I was told to look after Hawks Moor.'

'Blackmail?' Biatra said without thinking.

'It could be called that. Mrs Jarvis said it was just being compliant to their wishes.' Henson shrugged. 'But compliance only goes so far.'

'Do they know where Hugh is hiding?' Jago asked.

'The truth is Jago, Hugh isn't in hiding. They have taken him somewhere. Mrs Jarvis said it was for his safety, but I am not convinced. She is not an ordinary woman.'

'Where is she now?' Biatra asked.

'She is meeting the train at York and bringing someone to Whitby. She said you were to have a new guardian until all this was sorted out. The trouble is –'

Jago butted in. 'Ezra Morgan is still alive and so is Strackan. That is why they took the painting of the Vampyre Quartet.'

'That is the truth,' Henson said with a sigh as he pulled the cord tighter on his thick woollen housecoat. 'Everyone believed that he was dead, but the painting refused to change. They waited for weeks before they finally took it away. They don't want anyone to know.'

'Where is he?' Jago asked. 'I have dreamt of him many times.'

'No one knows. He has not been heard of since the time of the fire. What they worry about is that if he is alive, then who else? Kinross wanted to kill as many Vampyres as he could to cleanse the strain. It had nothing to do with the Lodge. Mrs Jarvis said that they were better off without him, now that there were so few of them left.'

'But didn't they find the bodies?' Biatra asked. 'I read in the paper that they had a funeral for Noel Kinross – he was the Prime Minister.'

'Propaganda. They had to bury something. Trouble is, the fire burnt so intensely that there was nothing left.'

'Vampyres burn, I have seen it with my own eyes,' Jago said, remembering the sight of Julius Cresco burning to cinders.

Henson handed Jago the Sinan and watched him unfurl the vellum.

'I know what you will do with that, but you will have to be careful. Mrs Jarvis will be watching everything.'

'When will she be back?' Jago asked. He looked at the scroll and saw that the ink on many of the names had faded away, leaving blank spaces.

'In the morning,' Henson answered.

'So many have gone,' Jago whispered soulfully, his eyes blinking in the candlelight as he scanned the list of names.

'This is the first time I have been in here for many years.' Henson smiled. 'When they took the painting and sealed the room I thought the Vampyre compass would be lost for good. Then Biatra came back and I saw her disappear behind the fire and knew she had found another way.'

Jago didn't speak; he ran his finger down the scroll, noting the number of empty spaces.

'Are they all the Vampyres who have died?' Biatra asked as she followed his finger with her eyes.

'Hundreds and hundreds,' Henson said. He tried to count the number of missing names on the scroll.

Jago stopped and looked up. His breath was panting in surprise and fear as he read some of the names on the scroll that, etched in black, were still clearly legible.

'Ezra Morgan – Toran Blaine – Vibica de Zoete – Ozymandias . . . They are all alive.'

Guardian

LATE IN THE EVENING of the next day the storm that had been darkening the sky finally broke over Hawks Moor. The rain fell in dark rods, rattling the roof tiles and battering the ground. Rivers of water cut deep valleys in the gravel road and spilled over the cliff top.

Jago looked out of the drawing-room window at the dark sky. He had spent the day waiting for the arrival of Mrs Jarvis. The hours had passed slowly. Biatra had sat by the fire and watched the flames. They had talked little. In the five years they had been locked away in a Scottish castle, Jago thought he had said everything. Now, as he waited by the window, he found it hard to fight against a deep desire to run and feel the rain on his face. He felt like a caged beast. He walked back and forth, looking out through the leaded glass panes. He wanted to race through the woods and along the beach, to dive through the waves and swim out to sea, never to return.

'Still no sign of them?' Henson asked as he brought more wood for the fire. 'I suppose the road from Whitby will be flooded. They could come tomorrow.'

'They are near,' Biatra answered without taking her gaze from the fireplace. 'They will be here soon.'

Jago never questioned how she knew. Since he had been blooded, he had also changed. He could taste things on the wind, his eyesight was sharper and he could hear the most distant sounds. Biatra was different to him: she could sense things that could not be seen and look at the thoughts of others as if they were dancers on a stage.

'Who is coming?' Jago asked. 'Did Mrs Jarvis say who it would be?'

'She never said a thing – just that she would bring a new guardian who would be better suited to looking after you both.'

'A new guard, more like,' Biatra grumbled. 'Turned Hawks Moor into a prison.'

'It's just until all this can be sorted out,' Henson answered. 'Anyway, who is to say you will still be here tomorrow?' Henson reached into his pocket a slipped a key into her hand. 'It's in the garage. Blaine's old motorbike. It has plenty of fuel – easily enough to get you to York. I wouldn't go to Whitby, too many people looking out for you.'

Biatra looked at the key and then at Jago. He smiled back.

'Not a word,' Jago said.

'Not a thought,' Biatra answered.

It was then that the headlights of an old taxi turned into the driveway of Hawks Moor. They faded in the darkness of the storm, the rain blotting out the light. The car juddered to a halt outside the front door.

'I'll go and see her,' Henson said, almost running from the room. 'You wait here and give nothing away.'

The door to the taxi opened quickly. A large black umbrella was pushed out as if to prod the clouds. It opened suddenly and covered the face of the woman who tightly gripped its long bone handle.

Jago could see her thin white fingers that gripped it securely. A long red nail tipped each finger. He watched as Henson paid the driver and shut the car door. Soon, he could hear them in the hallway.

'It is so good to be here. You must be Henson?' the woman asked in an English voice that sounded quite young. 'Terrible journey – road blocked for hours, flooding . . .'

Jago picked out the words he could hear. 'Not a problem. They are in the drawing room,' Henson said, his voice respectful.

The door opened. As the woman stepped inside she pulled the long pins from her hat and slid them into the lapel of her black jacket.

'Biatra and Jago?' she asked in matronly way. 'I am here to look after you. I am Mina Karlstein.'

Jago looked her up and down very slowly. He didn't care that she noticed. His eyes fixed on her face. She could be no more than twenty years old. Her lips were painted red, her eyes lined with kohl. Mina Karlstein was taller the Jago, with broad shoulders and an angular jaw.

'Have you seen enough? Do I have your approval?' she asked as she shook her woollen coat.

'He always does that, wants to see everything of a person before he speaks. He was like that before,' Biatra said, cutting short her words and not wanting to remember the time when he was not a Vampyre.

'I am twenty-five, a twin. I was born in 1698. My mother died of the plague. My doctor, who was also a Vampyre, saved me. Is that what you would like to know?' she asked humbly as Jago continued to stare at her. 'I wear these clothes for comfort and not for fashion. I only take blood that has been freely given and I never hunt.'

'Why are we here?' he asked, ignoring all she had said, not caring for the plain jacket and trousers she wore. Jago could not see her thoughts; they were just a cloud to him. For all he knew she could be lying.

Mina Karlstein looked at Henson. 'I thought that Henson would have told you by now?' she asked.

'He works for the Maleficarum. Why should he tell us anything?' Jago snapped quickly. 'So – why are we here?'

'You are here because it was no longer safe for you to be in Scotland with Hugh Morgan. He is now out of harm's way and cannot be found by *anyone*.'

'So we will be imprisoned here until you tell us that we can go?' Jago asked, not wanting to look at her.

'I am here to look after you. You have had a guardian before. Most of your life was lived that way,' she answered. 'I am sure you will get used to it.'

'It'll be fine, Jago. She doesn't look that bad,' Biatra added. She smiled at Mina. 'We're just getting used to all this.'

'The matter will be resolved soon. There are those from the Maleficarum who are trying to make sure that Hugh is always safe. Henson will be here with you and I have arranged for a delivery.'

'Cow's blood?' Jago taunted.

'As a matter of fact, no,' she answered smugly. 'It will be here in the morning. Can't have old Henson thinking we would be stalking him in the middle of the night, can we?'

51

'Henson can look after himself,' Biatra answered. 'If you see his room, he sleeps beneath a bow of holly and keeps a silver knife under his pillow.'

Mina Karlstein didn't think it was funny. She looked at Henson and tried to smile. Jago could see her eye Henson very warily.

'Force of habit, I'm afraid,' he said apologetically. 'My family were taken by a Vampyre a long time ago and things like that are hard to forget.'

'The Maleficarum hopes to be at peace with you, Henson. Don't forget you are being well paid for all you do for us,' she answered primly, her voice strained. Mina looked about her and nodded at each of them. 'It has been a long journey. I presume I have a room?'

'On the first floor, overlooking the bay,' Henson said as he gestured for her to follow. 'It is next to mine. You will be quite safe.'

Mina Karlstein shuddered as she turned to leave the room. The steel tips of her boots clicked on the stone floor.

'It would be good if we could talk in the morning – perhaps I could explain the rules,' she said as she followed Henson from the room.

'Rules?' Jago asked when he heard the door to her room close. 'Rules to keep us locked in this house and away from Hugh.'

'Let's see what she is like. She didn't look that bad to me,' Biatra answered honestly.

'I don't intend to stay longer than I have to,' he whispered, knowing that Mina would be trying to listen. 'We have to find Hugh and stop Walpurgis.'

'But how?' Biatra asked.

'He is human and can be stopped. We can hunt him down.'

'Is that your answer for everything?' she asked.

'It's what needs to be done.' Jago stacked more logs on the fire, then slouched back into the leather armchair. 'I will find a way.'

Jago didn't move from the chair. He still had the key to Toran Blaine's motorbike but was reluctant to leave without Biatra coming with him. As hour faded into hour he stared at the flames and embers until the night gave way. When dawn broke the sky had cleared. The house was still. Walking silently, the Sinan in his pocket, he went to the library. He checked the doorway of Mina's room but could hear nothing. The distant, faint sound of Biatra singing in her room trailed down the stairway.

Inside the library, Jago locked the door behind him and slipped the key into his pocket. He began to search the shelves for anything out of place. All the books looked the same, leather-bound with gold writing etched into their spines. There was no clue as to where he should be looking. All Jago knew was that somewhere Henson had hidden a box of papers. Jago hoped that within he would find the answers to his questions.

As he reached the end of the first aisle, Jago stopped. By the desk that faced the window was a small brass frog. It sat life-like on the polished wooden floor and stared at him through one bulbous metal eye. In all his time at the house, he had never seen the object before. Jago lifted it from the boards and saw that it covered a tiny hole, the size of his smallest fingertip. Without thinking, he placed the frog on the desk and then slipped his finger into the hole. The floor-board moved slightly as he flicked a catch behind. Suddenly the wood tilted as a slot in the floor opened.

Jago reached within, his hand fumbling in the darkness, and grasped a bundle of papers tied with a ribbon. He pulled them from the darkness, looked at them quickly and then hid them in his coat. Within a minute all was as it had been. Jago reached for the key in his pocket and turned to leave.

'I always worry about people who do things behind locked doors,' Mina Karlstein said as she stepped in from the balcony that overlooked the bay. 'It makes me think they have something to hide.'

'How –?' Jago asked, wondering how the woman had got to the balcony.

'I heard you, so I thought I would come and see what you were searching for. Is it something that you always do? Is it because you are a boy?' she asked intrusively.

'Do I have to tell you everything? Can I not have secrets?' he asked. 'Even Mrs McClure gave us freedom.'

'She told me that you were thoughtful and irksome and spent most of your time talking to the girl and thinking,' Karlstein answered as she closed the doors to the balcony behind her and looked around the library. 'Do you think I want to be here?'

'I care not,' Jago replied as he took the large key from his pocket and slid it into the lock. 'I will do what you ask and nothing more.'

In an instant the woman was at his side, her hand on the key.

'I don't want you to go, not yet. I feel that we have started badly,' she said as she touched his hand.

'It's breakfast, I still try to eat. It makes me feel –'

'Human?' she asked.

'Happy,' he answered.

'Perhaps the two are really one,' she replied as she moved away from the door and sat on the desk, flicking the switch of the reading light on and off.

'The bulb will explode,' Jago said as he turned the lock, 'and you could be electrocuted.'

'Would that be an end to your problems?' Karlstein asked. She picked a stiletto paper knife from the Toby jug by the lamp.

'It would be the start of yours,' he answered glibly as he turned the handle, trying to hide the bundle of papers stuffed into his jacket.

'They said that you would be like this,' Karlstein answered as she rolled the sleeve of her black jacket and pulled the cuff of her neat white shirt. 'What can I do to prove to you that I am on your side, Jago?'

'You could tell me the truth. I don't believe that we are here for protection. Hugh Morgan may be fooled by that, but I find it hard –'

His words were cut short by her abrupt reply.

'And if I told you the truth, what then?' she asked. 'Do you think you would be able to understand what it would mean for you?'

'I have now realised that Vampyres find the truth a hard thing to understand,' he said as he closed the door and looked at her.

Mina Karlstein was outlined in the light from the tall window at the far end of the room. It etched her in a murky shadow. She stood by the writing desk in her dark suit and looked as if she were a tall, slender man. Her hair was cropped short at the sides and cut high around the ears. It was piled on her head in a mound of thick black ringlets. She tapped the desk with her painted fingers as she smiled at him.

Jago saw her face change as she slipped her hand into the pocket of her jacket and pulled out a silver pyx.

'This is the blood of the plague doctor who saved my life. One day I was hoping to take it and change back to being human. I have carried it with me since the day he saved me,' Karlstein said as she held the pyx before him like a gift. 'I remember him well. He came to my house when my mother and sister were sick. He looked like a gigantic bird in his long black coat. As he climbed the stairs to my mother's room, at first I thought he was a monster. He looked at her and told me she would be dead within the hour. Then he told me of a way I could escape her fate.'

Karlstein slipped the vial of blood back in her pocket. 'He pushed me against the wall and bit my neck. It was on 15 August 1723.'

'And you would go back to being human?' Jago asked.

'I have considered it often,' she answered.

'Some of us do not have that chance,' Jago replied, 'because the woman who took my blood is dead.'

'What makes you think that?' Karlstein asked as if she knew more than she would ever say.

'The explosion at the house of Ozymandias . . . So many Vampyres died. Ezra Morgan, Toran Blaine, Vibica De Zoete, Noel Kinross – all dead.' Jago concentrated his mind on the sight of the burning steam engine so she could not see his true thoughts.

'There are only five hundred of us left throughout the entire world, Jago. This war has cost so many lives. Throughout the centuries our kind have survived pestilence and hardship. We have prospered where others have failed. But in five years of human warfare many of my friends are dead.'

'Didn't Kinross want to kill as many Vampyres as he could – isn't that why he planted the bomb?' Jago asked.

'He was deluded,' Karlstein said as she walked to the window and looked out across the remains of the labyrinth, tracing the outline of the passageways with her finger on the windowpane. 'The signs were there for many years. He had become obsessed with power and his own glory. Some say that he wanted war.'

'And now you keep me captive for even longer and you taunt me with stories of wanting to become human again.'

'The woman who took your blood was Medea – and she survives. She is as well as I am. She is in the same place as Hugh Morgan. She is also there for her own good. If you ever wanted to return to humanity it could be arranged,' Karlstein answered as if she would broker a deal.

'What would make you offer that to me?' Jago asked.

'You are very different from every other Vampyre that has lived – except for one . . .'

'Strackan?' Jago asked.

'Do you know who you really are?' Karlstein asked. She looked at him with piercing silver eyes that flickered red as she spoke.

'I am the son of Strackan,' Jago answered. A sudden breeze

stirred the dust from the bindings of the books around him as if the mention of that name brought them to life.

'Your true father,' she answered.

'So it is about me – all of this?'

'It is about you and what you are. The Maleficarum do not know what to do with you,' she said.

'Have they thought of killing me?' he asked.

'They are bound by a law that is as old as time. Murdering you could never be sanctioned and even if it was possible the Maleficarum would never allow such a thing.'

'So what is to be done with me?' he asked, sensing she was not telling him the truth.

'You are to be taken to a place far away from here. You will be kept there until they can decide your fate. You will never see Biatra again,' she said coldly.

'And if I don't go?' he replied.

'We will kill Henson and the girl. They are all that you have and we know you would never let that happen.'

[6]

Luna Negri

THE SMELL OF BREAKFAST filled Hawks Moor and lingered in the kitchen. Jago stood by the gurgling stove, clasping a cup of steaming coffee in his hands like a prayer. Henson was still in his room. Jago had wanted to wake him and tell him all that Karlstein had said but had decided to wait until they were all together. The last thing the guardian had said as he left the library was that she would tell Henson and Biatra at breakfast that Jago was leaving that morning. She had given no other details and Jago could tell from her pinched red lips that the woman would carry out her murderous threat if he refused.

He had not seen Mina Karlstein since he had left the library. It was still early and he could hear her walking the upstairs corridor as if she owned the house. He knew she was searching his room, hoping to find what he had taken from the library, and he laughed to himself. The papers he had discovered were still stuffed down the front of his jacket. When he was alone he would read them; he knew they must have some importance if they had been so well hidden.

It was not long before Jack Henson appeared at the kitchen door.

'Coffee, Jago?' he asked with a yawn. He looked about the room with eyes that asked where the new guardian was hiding.

'She is in my room and yes, there is coffee,' he answered. He put down his cup and took the pot from the stove.

'I had a strange dream. It was so bad that I got up and put another sprig of holly above my bed,' Henson said.

'We won't eat you.' Jago laughed as he handed Henson the cup of steaming black liquid. 'Biatra thought about it once but didn't like to take any of your blood as she thought you were so old you would need every drop.'

'Not you I was worried about,' he whispered in reply as he blew on the liquid to cool it down. 'I was on a train. It had stopped in a tunnel – there was a feeling of evil that was everywhere.'

'Too much cheese,' Jago answered. 'I have taken dreams too seriously.'

'Mina Karlstein was on the train; there was no one else but her and me. She was hunting me down through the corridors and passageways, her eyes streaming with blood.' Henson looked back and forth as if he re-lived the nightmare. 'It means something, Jago, I am sure of it.'

Jago looked beyond him to where the woman stood in the hallway, leaning against the frame of the drawing-room door.

'It means you are an old man,' Karlstein said as she straightened the lapels of her jacket. 'As a Vampyre I myself never dream. Sleep is just a closing of the eyes. Perhaps I have no need to work out my guilt through the phantasms of the mind.'

'Do you drink coffee?' Jago asked as he held out the pot.

'Only that which I have prepared myself,' she answered coldly. 'I think it would be a good time to explain what is going to happen and why we are really here.'

The woman looked at Jago. In turn, he smiled at Henson and raised an eyebrow.

'What do you want?' Henson asked her. 'Something's not right – I can feel it.'

'What is not right is that a man has got involved in our world,' Karlstein answered as Biatra turned the landing of the staircase and looked over the handrail.

She could feel the strained atmosphere. Her mind darted as she sought an explanation. 'What is it, Jago?' she asked, sensing his fear.

'I am going away,' he answered as he swallowed a lump in his throat. 'It's for the best. Mina told me early this morning when I couldn't sleep.'

'Then we will come with you,' she answered.

'He will go alone,' Karlstein said, annoyed by the interruption. 'It is all arranged. You and Henson will stay here. That is what must happen.'

'You can't stop us,' Biatra replied as she stepped towards the woman.

'Tell her, Jago.' Karlstein commanded. 'Tell your friend what will happen to her.'

'If I do not do what they say, Karlstein will have you both killed. I am to go away while the Maleficarum consider what will be done with me,' Jago answered.

He put the coffee pot back on the stove and slumped in a kitchen chair, folding his arms begrudgingly.

'Why do you need Jago?' Henson asked, stepping towards

61

Karlstein.

'Shall I tell him, Jago?' she asked.

'They know who my father is,' he answered.

'It doesn't take a fool to know it is Ezra Morgan,' Henson said.

'If that were the case then Jago would not be such a threat to our kind,' Karlstein answered.

'What do you mean?' Henson asked.

'She knows my father is Strackan,' Jago said calmly. 'They found out when Medea took my blood. Then Ezra Morgan told Kinross. That is why I could not be killed.'

'Why can't he stay here? He will do you no harm,' Henson pleaded.

'There is a place for such as him where no one can free him,' Karlstein answered. 'He will come with us this morning and you will stay at Hawks Moor.'

'You promised not to harm them,' Jago insisted earnestly.

'I will keep my promise. The girl will forget you in time and the man will die of old age long before you are ever set free,' she said with a smirk, twisting a curl with her fingertip.

'How long will we be kept here as prisoners?' Henson asked her.

'As long as it takes you to die,' she answered coldly. 'By looking at you, that should be fifteen years at the most.'

'And what of Biatra – what will become of her?' asked Henson. He looked at Jago, who sat on the kitchen chair with his face buried in his hands.

'When this crisis has passed and you are dead she will be put in the care of another guardian far, far away from here. She will be given a new name and a new life. Hopefully she will forget all about you,' Karlstein quipped arrogantly. 'It is quite tragic that you all got involved in this.'

'I had no choice,' Jago shouted. 'I was sired by a monster for his own good. He fooled my mother into thinking he was someone else, someone she loved. That is why I am here.'

'Save it, Jago. You will have your chance to speak before the Maleficarum,' she snarled.

'Where are you taking him?' Henson insisted as he gripped her by the wrist.

'Let go of me!' Karlstein shouted.

'*Where are you taking him?*' Henson repeated.

Karlstein twisted her wrist and threw Henson across the hallway towards the fireplace. He slid across the stone floor like a rag doll.

She screamed in anger. 'Don't ever touch me again or I will kill you!'

As Biatra thought for a moment and made ready to strike Karlstein turned to her. 'Don't think of it. I wouldn't hesitate to rip out your throat.'

'Just tell us where he is going,' Biatra said.

'Luna Negri – a place you will never know,' she answered.

'The prison of Luna Negri – the cave of the Black Moon?' Henson asked.

'I am surprised that a breather has heard of the place,' Karlstein said as she straightened the crumpled sleeve of her jacket.

'I thought it was just a legend . . .'

'Where is it?' Biatra asked, not giving Henson the chance to finish his words.

'No one knows exactly where. It is a guarded secret,' Henson answered as he slowly got to his feet.

'The cave of the Black Moon cannot be found easily. It will be a place you will never see,' Karlstein said as she looked at Biatra. Taking her by the chin she held her tightly. 'I never realised how pretty you really are. I might ask the Maleficarum if I can keep you for myself.'

'Touch her and I will kill you,' Jago shouted as he kicked the chair away from him.

'Have I struck a nerve? Do I sense love?' she asked.

'I promise you, Karlstein. If you ever touch Biatra, I will track you down,' Jago said, seething the words through his teeth.

'You make rash promises, Jago Harker. I would love to see the day that you tried,' she answered.

'Enough,' Henson shouted. 'There is no need for any of this. Please give us time alone with Jago so we can say our goodbyes. Even a Vampyre as cold-hearted as you can understand that?'

'If you insist,' she said softly with an arrogant smile. 'I hope it will help.'

They waited as Mina Karlstein walked up the stairs to her room on the landing above. Henson nodded towards the drawing-room door.

'We should be safe in there,' he said quietly, hoping that Karlstein wouldn't hear him.

'We can't let them take Jago,' Biatra said as Henson closed the door to the room.

'You have no choice,' Jago answered. 'They will kill you both if I don't do what they say.'

'We have to think of a way. What if they decide to kill

you?' Henson asked.

'Then that will be that,' Jago replied, as if resigned to his fate.

'How far is the cave of the Black Moon?' Biatra asked.

'I thought it was just a legend. When I was searching for the killer of my wife, I had heard there was a place where the Vampyres would imprison those who stood in the way of the Maleficarum. I was told that Luna Negri could only be found on the darkest night of the month, just before the new moon.'

'Then we could find Jago if they take him there,' Biatra said.

'We would have to escape from Mina Karlstein,' Henson added.

'We have done it with others before. She is no different,' Biatra said as she held Jago by the hand.

'I think it is the place where they have taken Hugh. Karlstein spoke to me when she found me in the library,' Jago said as he slipped the papers from inside his shirt. 'I found these under the floorboards.'

'What are they?' Biatra asked as she looked at the faded papers with their torn edges.

'They are deeds of sale and a letter. That is the handwriting of Ezra Morgan,' Henson said. 'I would recognise it anywhere.'

Jago handed the papers to Henson. He read them quickly.

'He sold Hawks Moor a hundred years ago,' Biatra said as she read the first line of the deed.

'More than that,' Henson answered. 'All the money was placed in the Bank of Perazzi in London. And here,' he said as he pointed to a single line written in an almost illegible scrawl. 'Hawks Moor is to be the dwelling place of the Morgan family until they are all dead.'

'Why would he want to sell the house?' Jago asked as he looked at the other papers.

'That I don't know, but it now makes sense. If Morgan did have the Oracle diamond then the Maleficarum would want it. A device to know the future would be highly prized. With you and Hugh out of the way, they can do what they want.'

'And are we just to let him go? Couldn't we escape *now*?' Biatra asked as Henson looked at the letter again, his eyes scanning the parchment feverishly.

'I would not have you risk such a thing,' Jago answered.

'It is the address that is interesting. Ezra Morgan was living abroad when it was written. Look – Chateau Cap Estel.'

Outside the window, a long black car drew up. The doors slammed angrily as two men in leather coats got out and looked about them.

'They've come for me,' Jago said as the shadows crossed the window. 'Take the papers, hide them.'

'What will you do?' Biatra asked.

'I will have to go with them. There is no other way,' Jago replied.

The door to Hawks Moor opened. The men came inside and stood by the fire.

'Mina! Mina!' one of them shouted as Jago walked from the room.

'So you must be Jago Harker?' the man said as he took off his fedora hat and smiled. 'We have come to take you away. There is no need for you to know our names. We will not be doing much talking.'

He nudged the other man and they both laughed. Jago looked at them both. He could tell instantly that they were companions. They did not have the look of the Vampyre. Their clothes were old and threadbare, their shoes unpolished and tatty. Each man looked as if he had not shaved, and as they stood by the fireplace Jago could smell their cold sweat.

'You are late,' Karlstein said as she walked down the stairs. 'Have you said your goodbyes?' she asked Jago.

'I am ready to go,' he answered as he looked back at Biatra and Jack Henson. He could see that Biatra wanted to cry. She kept gulping her breath and squeezing her hands tighter and tighter.

The man nearest the fireplace took out a pair of silver handcuffs and let them dangle from his fingers.

'There will be no need,' Karlstein said as she stood next to him. 'We have come to an arrangement.'

She looked at Jago and he nodded, the agreement complete.

'We will see you again,' Biatra said as she reached out for his hand.

'For that I will pray,' he answered as their fingertips touched briefly.

'That is to be seen,' Karlstein said as she pushed his shoulder. 'Is everything arranged?'

'Just as you said,' the man answered as he took hold of Jago by the scruff of his sleeve. 'You weren't thinking of trying to run, were you?'

'Where to?' Jago answered. 'This was my home.'

'And now the fox has nowhere to lay his head,' the other man joked as he opened the door and looked back at Biatra and Henson. 'We will take good care of him.'

'Don't trust them, Jago,' Biatra shouted as he was led outside.

'They won't harm him,' Karlstein said as she pulled Biatra back from the doorway.

The two men dragged Jago across the gravel to the black sedan parked near the drawing-room window. The taller, shabbier man opened the back door and pushed Jago inside. He looked back to the doorway and waved at Mina Karlstein as she held the old brass handle and stared out.

'We will call you from London,' the man shouted as he got into the car and started the engine. 'Hotel Julius.'

'The Vampyre hotel,' Henson muttered under his breath. 'Thought as much.'

'You know so much about our ways, Henson. You must be a very bitter man,' Karlstein said as she stroked his face mockingly.

'I suppose you have never lost anyone you have loved,' he answered honestly.

'I have never loved and that makes life a whole lot easier,' Karlstein replied. She smiled at Biatra. 'Although I could make an exception . . .'

Biatra stepped away from the woman and took one last glance out of the open door as the sedan drove off. As the car turned on the gravel drive she saw Jago looking from the back seat of the car, the house reflected in the glass. Biatra waved as she caught his eye. Jago smiled. Deep in his pocket, he still had possession of the Vampyre compass, and he also had the key given to him by Hugh Morgan.

'Soon,' she whispered, hoping he could hear her.

'Looks like a puppy on his way to be put to sleep,' Karlstein laughed as she slammed the door. 'You won't be seeing him for a long time – if at all.'

Hotel Julius

IN ROOM 203 of the Hotel Julius, Madame Arantez stared up from the bed and traced the jagged crack across the ceiling with her eyes. She wondered what was on the other side and who was in the room above. She had heard their footsteps throughout the night.

She had lain awake, listening to Walpurgis talking in his sleep as he relived an old nightmare. Arantez had watched the hands of the clock move from hour to hour as she waited for him to wake. She had traced her fingers over the smooth contours of his chin and down his neck and yet he still slept. Above, a door had slammed and she had heard whoever was in the room drag a heavy case across the wooden floor. It was obvious that, like her, they hadn't slept.

Walpurgis stirred, and she closed her eyes and made out she was asleep. He got up from the bed and went into the bathroom.

Light broke in through the plain wooden slats that shuttered the window from the noise of the street. She knew it was late; Walpurgis had slept in and Ozymandias would be furious with her. Somehow it didn't seem to matter, she thought to herself, as she heard the sound of hot water pouring from the tap and splashing the white porcelain tiles of the ornate bathroom.

'You have been ages,' she shouted to Walpurgis as he began to drone out some old song. Wafts of steam billowed into the bedroom in ghost-like clouds. 'How long will you be?'

'It's only the second bath I have had in over five years. There was no running water in the prison camp,' Walpurgis shouted back as he wallowed under the shower, chest deep in water. 'I ordered breakfast before we came up from the lobby. It should be here soon.'

'I don't eat,' she answered coyly.

'They didn't have blood on the menu,' he said as he submerged himself in the hot water and washed the soap from his hair.

'Ozzy is frugal with that. He rations all of us so he is in control. I think he likes it,' she answered as she got up from the bed and slipped on a long white robe that trailed on the floor. Walpurgis didn't hear. He was under the bathwater, holding his breath and counting the seconds. 'Am I that boring?' she asked as she looked into the bathroom and saw his rugged outline beneath the water.

She turned and walked to the window. Opening the slats of the wooden blinds, she looked down on the street below. There was the usual scurry of working people snaking in and out of Dean Street. A woman in a red dress stood on the corner of Old Compton Street and looked nervously back and forth. Arantez studied her for a while, wondering what she would taste like and if she would be hard to catch. It was always the same when she had the hunger. She would begin to see people as prey. The veins in their necks would pulse like

71

fascinators. Arantez would study them intently, looking for any sign of weakness. It was a feeling that came from within, an ancient desire to drink blood.

Even now, when she looked at Walpurgis she had to steel her mind not to want to rip out his throat. Five years in a prison camp had toned each muscle of his body to fine sinew. He looked like a well-worked horse, the veins visible under the skin, running over the layers of muscle. He hadn't aged as much as she thought he would have done. When Walpurgis had vanished in 1939, Arantez believed she would never see him again. He had come into her life for three weeks and then early one morning had told her he was going on another expedition in search of an artifact. He had packed his rucksack and walked out of the door without looking back.

'Looking at the menu?' Walpurgis joked as he stepped from the bathroom wearing just his trousers. 'Do you ever look at me that way?'

'Every moment I am with you,' she replied as she smiled at him, her eyes focused on the crystal pearls of water that trickled down his neck.

'Do you feel different since . . .' he asked, not really knowing how to ask the question.

'I am glad it happened,' she replied eagerly. 'I never thought I would see the world in such a way. Everything comes to life – the colours, the sounds. I even know how people are on the inside, especially if they are frightened.'

'And how am I?' he asked as he stood next to her, an arm hooked over her shoulder as he looked into the street.

'Do you ever get frightened?' she asked.

'When you have no fear of death, what else is there to

72

be scared of?' he answered as he pulled away. 'I don't like spiders, enclosed spaces, Vampyre women and shaving,' he joked as he walked back into the bathroom.

'In that order?' she asked, her eyes following him closely and counting the pulses in his neck.

'Well, I suppose Vampyre women are an exception,' Walpurgis said as he gave her a broad smile.

She thought he had American teeth. They were perfect and bright white. His smile dazzled against the sunburnt skin and broad lips.

'Ozzy insists that you read everything that is in the envelope,' she said as she heard him take the razor from the box and sharpen it on the leather strap that hung behind the door. 'He wants the Oracle diamond more than anything else in the whole world. He told me to get you to read the papers.'

'He didn't need to pay me, I would have gone after Hugh Morgan anyway. I hate getting cheated out of a deal,' Walpurgis replied as he lathered his face with a badger brush and then pulled the sharp steel across his face.

'He told me he couldn't understand how you could hate Vampyres so much and still trade with them,' Arantez said as she sat on the bed and watched him in the reflection of the mirror.

'You go where the money is. I got paid a thousand pounds a year as a lecturer at Cambridge. I can make twenty times that much selling some old bit of stone to a delusional fool that drinks blood.' Walpurgis grunted the words as he wiped the blade on the towel. 'I get them what they want and they pay me well.'

'Then you kill them if they cheat on you?' she asked.

73

'When I found the Oracle diamond, Ezra Morgan promised me as much money as I wanted. He went back on the deal. I am only getting what is mine. If I don't fulfil the contract then all the others will think I have gone soft. Before I know it, every one of them will be ripping me off.'

'Found the diamond? I thought you stole it?' she asked.

'Found? Stole? Appropriated? They are just words that mean the same thing.' Walpurgis finished shaving and wiped the remnants of the soap from his face.

Arantez watched him put the blade neatly on the glass shelf and wash out the brush and place it precisely an inch from the razor.

'Still like everything just so?' she asked.

'Has to be that way. Can't sleep if I know something is out of place.'

Before she could answer there was a knock at the door. Walpurgis looked at her and shrugged his shoulders. 'Must be breakfast. Would you . . .?'

She opened the door and was thrust aside by a waiter pushing a tall trolley filled with steaming teapots and covered dishes that smelt of eggs and bacon. He held out the pad and asked her to sign as his eyes darted about the room.

'This is Room 203 – Walpurgis?' he asked.

'Sure,' Arantez answered as she tried to work out his accent. He wore a crisp linen shirt and shiny leather shoes.

'Just thought . . .' the waiter's voice trailed off as he backed out and closed the door.

'Times are changing,' Walpurgis said as he looked at the breakfast tray. 'He didn't ask for a tip.'

'Perhaps he knew you were so mean and would kill him

for a dollar?' she said as she took the silver lid off a plate of eggs and bacon and allowed the aroma to swell around them.

'Perhaps I will,' Walpurgis replied as he put on his shirt. He took a bite of toasted bread and then wiped his fingers on the towel.

'Looks disgusting,' she said as she watched him chewing.

'I remember you said to me you would never become like them and that you would always remain a companion.'

'That was before. Ozymandias paid me well for my blood. I thought that's how it would always be.'

'And the Oracle diamond – what is he going to do with it?' he asked.

'I heard him say that he would use it to take over the Maleficarum. He wants to rule us all like some ancient king. He's even bought himself a Scottish baronial title. If he knew the future then he would have something that no other Vampyre possessed.' Arantez pushed a slice of bacon with the tip of her finger as if it was some hideous thing.

'I have something no other Vampyre has,' he answered quietly.

'What? More strange artifacts?' she asked.

'You,' he replied even more softly.

Arantez closed her eyes, not wanting to look at him.

'Dangerous words, Heston,' she answered as he kissed her. Arantez pulled away and walked across the room.

It was then that there was another knock on the door. It was urgent, demanding, and came again and again. 'Let me look,' she said before Walpurgis could stop her. She put her eye to the circular lens in the centre of the door. 'It's just the waiter . . .'

It was the last thing she said. The wood splintered as a long silver blade pinned her to the door. Walpurgis saw it twist as it was pulled back and the wood cracked and groaned. Arantez looked at him through dead eyes, glazed and unseeing. She sighed as her body slumped back.

'Arantez!' he shouted as he grabbed the handle.

The door burst open as the waiter kicked at the lock. With great strength, the man pushed the body of Arantez out of the way with his foot. He stood in the doorway holding the sword in his hand.

'Heston Walpurgis?' he asked as he glanced momentarily at the dead body next to him.

'Who wants to know?'

'I was told to tell you that you are a cheat and a liar. Then I was asked to kill you. Understand?' the man asked in a broken accent from the farthest edges of Europe.

'Who do you work for?' he asked.

'The Oracle,' the dark man answered, twisting the sword back and forth in his hand.

'Then I will tell them how you died,' Walpurgis answered as he stood his ground.

Without warning, the man swung the sword through the air and lashed out at Walpurgis. It smashed into the bed, slitting the crumpled sheets and the mattress. Walpurgis rolled forward, grabbing the gun from under the pillow and shooting as he slumped to the floor on the far side of the bed. The silenced bullet smashed into the wall just above the head of the assassin. Walpurgis steadied himself and took aim again.

Before he could fire the man turned and ran into the corridor. Walpurgis looked at Arantez and then gave chase. A deco-glass door halfway along the corridor swung back, but he could see no one. He ran on, pushing his way through door after door, his bare feet sliding on the polished wooden floor. Through one door and then another, he ran until he came to the landing.

The sword came from the darkness, cutting through the air before Walpurgis could see it. The blade sliced into the wall just above his shoulder. It held fast as the assassin kicked at him. Walpurgis fired the pistol. The bullet thudded, the man groaned. He fired again as the sword was pulled from the wall and down his arm.

Lashing out with his hand, Walpurgis aimed blind blows. He felt the pistol smash against flesh. Then there was nothing but a wisp of smoke and he knew he was alone. Back towards his room he could hear pounding footsteps. He chased after them along the darkened corridors. Doors swung back and forth. The footsteps ran on, always out of sight. Then Walpurgis slowed to a walking pace. He knew the man could not have run further than this. He tried each door that he passed until he came to Room 213.

The door was slightly ajar. It was as if it had been purposefully left that way. A a small chink of light came from within, and a radio inside the room whispered some jangling dance music. Walpurgis pushed on the door. It opened slowly. The room was completely empty. He looked at the neat pile of clothes and ebony walking stick on the bed, criss-crossed by slats of light from the window. Standing back, he fought the desire to go inside and find the assassin. He knew the man was hiding somewhere, waiting for him.

Walpurgis pushed the door further open and tried to look

under the bed. Like a childhood nightmare, he waited for a hand to dart from the dark underneath and drag him down. He stepped forward, catching his reflection in the mirror.

Suddenly from behind he felt a rush of air. The door of Room 212 opened quickly. He ducked as a blade stabbed the air above him. Falling to the floor, he turned and kicked at the legs of the man. He heard him fall as he grabbed the door and slammed it shut.

The sword smashed through the door again and again with the power of a monster. It ripped at the wood, tearing splinters as it cut the air and passed his face.

'When will you die?' the man shouted as he kicked at the door.

Walpurgis waited a split second and pulled the handle. The man fell into the room, sword outstretched, and stumbled across the floor. Walpurgis kicked at him, knocking him further towards the bathroom. The man fell as the sword buckled backwards and pierced his leg.

Standing over him as he gripped the wound, Walpurgis laughed.

'I think you have some explaining to do,' he said as he tucked the gun into the belt of his trousers.

'I will say nothing,' the man answered as Walpurgis took hold of the sword and the man's leg and dragged him from the room.

'Think we should talk in my room. I can introduce you to Madame Arantez – the woman I loved – the woman I would have married.'

The assassin looked up, the pain so intense he could not speak. He could tell from the glare on the face of Walpurgis that he would not live to see another night. Once back in his room, Walpurgis locked the door.

'What do you want to know?' the man asked as the pain subsided and he was dumped in the bathroom of Room 203. 'Words for my life?'

'Depends what you can tell me.' Walpurgis took hold of the man by his jaw, forced open his mouth and slid two fingers to each side of the tongue. 'Thought you were a Vampyre. Why are you after me?'

'I was ordered,' the man answered. 'What about the deal?'

'Words for life?' Walpurgis asked as he slipped the sword from the leg of the man and wiped the blade on the towel. 'Haven't seen a sword like this in a long time.'

'Deal?' the man insisted.

'If you must,' he answered. 'As long as you don't come back to kill me.'

The man laughed, his brown almond-shaped eyes sparkling at the thought.

'You are a wanted man, Mr Walpurgis,' the man panted. 'There is more than one gathering that would like to see you dead.'

'And?' Walpurgis asked.

'I was told to give you a message and then kill you. The Oracle insisted that I –'

The man made a sudden grab for the sword. Walpurgis snatched the blade and stabbed the man as hard as he could. The body slumped to the floor. Walpurgis lifted the man by his hair and dumped him in the bath. He wiped his hands on the towel and went to the telephone.

'Room service?' he asked softly. 'I take it the Hotel Julius still offers the same service when there has been an *accident*?' He breathed hard. 'Good . . . well, in fact it is two *accidents* that need to be disposed of . . . very well, five minutes.'

Walpurgis sat on the bed and after staring at the body of Madame Arantez he took the envelope she had brought and looked inside. There were several photographs, each marked with a name. Hugh Morgan – Biatra Barnes – Jago Harker. He held the last sepia print in his fingertips and looked at the face, studying each contour and line. It was an old school photograph of a boy in a flat cap. 'You will be the first. If you had not taken my Arantez this would not have happened.'

Walpurgis dropped the photograph to the bed, sat back against the pillows and closed his eyes. He knew that room service would soon come along. It would cost five hundred pounds for their silence. But this was the Hotel Julius, the Vampyre hotel. People died here all the time and, if rumours were to be believed, blood was their business.

[8]

Laundry

WALPURGIS LOOKED BACK into his room and checked all was well before he turned the key. It was late evening and already the noise from the street was too loud for him to sleep. Room service had arrived with a laundry basket and taken away the bodies. Taking one final look at Madame Arantez, he had kissed her on the forehead as they wrapped her in a blanket and took her from the room. He had paid them with the money he had taken from the pocket of the assassin.

He didn't know what to do with the evening. He thought of catching the midnight train to York, hiring a car and then arriving at Whitby in the morning. He thought it would be best to start his search for the Oracle diamond at the place he had handed it to Ezra Morgan before the start of the war. Walpurgis hadn't liked Hawks Moor. He felt it was cold and murky, always swirling in sea-fret.

As he walked down the narrow stairs towards the lobby, he tried to think of how long it would take to get to the north. Instinctively, he patted his pockets to see if he had everything he needed. Money, pistol, knife – he felt each one. Opening the door from the dark stairway, he stepped into the lobby and saw an old man on the long studded leather seat under the window. The man looked up from his newspaper and stared at him. To his left the redhead behind the counter got up from her chair and smiled at him.

'Everything to your satisfaction?' she asked with a smile of her ruby lips.

'Perfect as always, Julia.' Walpurgis said. 'I may not be back tonight, but I have left everything in my room.'

'I will make sure that it is there when you get back,' she answered, careful not to say too much.

'When do you finish work?' he asked as he leant on the counter and dangled his key in the tips of his fingers.

'This is the Hotel Julius. I never finish and will always be here for you,' she said as the door opened.

The lobby filled with the smog of the cold London night. It smelt of cheap diesel and wood smoke. Walpurgis gave no attention to the man now standing on his right. He looked at Julia and then picked an information card from the rack.

'We have two rooms booked for tonight,' the man said. 'They should already be paid for.'

Julia looked at the large double-paged book on the desk and ran her finger down the list of names.

'Two rooms in the name of Bathory?' she asked in her usual way of ending even the most straightforward sentence with a question.

'I am Nicholas Bathory,' the man answered, as if he had been rehearsing the words for hours.

With her usual slickness, Julia handed Bathory the keys to the rooms. The man looked at the fob and nodded before turning and walking out of the hotel.

'Breather,' Julia said as he went out of the door.

The man holding the paper laughed.

Walpurgis followed, soon engulfed in the fog outside. On the edge of the pavement was a black sedan. Bathory leant into the open window.

'The rooms are ready. I will take the boy. You go and park in Brewer Street. Usual place.'

There was something about the conversation that intrigued Walpurgis. He looked in the window of the bookshop next door and tried to listen. Like him, the man was human and yet he was allowed to stay at the Hotel Julius. That was a privilege that not many warm-bloods could enjoy. Walpurgis knew that Hotel Julius only accepted those invited and then only once the reclusive owner had agreed.

That made Bathory interesting to Walpurgis, but there was something else about the man that he found intriguing. He wore a long coat that was hand-stitched. His shoes were dirty and scuffed and his face looked drawn, as if he hadn't slept. Walpurgis thought he looked a mess, and from the bulge under his left arm he knew he was carrying a gun.

He watched out of the corner of his eye as Bathory opened the car door and pulled the boy from within. Walpurgis turned to walk away, having thought he had seen enough. Then he stopped. Standing on the pavement, covered in an old coat and with his hands chained, was Jago Harker. He recognised him immediately. There was no mistake. The boy looked older, almost a man, but it was definitely him.

Walpurgis swallowed hard with excitement. He felt the pistol in his pocket and for a moment thought he could just gun Harker down in the street. He looked around; the mercurial smog would give him plenty of cover. He would just be a vanishing shadow in the thick mist. Walpurgis pulled back the hammer of the gun and made ready.

Harker suddenly looked at him. Walpurgis stopped and turned back to the window of the bookshop. When he looked again, Jago Harker had gone.

Walpurgis stood on the crowded pavement as if he were a stone in the tide. He waited, trying to gather his thoughts. He watched as the driver of the black sedan appeared out of the fog from the direction of Bourchier Street. For the first time in his life he could feel panic twist his stomach. The man passed by without even looking at him. Walpurgis tried to take in as much about him as he could. He could see that the fingers of the man's right hand were stained with nicotine, that his face was swollen on one side and that he hadn't shaved for at least two days. Like the other man, he also wore shabby shoes and fine clothes that were in need of repair. They were badly fitting and looked as though they had been borrowed from someone far larger than he would ever be.

The man went inside Hotel Julius. Walpurgis could see that Jago Harker was some kind of prisoner. The clasps of the handcuffs had been easy to see under the cuff of the leather coat.

After waiting several minutes, Walpurgis went inside the hotel. The old man with the white hair and newspaper had gone. Julia stood at the far side of the counter and looked up when he walked in.

'Back so soon?' she asked. 'Couldn't keep away?'

'Too irresistible,' he answered as he looked to the doors of the empty bar. 'Think I'll go and try to sleep.'

'Haven't done that for half a lifetime,' Julia answered as she flicked back her hair.

Walpurgis wondered how old she really was. The thing with Vampyres was that they might look young on the outside, but all those years of stolen life made them different inside. Julia looked like the old photograph of his mother that was always on the lid of the piano. She was a woman he had never known. Evie Walpurgis had died three days after he had been born; his father had been arrested for her murder, and from then on Heston had lived with an aged aunt twice removed, sharing his early life with her and a toothless spaniel. They had all lived together in a large and draughty house on the outskirts of Cambridge. It was there that he had looked at the photo of his mother day after day. He wanted to cheat death and find her, be with her again. Great Aunt Poppy had told him that his mother had gone to the *other side* . . . She had tried to describe the place and made it sound more like Worthing than Heaven. From then on, he had searched for some way to bring the two worlds together. GAP – as he called Great Aunt Poppy – always talked of death and mostly at breakfast. She would sing, play the piano and try to channel the spirit of some great but dead composer. Walpurgis would sit on the chair by the window and stare at the image of his mother. Now he stared at the receptionist in the same way. She was uncannily similar, even to the way in which her hair fell to the shoulders.

Julia could obviously not read minds. She smiled at him and handed over the key to his room.

'The guy who checked in, the *breather* – Nicholas Bathory.

What room is he in?'

'Confidential,' she replied. 'You know we never give out the room numbers of our guests.'

Walpurgis reached over the counter and taking her by the lapel of her jacket pulled her closer.

'I was just interested. Didn't want *us* to be disturbed,' he said in a low breath.

'Rooms 107 and 109, first floor, opposite the laundry. It is quite cheap and they aren't having their bill paid by Mr Ozymandias,' she replied as if that made all the difference.

Walpurgis touched her on the lips, his finger sticking to the gloss momentarily.

'Good to know where the laundry is,' he said wryly as he opened the door and walked up the stairs.

Walpurgis turned on the first landing and soon he was outside the rooms. He listened to each door. He could hear Bathory talking inside Room 109. Walpurgis checked the gun in his pocket and tried to think where they would be in the room. He would use three bullets and shoot Jago Harker last. That would be after he had questioned him about where he would find Hugh Morgan and the diamond.

The handle of the wooden door shuddered as someone inside slipped the bolt. Walpurgis jumped back into the dark doorway of the laundry. The man stepped outside and looked up and down the corridor. Walpurgis watched him from the shadows and then, like a cat, struck out. Before the man could scream or even make a sound he was dragged across the corridor and into the laundry.

With a sudden, sharp crack of the neck, the man was on the tiled floor unable to move. Walpurgis dragged him through the room draped with sheets and towels that hung from rails on the high ceiling. A single clear glass bulb lit the room. A small, black fly that had forgotten the season buzzed irritatingly around the bright glass.

He could see the door to another room close by, and he dragged the body within. He flicked the switch and, as the light flickered and grew brighter, he looked around him. There, hanging from hooks on a steel rail, were several bodies. Some were attached to thin, metal pipes connected to a pump. He recognised the bodies of Madame Arantez and the assassin. Walpurgis pulled a hook and chain from the rack above him and slipped it under the neck of the man, then he hauled on the chain until the man hung from the air. The pumps chugged and churned as they sucked the blood from the bodies. Walpurgis followed the clear glass pipes with his eye as they crossed the ceiling and ran down into a boiler on the far side of the room. The room looked like the workings of an elegant Neapolitan ice-cream factory. Everything was meticulously clean and tidy; the bodies hung in order of size, their hair brushed and clothes pressed. Even the body of Madame Arantez looked as though it would come alive.

Leaving the man hanging from the hook, Walpurgis sneaked back to the corridor outside Room 109. He listened to the door. There was silence. He thought of what he would do. Then he heard a muffled voice within.

'There's a man outside with a gun,' he heard Jago Harker say. 'He's planning to kill you and then me.'

Bathory laughed.

'You expect me to believe that? You a mind reader? I heard that Vampyres could guess what you were thinking. Perkins will be back soon and he will see him,' Bathory gloated. 'Tomorrow I hand you over to the French. Then life gets back to normal.'

'Why aren't you taking me?' he asked.

'Don't like crossing water. Superstitious that way, me and Perkins,' Bathory answered. 'You're going all the way to Luna Negri – that's almost to the other side of the world.'

'I can hear him, he's outside. There is someone in the corridor,' Jago insisted.

'If I take a look and there is no one there, you will be in trouble,' Bathory answered begrudgingly, not wanting to look. 'This is the Hotel Julius – only special people can stay here and it is the safest place for your kind in London.'

Bathory went to the door. He looked through the miniature spy-hole but could see no one. Turning the key and then twisting the handle, he pulled the door open. The corridor was empty; the dim light at the end by the stairs flickered in its oyster glass. 'Told you, kid. Your mind reading isn't what it should be.'

'He was hiding,' Jago answered as Bathory slowly closed the door.

'Hiding?' Bathory asked angrily. 'See for yourself,' he said as he pulled open the door. 'Look – no one.'

Jago shuffled on the bed uncomfortably. His eyes stared into the darkness of the corridor. Bathory could see the reflected image of a man within them. He turned slowly as if a ghost stood behind him.

'I would always listen to young Vampyres, Mr Bathory. They have yet to learn to lie and will always tell the truth,' Walpurgis said as he held the pistol with the silencer towards

88

the man.

'Take him – if it's him you are after,' Bathory answered as he raised his hands, his fingers twitching nervously. 'My friend will be back soon, went to get something from the car.'

'He's taking his time, probably hanging around one of the rooms.' Walpurgis laughed to himself. 'I don't think I will worry about the time.'

'I have money and an account at the Bank of Perazzi. Take whatever you want,' Bathory pleaded.

'Why is he your prisoner?' Walpurgis asked as he closed the door behind him and with one hand slid the bolt.

'We were told to take him to Dover and put him on a boat for France,' Bathory replied.

'Who by?' he asked.

'The Maleficarum – do you know of it?'

Walpurgis smiled, raised the pistol and pulled the trigger. Bathory dropped like an icicle from a gutter. He put away the gun, unscrewing the silencer and slipping it into the pocket of his coat. Without speaking, he took hold of Bathory by his dirty shoes and dragged him from the room.

Jago couldn't move. The handcuffs on his wrists were chained to the bed.

Soon Walpurgis returned. He looked at Jago as if he was trying to make sure he had the right person.

'I take it you are Jago Harker?' he asked.

'And you are Heston Walpurgis?' Jago asked.

'It is so good not to have to introduce myself. Did Hugh Morgan speak of me?' Walpurgis asked as he took a small key from the pocket of his coat and released the handcuffs. 'You could save yourself an awful lot of suffering if you were to answer me honestly.'

'So you are going to kill me?' Jago asked.

'As soon as you tell me what I want,' he answered.

'I don't have the diamond. Ezra Morgan is dead and I have no money.'

'Ezra Morgan promised me one million pounds. Do you know how much that is?' Walpurgis asked.

'More than I will ever have,' Jago answered.

'Ezra Morgan was one of the richest men in the world. Before the war he bought as many artifacts as he could and hid them all over Europe.' Walpurgis coughed as if the words burnt his throat. 'That's what Vampyres do when they hear of war. Money can lose its value, but gold, silver and great paintings keep their worth. I know the diamond is hidden somewhere.'

'We don't have the diamond. The only time I heard of it was when Jack Henson read your letter to us.'

'So Morgan has read the letter?' Walpurgis asked as he slumped into the leather armchair by the door.

'Hugh Morgan is a prisoner. The Maleficarum have locked him away to keep him safe from you. That's where they were taking me. Some place called Luna Negri.'

'Luna Negri?' Walpurgis asked. 'Are you sure?'

'That is what a woman called Karlstein said,' he answered.

'Mina Karlstein?' Walpurgis asked, his interest aroused. Jago nodded. 'Then this just gets better with each second.'

'Is that all you need to know?' Jago asked, trying to see what was in the mind of the man.

Walpurgis thought for a while. 'Did they say how they would find Luna Negri?' he asked.

'Only that I would be handed over to the French and they would take me,' he answered.

'Shame I killed him,' Walpurgis whispered. 'Bathory could have been useful.' He got up from the chair and looked at Jago closely. 'Why are they so interested in you?'

'My mother was a brood mare. I was born for a purpose. That's what Ezra Morgan said. It was because of my blood.'

'And they want to keep you safe?'

'Locked away until they can decide what they want to do to me.'

Walpurgis spoke his thoughts out loud. 'Perhaps you really are worth more to me alive than dead.'

9

The Bank of Perazzi

A N HOUR LATER, Jago was in Room 203. He sat in the leather chair by the window and watched as Walpurgis packed a small bag with two shirts and a pair of trousers. They were precisely placed and then re-arranged several times until he was completely happy with where they were. In all this he never looked at Jago, who eyed the man warily, knowing that he cared nothing about his life and that he was only *useful* to him. Jago found it hard even to sense what Walpurgis was thinking. He found that this was often the case with people who had spent a lot of time around Vampyres. The constant prying around the edges of their mind made them suspicious and often, without even trying, they began to hide their thoughts.

Walpurgis didn't speak as he pulled a sword from underneath the mattress of the large bed that dominated the room. He measured it against the length of the bag and then sighed as he threw the blade on the bed.

Jago knew what the blade was for. He had seen them several times before. They were always made of silver and always long enough to penetrate the body from side to side. Vampyres could not be killed by means that would end the life of most humans, but even the most meagre and paltry wound from a silver blade would soon bring sickness and even death. He had seen the look of horror on the face of Ezra Morgan when he had stood before him with the blade given him by Jack Henson. The terror could be felt in the room, such was its power. Now, as Jago stared at the blade, he felt the same. It was a rising panic; he felt as if he were surrounded by venomous snakes. It made every nerve in his body quiver. What made it worse was that he knew Walpurgis would not hesitate to kill him.

'What do you do?' Jago asked. 'Why did you sell the diamond?'

Walpurgis looked up. 'I am an archeologist of sorts. I specialise in that which is of myth and legend. Artifacts – objects of superstition and the occult. I find them and sell them on.'

'But why to Vampyres?'

'They have the most money and ask the least questions. One thing I have found is that they love things of beauty and if they are told the object has power then they find that even more attractive. Beauty and power – what more could they ask for? They keep their money in the Bank of Perazzi on Ludgate Hill. I try to take as much of it as I can.'

'What are you going to do with me?' Jago asked when he saw that Walpurgis had finished packing the case.

'I am going to trade you with someone I know. They in turn can do with you what they like,' Walpurgis answered as he pulled the price tag off the handle, holding together the two sides of the leather bag and twisting the gold lock. 'Ozymandias was insistent that I kill you. That makes me think you could be useful. What you have to remember, Jago, is that in life there are always two sides to everything. I want my money from Ezra Morgan, and as he is dead I will take the life of his son . . .'

'He isn't dead,' Jago interrupted quickly. 'He is still alive.'

'What?' Walpurgis asked flicking back the locks of hair that had drooped across his forehead. 'Alive? How do you know?'

'At Hawks Moor there is a painting of four Vampyres. They are called the Vampyre Quartet. When each Vampyre is killed, their faces appear in the painting. Ezra Morgan's face did not appear. His name is still on the scroll of the Sinan.'

'You know about the Vampyre compass?' Walpurgis asked. 'That is a relic I would love to see. It would make my life so much easier. Vampyres are sometimes the most awkward beasts to catch.'

Jago hoped he could control the expression on his face. He felt in the deep pocket of his leather coat, touching the scroll and the compass.

'I have only heard of it, but the Maleficarum say his name is still there,' he answered as he tried to hide his anxiety.

'That alters the case,' Walpurgis grunted. He looked in the mirror, adjusted the collar of his white linen shirt and straightened the knot of his tie. 'If Ezra Morgan isn't dead –'

'Then the debt isn't passed to his son?' Jago asked.

'The contract for the Oracle diamond was quite clear. If Ezra Morgan didn't pay then I could kill his son. That still stands. What makes things difficult is that the Maleficarum have hidden him away.' Walpurgis paced with his thoughts around the room, his hand jerking in the air as if he conducted a silent orchestra. 'Now – should I go after Ezra or his son?'

The man stopped suddenly and looked in the full-length mirror that hung against the grey walls by the door. Jago could see he was deep in thought. Walpurgis struggled with the many voices in his head as he wiped his face with the tips of his fingers and traced each lined contour. 'Something makes me think I am being cheated and Heston Maximillian Walpurgis does not like to be cheated.'

'What about me?' Jago asked, wondering if he could escape.

Walpurgis turned as if he suddenly realised there was someone else in the room.

'I think I have changed my mind. You would only get in the way and I am not sure if keeping you alive would be the best thing,' he answered. 'If you wouldn't mind going and standing in the bathroom?'

Walpurgis rummaged in the pocket of his coat and pulled out the gun. Then quite awkwardly he found the long silencer and screwed it into the tip of the barrel.

'You're going to kill me?' Jago asked as he got to his feet. 'But I thought I would be useful to you?'

'Things change, Jago. I can see that you have not been in your current condition for very long. Perhaps it would be best for you to meet your maker before the poison destroys your soul,' Walpurgis answered coldly. Drops of white spittle stuck to the sides of his mouth.

'But what have I done to you?' Jago asked.

'You are an aberration of nature, Jago. An inconvenience of life, a bacillus on the sidewalk of the world, a scruple in time.'

Walpurgis paused as he checked the gun. 'You are already dead, Jago Harker. The moment you were bitten the life was taken from you.'

'But –' Jago tried to protest as he stepped closer to him.

Walpurgis lowered the gun and spun the chamber as if counting the bullets. 'Do you remember a woman driving a van? She worked for Ozymandias?'

'Yes,' he answered.

'You took her blood?'

Jago nodded hesitantly as he stepped into the trap. 'It wasn't like that,' he replied, his mouth dry, throat gulping.

'I knew that woman, Jago. When I was in prison during the war I thought of her often. On black, cold days when I thought the sun would never rise, the memory of her was one of the few things that brought me light. You took her blood and now she is dead.'

'I saw marks on her neck. She had already been blooded. There was a bite. It was fresh. I saw it,' Jago snapped back as he looked for a way of escape.

'Step into the bathroom. It will be easier to clean up the mess and I don't want to get blood on the ceiling.' Walpurgis flicked the safety catch off the pistol. 'I always buy silver bullets. Even a flesh wound will ultimately bring about your death.'

'She was already changing. I could see it. She worked for Ozymandias,' Jago argued.

'It will do you no good. My mind is set like flint and will not be changed.' He answered casually, as if he were inviting Jago for tea. 'It shouldn't take long. I am quite used to doing this.'

96

'She was a Vampyre. I could taste it in her blood.'

'Please calm down,' Walpurgis commanded as if he spoke to petulant child.

'It's true,' he said as he moved closer to the bed, his hand near to the hilt of the sword.

Jago saw the look change on the face of Walpurgis. His eyes widened as if he had never been challenged this way before. He took three deep breaths and shuddered slightly as if he tried to contain the rage that was about to explode within him. He seethed and moaned to himself as if tormented by an argument within. He lifted the pistol and aimed it at Jago.

'What will be your final words?' he asked.

Jago grabbed the sword and at the same time knocked the gun to one side. Walpurgis leapt forward, pushing Jago against the wall. With one hand holding the gun, Walpurgis pushed his arm against Jago's throat. He raised the gun but Jago kicked out as hard as he could and Walpurgis buckled with the blow and stepped back. Before he could aim again, Jago dived towards him. Walpurgis fell back against the door to the bathroom and the sound of splitting wood stopped the fight.

Walpurgis dropped the gun to the floor. He held the sword that had sliced through his leg and pinned him to the door. Holding in a scream, he looked at Jago.

'It didn't have to be like this,' Jago said as he picked up the gun at his feet and pointed it at Walpurgis. 'We could have helped each other.'

'Dreams, dreams,' Walpurgis answered. 'You will be dead by the morning. Once the Maleficarum find you escaped they will come for you. The bodies of your companions hang

97

in the blood-room of the laundry. When they find them they will think that you killed them and that will be it. I never thought I would be outsmarted by someone so young.'

'I want to find Hugh Morgan and the diamond,' Jago answered as he watched Walpurgis struggle to stop the flow of blood.

'Just get it over with – but not in the head.' Walpurgis pulled open his shirt. 'Make it quick and don't miss.'

'I am not going to kill you,' Jago said as he looked at the pool of blood that trickled across the floor. 'I will leave you here, on one condition – that you don't come after me.'

'I don't know if I could promise such a thing,' he replied.

'Then at least, give me a head start. If you have a soul, remember that I allowed you to live,' Jago said as he could see Walpurgis weaken.

'If our paths cross I will remember that,' he answered. 'If I were you it would not end this way. What you do is a sign of your weakness. They will find it and use it against you, Jago Harker. A Vampyre is a killer born and bred. Remember that as you search for your friend.'

'I will find him and the diamond and then your debt will be paid.' Jago took the six bullets from the pistol and stood them neatly on the cabinet. He twisted the rod and released the chamber, sliding the hammer spring.

There was a sharp knock on the door. Jago looked at Walpurgis.

'It's Julia, the woman from reception. I arranged to see her,' he said. 'She won't go away, she knows I am here.'

Jago went to the door and opened it slowly. The woman stepped nervously inside.

'You came to see Walpurgis?' he asked as they stood in the small lobby of the room. 'He's in there.'

'What have you done to him?' she asked as her eyes picked out the fine flecks of splattered blood that glowed like red crystals on his leather coat.

'He's alive,' Jago replied. 'Have you eaten lately?'

The woman smiled her ruby smile; her brow arched, wrinkling the thick white powder that covered her face.

'That's the risk they take when they stay here, I suppose,' she whispered as Jago slipped from the room.

He was soon in the street. The night was dark, the fog thick and brooding. As he walked along Dean Street and then Old Compton Street, he kept looking back. Jago didn't care what would happen to Heston Walpurgis; he thought the man was mad and dangerous. Sadly, he knew that he had not seen the last of him. Somewhere in his future, Walpurgis would be there, waiting.

It felt strange, being back in London. Jago knew the streets well. He had walked them every day of his life before he was evacuated at the beginning of the war to Whitby. Every Saturday he would walk from Brick Lane through the City to the West End. He looked at all the wealthy people as they sat in cafés, eating bowls of ice cream covered in sauce and drinking hot frothy coffee in Italian restaurants. Once he had stood and gawped through the window of Giovanni's in Wardour Street, staring at a young couple. Eventually the man got up and came outside, clutching the half-eaten bowl of frozen whipped cream. 'Do you want some?' he asked. 'You can't stop looking at it.'

Jago had taken up his offer and eaten the ice cream. It had tasted of everything that he thought it would and more. He had taken the final spoonful and let it melt on his tongue before he thanked the man.

As he walked towards Southampton Row, Jago savoured the memory. It was one of the few he could remember. Since Medea had taken his blood, all that had happened before had become vague and meaningless. It was as if he had some strange disease that corrupted all that had been good. Starting with the memories of his childhood, it took away the Christmases and birthdays, the laughter and smell of the freshly cut grass in Belsize Park. Jago had to search hard to think of any good thing before that time and with each day the condition grew worse.

Now he tried hard to picture the face of his mother, the apartment they shared and her things on the mantelpiece. If he had thought of them before Jago would have said they were trivial, fripperies that mattered not. Now, in the cold and loneliness of that London street, they meant everything.

As he walked, he counted his steps. Each pace was a yard further from Walpurgis and the Hotel Julius. He knew he was near the river – the bombed-out factories and stench of sewage told him that. Far away he could hear the sound of boats on the Thames. These were the night boats that took the garbage out to sea. They dumped the old beds, dead cats, waste helpings of potatoes and scraggy ends of bread at Northfleet. The rubbish would often float back on the tide and swirl in the river by the Isle of Dogs. Often it was so thick that seagulls could walk upon it. They would chew and pick at anything they could find until the tides dragged it down into the mud. He smiled; this was another thing from his childhood that he could remember.

At the third hour of the night, he stopped at Temple Church. There was a group of men sleeping on the steps. They looked ragged and tired, careless of his passing by. He waited in the shadows of the trees and looked at the bombed-out offices of Temple Court.

He was hungry. The pain gnawed at his guts and twisted them around. Jago watched a man stagger from the group. He was drunk on Buckie and held the empty bottle proudly in his hand. The man whistled and murmured an old song as he fiddled with the buttons of his trousers and tried to hold himself up against the wall.

'Your lucky night,' Jago whispered to himself as he pulled up the collar of his coat and walked away, leaving all thoughts of feeding from the man far behind. 'Would rather wait.'

Following the line of what was once Tallis Street, he turned on to Bridle Lane. He knew it well. Gone was the coffee grinder with the blind monkey. The bombing had broken the backs of every building. They stood like dead carcasses of iron and stone. Their insides were crushed and filled with mounds of rubble. On the door of one shop was a red sign, the words plainly legible: DANGER UXB . . .

Ludgate Hill was empty of people. The City was always like this at night. Jago could hear the faraway bells of a solitary fire engine as it rattled through the streets. He counted the doors of the cold grey buildings that lined the hill. By each was a brass plate that gave the number and the name, and he read each one as he walked by. There was no sign of the bank he was looking for.

It was only when he crossed the road to the corner of Old Bailey that he saw a small red door set back into the wall. It was half the size of any man and the small brass handle would easily fit into the hand of a child. Anyone passing at walking pace in the light of day could easily miss it. Only at night, when there were no distractions, could it really be seen.

Jago looked back down the road from where he had come. He was still alone. Stooping down, he read the small brass plaque that gave the name of the business that lay within: BANCO PERAZZI – OPENING HOURS BY ARRANGEMENT – PLEASE KNOCK.

10

Fredrico Lucca

THE SKY DARKENED over Ludgate Hill as thick black clouds billowed in from the flatlands of Graves-end. As Jago stood outside Banco Perazzi the first drops of ice-cold rain fell to the dirty pavements. The iron gutters began to gurgle as the water oozed from the high roof of the bank. From St Clement's he heard the chiming of the clock and, escaping from the storm, he hid in the broken-down doorway of a tobacconist's opposite the bank.

The rain beat down in rods and bounced on the stones of the empty street. It brought with it a smell of sweet, sickly treacle as it washed the grime of a thousand footsteps and grubby lives into the sewers. It pounded hard, each drop bouncing up when it struck the road. Jago covered himself in old newspapers that had been piled in the corner of the doorway. As the raindrops fell he edged deeper and deeper into the shadows, feeling ever more alone.

Looking out, unable to sleep, he saw a solitary figure. It kept close to the buildings of Old Bailey. As it drew closer, Jago could see that it was a man. He carried a raven-black umbrella edged with twisted tassels like the trimmings on a funeral horse. The man walked with an uneven gait, as if he had carried a limp from birth. Every third step he would lift the umbrella to see the way ahead. Jago could make out a small grey beard, a black hat and round glasses. The man looked across at him and smiled. He nodded, shook his umbrella and then looked up to the sky.

Approaching the door to the bank, the man hesitated and again looked at Jago, as if he was making sure he hadn't moved. Then, propping the umbrella against the wall, he slipped a key from his pocket, opened the small door of the bank and quickly slipped inside. For an instant, Jago wondered if he had dreamt seeing the man. Then, shaking the papers from him, he got to his feet.

Old Bailey was still empty and Ludgate Hill ran like a small river as the storm water bubbled from the drains and washed out the rats. Jago ran across the road and knocked on the door of the bank. Almost instantly, a small grille opened in the door. A man peered out in such a way that only his eyes could be seen.

'Yes?' he asked as if it was quite usual to have callers at this time of day.

'Is this the Bank Perazzi?' Jago asked.

'What does the sign say?' the man asked.

'Banco Perazzi,' Jago answered as he looked at the sign and the carved wolf head beneath.

'Then it must be,' the man answered coyly, as if he were enjoying the conversation. With that he slid the grille shut. Jago knocked again. 'Yes?' asked the man.

'Can I come in?' Jago asked.

The eyes looked him up and down as far as they could and then stared at his face.

'Why should you want to come in here? This is not a lodging house for waifs and strays. Nor is it a prison for the world's criminals. This is a bank.'

'It's my family bank,' Jago answered.

The man sighed in disbelief. 'Then if it is your family bank you will have a key to the vault and as you should know the key must be kept with you at all times . . . Do you have such a key?' the man asked, believing his words to be futile.

Jago undid the collar of his shirt and pulled the thin cord that hung around his neck. The brass key dropped into his hand. He held it for the man to see.

'I was given this key by my brother,' Jago answered, not knowing how else to describe Hugh Morgan.

The man looked at him suspiciously.

'Does the *brother* have a name?' he enquired civilly.

'Hugh Morgan,' Jago answered as he felt the water soak in through the sodden leather of his shoes.

The grille on the door slammed shut. Jago heard several locks turn and bolts slam. A chain slipped from the door and an iron bar scraped across the inside of the wood. Then he heard the sound of what he thought was a large stone being pushed out of the way.

Slowly, carefully, the door opened. Jago could smell the scent of lavender. It billowed through the small entrance as if it were a summer's day.

'And you are?' the man asked as he waved Jago inside.

'Jago Morgan,' he answered as he stooped through the tiny doorframe into the lobby of the bank. Jago had never seen a room like this before. The walls were clad with yellow wood inlaid with silver. The floor was made of white marble marked out with lines of jet in the shape of a five-pointed star. In the corner was an electric fire that glowed warmly. It was more like the entrance to an Italian villa than an old bank.

'I have known Ezra Morgan for many, many years and didn't know he had a son called Jago,' the man said.

'I didn't know myself until the start of the war,' Jago answered. He realised this was the same man who had walked down the street with the umbrella. 'It came as quite a surprise.'

'It is strange that you should hide in the doorway of a bombed-out shop when you come from such a prestigious family,' the man said. 'How is Eagle Moor?'

'I don't know that place. We live at Hawks Moor, south of Whitby,' Jago answered.

'So you do,' the man answered as he stroked his beard, obviously wondering what to do with the boy. 'I am Fredrico Lucca. I am the manager of the Banco Perazzi. In fact, I am the only employee. We have such a limited number of customers that I can do the job alone. Did you know this is a *special* bank?'

'Hugh told me that I should come here when I was in London,' Jago answered.

'Then I shall take care of you,' the man said. His eyes widened warmly and his face broke into a smile. 'You look wet and hungry. Before we do business I shall take care of those things for you.' He beckoned Jago to follow. They walked from the lobby along a wide corridor that seemed to go on for ever to a door made of solid teak inlaid with red beading. 'This is my sitting room. Not every customer gets to see this

106

place,' he laughed.

Lucca opened the heavy door and pushed against the wood. It moved slowly as it opened wide. Jago gasped.

'Bloody beautiful,' he said out loud as his thoughts escaped through his mouth.

'Indeed,' Lucca answered proudly. 'Even I think it is beautiful.'

Jago looked around him. The room was vast. It was as high as it was long. The walls were covered in gold leaf and stretched up to a cornice of marble, carved with the faces of angels. Hanging from the ceiling was a gigantic chandelier that glistened and shone in the electric light. Such was the glow that the room appeared to be without shadow. By the white, rococo fireplace was a gold-framed sofa covered in red velvet.

'I will get you a chair,' Lucca said, and he lifted a plain dining chair from behind the door and placed it opposite the sofa.

'Do you live here?' Jago asked, in awe of his surroundings.

'Occasionally,' Lucca answered. 'Sometimes I find it overpowering . . . Would you like a drink?'

Jago nodded as Lucca scurried from the room, the limp now vanished. Soon he returned carrying a silver tray. Placing it on the small table next to Jago, he poured a glass of wine from a tall decanter.

'I don't like to –' Jago muttered, not wanting to be impolite.

'This isn't wine, Jago. You need something more than that. I take it from the look in your eyes that you have not eaten for some time?' Jago looked to the floor, not knowing what to say.

'I can see you are a Vampyre, Jago. You are in good company.'

Jago took the glass warily. He sniffed the rim. It was blood.

'How did you know I was hungry?' he asked.

'I could hear your stomach rumbling when we were at the door. When I saw you in the street I had an inkling that you were waiting for me but I could not be sure. From the state of your clothes I would say that you have been travelling for some time, and . . . you have the scent of human blood on your coat.'

'Am I like a book for everyone to read?' Jago asked. He sipped from the glass and felt the blood trickle like nectar down the back of his throat.

'If you have lived as long as I have then you can see a great many things,' Lucca said as Jago stared at the two creatures that had appeared on the back of the sofa behind the man. Lucca laughed as he noticed Jago glaring at him. 'Meet Marco and Carlo . . . my ancient *mucaca fuscata* – snow monkeys. Marco is the one with the black mane.'

Jago had never seen such beasts before. They sat on the back of the velvet sofa like a pair of disgruntled old men angry at life. Their beards trailed over their sour faces and with every twitch of their flat noses they would curl back their lips to bare their dirty brown teeth.

'Monkeys?' Jago replied, his word as puzzled as the look on his face.

'I once lived in Florence and supplied money to Yan de Blannen. He gave the creatures to me as a gift and a reminder never to lend money to a blind warrior.' Lucca smirked as if he remembered pleasant times. 'That was in August 1346.'

'That was six hundred years ago,' Jago answered.

'Is it that long? How time flies.' Lucca turned to the monkeys. 'Did you hear what young Jago said? You are six hundred years old.'

'How have they lived so long?' Jago asked as Marco slid from the back of the sofa to sit cross-legged next to his master.

'They are like you and me. I fell in love with them and they have been such good company that I decided to see if the venom could prolong their lives. I decided it had worked when they had outlived my first companion. I am sure that they understand every word I say.' Marco shivered agreeably as he held on to Lucca's arm and picked through his grey beard with fine claws. Carlo sat on the back of the sofa and glared at Jago as if he were an unwelcome guest.

For three hours, Lucca told him of his life in Florence and his travels through Europe and the history of the Banco Perazzi. Jago listened as he sipped from the glass and grew stronger. Soon, the first glimpse of morning etched the corners of the damask curtains that covered the windows. 'And that is how I came to be here and how our lives have crossed.'

Jago sighed, finally feeling dry, full and content. The two macaque monkeys had curled up beside Lucca and appeared to be fast asleep.

'What do they eat?' Jago enquired.

'Blood, human blood . . . They guard the bank when I am away. No one in their right mind would ever dare to break in. Whilst the war was on I had an endless supply, but now I don't know what I will do.' Lucca suddenly looked at his watch. 'Marco, Carlo . . . it is time to show this young man the vault.'

Jago remembered why he was there. He pulled the cord and held the key in his hand as if it were a golden ticket.

'I would like to see what is in the account,' Jago asked.

'Then I will have to check the ledger. Marco and Carlo will take you to the vault and show you the box. All you have to do is tell them the number on the key.'

Jago had not seen a number. He examined the key until he found the minute etching on the stem.

'Number eleven,' he answered.

'Saint Augustine said that eleven was the blazon of sin. It is a symbol of rebellion – well, that is if you believe in numbers,' Lucca joked. 'Take Jago to the vault and find the casket of eleven. I will look in the ledger and discover your wealth.'

With that, Lucca got up from the sofa and walked ably from the room.

The macaques held each other as they looked at Jago and then Marco, the larger of the two, jumped to the floor and coughed. Carlo slinked behind him as if it was all too much trouble and that the young man in their midst was an irrelevant inconvenience.

Jago followed the beasts back down the corridor. Marco grappled with the handle of a large door as Carlo pulled against it. The door opened to reveal a metal staircase that dropped to a floor below. The monkeys slid down the banister, hanging from the stairs and dropping to the floor. Jago trod each metal step warily. Soon he was in the basement of the bank.

It was a cold room, dark and foreboding. The walls were filled with racks and each rack was filled with wooden caskets. It was smaller than the lobby and yet it echoed like a cavern. Tessellated into the tiled floor was the head of a bull. Jago knew this sign from the room where Medea had taken his blood.

Carlo climbed a wall as if it were a tree; he reached for a box and with considerable strength pulled it from the wall. He dragged it across the floor and placed it roughly on a long table in the middle of the room.

Marco held out his hand to Jago and chattered wildly. Then, before he could do anything the monkey jumped, snatching the key from around his neck. He ran to the table, slipped the key in the lock and opened the box. As if he had completed a circus trick, Marco somersaulted backwards, clapping ferociously as he landed on his feet.

Carlo sat in the corner of the room and picked his nose as he watched every move Jago made.

'I suppose you two would like to see what is in the box?' Jago asked the mute twins. 'Then again, you most probably already know.'

Carlo bared his teeth and squawked.

'We try to keep the contents of each box a secret, Jago,' Lucca said as he came down the steps behind him. 'It is a party trick that my two companions know the numbers of the boxes. Since the end of the war, many of them will remain locked for ever. There are not many of us left and I fear for the future.'

'I have been told there are only five hundred in the entire world,' Jago answered, wanting to look into the box alone.

'And yet, there is good news. Since the death of Ezra Morgan, nine million pounds has been paid into his account. That makes a total you share with Hugh of thirty one million, eight hundred and seventy thousand, four hundred and forty-three pounds, ten shillings and nine pence halfpenny,' Lucca said in one breath. 'You are a very wealthy lad. All I need is a signature from your brother and you can take your money.'

'Hugh has gone away,' Jago answered.

'Then the money has to remain in the bank,' Lucca insisted, his tone harsher.

'I need a million pounds to pay off a debt that Ezra Morgan refused to pay,' Jago said.

The macaques bristled excitedly, jumped on the table and looked in the box.

'You can have whatever is in the box because you have the key. What is in your account must stay there, debt or not,' Lucca answered apologetically. He took out a pair of gold spectacles from his pocket and hung them on the bridge of his long nose. 'If it is another Vampyre, I can arbitrate in the debt and assure them the money will be paid.'

'It is not one of us,' Jago murmured. 'It is a man called Heston Walpurgis.'

At the mention of the name, Marco leapt from the table and snarled at Jago. His brother stood his ground, teeth bared and ready to strike.

'Not a name to mention in this place, Jago. That man has caused much trouble in my world. I advised Ezra not to work with him. He is a charlatan and a fraud. Much of what he sells is just worthless junk.'

'He said he will kill Hugh if the money is not paid,' Jago answered.

'Ah, the flecks of blood on your jacket – who do they belong to?' Lucca asked.

'Walpurgis. At the Hotel Julius.'

'I thought so. Is he still alive?'

'I only injured him,' Jago replied, knowing he had said too much.

'Then like any wounded animal he is even more dangerous.' Lucca clicked his fingers and silenced the gibbering and barking of the macaques. 'Marco, Carlo, we will leave this man to see the box alone. It's not for us.'

Lucca clicked his fingers and climbed back up the spiral staircase. The beasts followed, getting to the top before him and swinging on the bars until he called for them to stop.

Jago was alone. He moved the table candles closer to the box and then looked inside. Wrapped in a silk cloth was a gold case. The cover sprang back as he opened the case quickly. There in the lid was a picture of his mother. It was taken at Tower Bridge by the river. She held a small child in her arms and smiled at the camera as if she was in love.

In the box were ten gold coins. Next to them were two envelopes, one written out to him and the other to Hugh. Jago took the letter addressed to himself and opened it. Inside was another key. It was the size of his finger, with two small prongs at each end. Attached to the key was a small tag on which was written: *Banco Perazzi – Number Seven.*

Jago searched the walls and found the box. He placed it on the table and used the key. The lid opened easily and he looked inside. There, wrapped in newspaper was the handle of an old knife. It was gold, encrusted with jewels, and fitted snugly into his palm. Jago held the knife handle in his hand. As he squeezed it the handle seemed to cling to him as if they were one. Suddenly a blade shot from within. It was silver and sharp as a stiletto. Inscribed on the blade was a name: *ERASMUS STRACKAN.*

[11]

Mucaca Fuscata

AS LUCCA RETURNED, Jago squeezed the handle of
the knife again and the blade slid within, out of sight.
He put the handle deep into the pocket of his leather coat.
Marco and Carlo swung down the banister of the spiral
staircase and landed on the table as he closed the lid of the
box and locked it again. The monkeys screamed angrily and
picked at the stone floors.

'One thing leads to another?' Lucca asked. 'I have been
thinking that I would like to help you, but it may take some
time. There could be a way of paying Heston Walpurgis and
getting him off your back for good. Did he say what Ezra
Morgan had purchased from him?' Lucca asked inquisitively.

Jago didn't know how to answer. Lucca was a Vampyre.

'He mentioned a diamond. He said that whenever there
was a war, Vampyres always put their money into objects of
value.'

'I know that to be so true. When Napoleon ravaged Europe
I recall that half the money was taken from the bank. People
feared it would become worthless. It was then that I decided
to open a repository.'

'For what?' Jago asked.

'For all the things of value that they wanted to keep safe. A bank is not just for the keeping of money,' he answered as the macaques prowled closer to Jago, their eyes wide and teeth bared.

'Did Ezra mention a diamond to you?' Jago asked, wondering if he could help him find it.

'That would be confidential. I would have to have a letter of authority signed by Hugh and then I could divulge that information,' Lucca answered. He rubbed his beard, his eyes darting around the room. 'If you were to stay for a while I could see what I could do. I really want to help your situation.' Lucca stopped suddenly and looked at him. 'How did you find yourself in London again?'

'I came to the bank. To sort out my finances. I am looking for my brother.'

From his answer, Lucca could tell he was lying. 'Very well – how would you – what would you . . .' Lucca took a deep breath. 'You are lying, Jago Harker,' he said eventually. 'I know who you are and your story is not quite convincing.'

Lucca stepped back towards the staircase, the macaques protecting him with their coughs and snarls. Marco stood to full height and lashed out with his claws.

'It's true,' Jago insisted. 'I have the right to this – I am looking for Hugh Morgan.'

'You have escaped from the Maleficarum. Whilst you were down here, I spoke to Mina Karlstein. She thought you were at the Hotel Julius.'

'Why did you do that?' Jago argued as he looked for a way to get to the stairs before Marco or Carlo.

'Any mention of your name will attract interest. I jour-

116

neyed north on the night of the Lyrid of Saturn. I came to Hawks Moor to watch a once-in-a-lifetime event and you spoilt it for us all. When the wave struck the coast I was lucky to survive. Since that time, the name of Jago Harker has always been on my lips.'

The monkeys jumped back and forth screaming and howling as if they were about to attack.

'What are you going to do?' Jago asked.

'It is not what will I do – but what have I done?' Lucca answered as he backed further up the staircase.

'Let me out of here,' Jago demanded.

'Not possible. They are on their way from Hampstead. They will be with us soon,' he replied. Marco and Carlo swung on the staircase.

'I can't stay, I have to find Hugh Morgan.'

'Hugh has already been found. He is quite safe. It is *you* that has escaped and now that is soon to be rectified,' Lucca answered, his voice monotone and sharp.

'But you don't understand. I have to find Hugh.'

As he spoke, Lucca clicked his fingers twice. The macaques were suddenly silent.

'On my next instruction, they will rip you limb from limb and eat your bones, Jago Harker. You are becoming quite troublesome and it needs to stop *now*,' Lucca insisted as the macaques waited at the foot of the stairs for his instructions. 'I want you to follow me. You will be safe. They will only attack if I give the command.'

'Where are you taking me?' he asked.

'There is a room. Made for occasions just as this. You will be kept there until *they* arrive.'

Jago did as he said. The macaques reluctantly crawled aside, hackles raised, as he followed Lucca up the spiral steps and into the corridor. The two beasts crept behind him, keeping their distance.

Lucca walked ahead, not turning back, knowing Jago would do what he asked. The creatures would see to that. He had never known anyone dare take on the beasts. He led on, along the passageway with its marble cornices and dangling candelabra. Then, as he reached the lobby with its curved staircase to the upper floor, he flicked the handle of a small wooden door.

'How long will I have to stay?' Jago asked, certain this was a prison.

'Time is in our hands now, Jago. They should not be long.' Lucca stared at Jago, counting in his heart the slow passing of each second. 'If you would care to step inside.'

Jago looked into the room. It was small and dark; the air appeared thick with smoke that ebbed out into the passageway like a tide.

'What is this place?' he asked.

'It was once the place where we would hide. Now it is used to keep people until we decide what to do with them,' Lucca answered as he waved his hand for Jago to enter.

'Where shall I sit?' Jago asked.

'Sit?' answered Lucca, thinking the question strange 'Where shall you *sit*?'

'I can't see,' Jago said, stepping closer to the door.

Lucca peered in as he held the doorframe to steady himself. The macaques bristled in anger as if they could sense what was to come.

118

'I'm sure it will be quite comfortable for you,' Lucca replied.

Jago struck. He kicked the man in the back and then pushed him into the room. The door slammed shut. Jago slipped the catch and locked the door.

'See how you like it,' he shouted as he ran towards the lobby.

The macaques hesitated. Marco leapt at the door, pulling on the handle, as Carlo screamed for his master to be released.

'*Kill him!*' Lucca shouted.

Marco leapt from the door and looked around him. Jago was already at the front door of the bank. He screeched to Carlo as he saw Jago trying to escape. Then, puffing himself up to his full height, the monkey set off at a fast pace.

Before Jago could open the door, Marco leapt across the tiled floor and landed on his back. He dug his jagged claws into the leather coat, and Jago screamed as the talons punctured the skin. Then came the first bite. The monkey ripped at the leather coat with its teeth as Jago twisted to be free.

Carlo was striding across the lobby towards him, gibbering and snarling. The monkey ran faster as Jago turned. Then it leapt for his throat. As the beast flew through the air, Jago ducked and rolled on the floor. Marco was thrown from his back. Quickly he got to his feet and began to run. Taking the stairs two at a time, he was soon on the ornate upper landing. It bowed round in a gentle arch, following the corner of the building. Its gold walls were hung with ancient pictures in gilt frames. Jago ran, the macaques chasing faster. Ahead he could see an open doorway and stairs beyond.

The monkeys ran across the furniture, knocking large Chinese vases to the ground, smashing them out of the way to get at Jago. He dared not look back, fixing his eyes on the doorway ahead. Three more strides, he thought to himself.

It was then that Marco struck, grabbing Jago by the leg. He fell to the floor as Carlo pounced. Jago slid across the floor and smashed into the wall. The monkeys were upon him. They snatched at his leather coat with their talons. Marco lashed out at his face. Jago dug his hand deep into his pocket and clutched the handle of the knife, and the blade leapt instantly in his finger. He stabbed Marco in the upper arm, the blade slicing through the bone as if it were crusted bread. The monkey screamed as its blood splattered the walls. Carlo jumped back as his companion fell to the ground holding its wound, its eyes wide and fearful.

Jago looked at the beast. It was as if whatever possessed the creature had been exorcised. Gone was the menace of its stare. No longer did it look as if it were a monster. Marco cowered and whimpered, holding out its hand to Jago. A single tear rolled down its cheek, as if it knew it was dying. In that moment Jago saw what he had done. He held the knife in his hand and looked at the blood-covered blade. Marco cried as Carlo came to him and encircled his companion in his arms. Together they sat shaking and fearful, never letting Jago out of their glare.

He could see that the monkey was dying. He could feel the pain of guilt wrestle in his mind, twisting his thoughts, and he didn't know what to do. He got to his knees and reached out towards Marco with an assuaging hand. The beast responded, reaching out with his fingers until tip touched tip. Jago reached further and gripped the hand, hoping the macaque would know the guilt he felt.

It was as if Marco smiled – no longer like a dumb beast, he smiled as if he were a creature with a soul. Jago felt his own pain as he watched the creature slowly dying. He moved closer. Carlo edged back, fearful Jago would strike at him.

'Don't worry,' Jago said softly. 'I didn't mean . . .'

Marco hunched his shoulders and shivered as Jago touched the wounded shoulder. The creature sighed as if death was upon him. Jago looked at Marco as the monkey surveyed his face with a sentient stare.

Then, without warning, Marco spat hot blood into Jago's face. It leapt towards him, dragging its broken arm as it bit at his neck. Jago fell back, taken by surprise. The monkey ripped at his face with his claw as Jago fended off the blows.

He knew the other monkey was making ready to jump at him. He could see the beast hanging from a candelabrum on the wall, waiting to drop. Taking the knife, he stabbed Marco again. The beast let out a final piercing scream and slumped on his chest. The blow was fatal. Carlo hung from the wall and bared his teeth. He turned his head back and forth as if he could hear something far away.

Jago threw the dead monkey from him and got to his feet. He edged back to the doorway. From outside, in the empty street, came the slamming of three car doors. The monkey chattered excitedly as if it knew what was to come.

Stepping to the window, Jago looked into the street. There below were three sedan cars. Six men and a woman crossed the road towards the bank. He looked at the woman's face and instantly saw it was Mina Karlstein.

Carlo backed away and ran slowly towards the lobby. Jago didn't follow. He knew he had to get out of the bank. Taking the stairway, he spiralled down to the floor below. The corridor led to the back of the building. From far away he could hear the door open and voices echoing through the building. A man shouted as the cell was opened and Lucca was set free. It was as if they were coming closer and were somehow all around him.

His pace quickening, Jago ran through the darkened corridors until he reached a large wooden door. He twisted the iron key and pulled the door. It opened easily and Jago stepped inside. In the shadows of the room in the dim light that fell from a high crescent window, Jago could see stacked wooden cases. They were laid out in aisles and went on and on in what he could now see was a vast warehouse. Jago knew that this was the repository that Lucca had spoken of.

Making his way speedily to the far side, Jago cut back and forth through the aisles. Each case or box was marked with a name, a date and its contents. He read them as he walked by. Some were filled with paintings. Jago read the names of Goya, Titian, Holbein and Caravaggio. Other boxes were filled with silver and gold. On one it just read: *Lion's head – gold teeth – ruby eyes*. He could not find the name of Ezra Morgan, or any mention of the Oracle diamond.

Jago gave up his search as he heard the door open and footsteps come into the repository. On either side, men searched in and out of the artifacts. He knew that he could not escape. Then he looked up. On a box high above him sat Carlo. The monkey stared down.

He buried the knife in the lining of his coat next to the

Sinan. He hoped it would not be found. The monkey began to chatter and call out. Jago ran. He twisted in and out of the aisles, trying to get to the door before those who now pursued him. Carlo followed, jumping from box to box and shouting as he gave chase.

Jago reached out, took the handle and pulled. The door opened.

There, standing in the entrance, wrapped tightly in her black coat, was Karlstein. She was the same in every way as Jago had seen her before but strangely, her hair was different. Gone were the shaved sides and mass of ringlets piled on top. Now her hair was bleach-blond and cut long, held back by a gold brooch.

'Jago Harker, nice to meet you,' she said with a smile. 'I have heard so much about you and none of it good.'

'Mina Karlstein?' Jago asked.

'No – her twin sister, Lana Karlstein.' The woman laughed.

Whatever came next, Jago could not remember. There was a sudden jerk of her fist, the light dimmed and then he woke in the fine room in which he had talked with Lucca. He lay on the velvet sofa and felt the pain in his face. Lana Karlstein sat on the chair by the fireplace. Lucca stood next to her, clutching the body of the monkey as if it were a child.

'You killed him,' Lucca snarled, his face flushed with blood, his hair ragged and pulled across his brow. 'There was no need for any of this. You are a fool – that is what you are, Jago Harker.'

'Lucca was quite attached to Marco. He was a good companion for hundreds of years,' Lana answered as she studied Jago. 'I have never known one who looks so frail cause so

123

much concern in our world.'

'I didn't ask for any of this,' Jago said as he tried to sit up. 'You have taken away my life.'

'If you had just done what was expected, none of this would have happened. Do you know that many of us blame you for the death of all of our friends? They say that it was because Noel Kinross became so obsessed with you that he decided to kill as many Vampyres as he could with that stupid bomb. Then we are told that we cannot kill you, because you are *special*. Yet no one in the Maleficarum will tell us why.'

'And now you want to lock me away at Luna Negri?' Jago asked as he looked at Lana and realised her face was identical in every way to her sister's. Even the red lips and kohl-lined eyes were alike. It was just the hair that set them apart.

'That will be the best place for you. I spent some time there myself for a minor misdemeanour. Twenty-seven years to reflect on what I had done was a small price to pay,' Lana said as she took the remnants from the glass on the table next to her and sipped the drink.

'Your sister promised to keep my friends safe,' Jago said.

'You promised not to escape,' Lana answered as Lucca rocked the corpse of Marco back and forth and hummed gently as if to rock it to sleep.

'I didn't. A man called Heston Walpurgis came. He killed your companions and took me captive. I managed to escape.'

'Escape? From Walpurgis? I can hardly believe it,' she answered, her eyes glaring in disbelief. 'He would kill you. He knows who you are.'

'Walpurgis wants a diamond and thinks we have money to

pay him,' Jago answered.

'So it was true,' Lucca said. 'It was Walpurgis. He has the blood on his jacket to prove it, Lana.'

'Then Walpurgis is an added complication. We should find out who he is working for,' Lana said. 'Walpurgis is a mercenary. He never works for himself. We should visit Hotel Julius.'

'Where will you take me?' Jago asked Lana Karlstein, who appeared to be more relaxed than her sister and smiled at him constantly as if intrigued.

'Don't worry, Jago. We will take good care of you. You should fear Walpurgis more than the Maleficarum. He has never let anyone get away from him before and no matter where in the world you are, if you have hurt him, he will demand an eye for an eye at the very least . . .'

12

Crillon de Paris

IN THE PRIVATE COMPARTMENT of the evening train to Paris, Jago tried to look out through the gaps in the shuttered window. When they had left the bank Lana Karlstein had waved goodbye to Lucca, who still clutched the body of Marco as he stood in the small doorway. A car had taken them through London to a small station on a disused railway. From there, a single coach drawn by a steam engine had taken them to the coast. A waiting boat crossed the Channel and now another train took them across the flatlands of France.

Lana Karlstein sat uncomfortably close to him on the plush leather couchette. She had talked all the way from London, telling Jago the intricate and often violent details of her life. Lana seemed to know the identity of everyone. She was a hunter and seemed to enjoy the chase more than the kill. Jago had been particularly intrigued about the man in Paris. He knew that was where they were taking him for the night – he had heard one of her companions say this to the guard on the train. The man had helped them into the private compartment and for his troubles was given a large banknote pressed into the palm of his hand.

As they had left Calais, Lana had snuggled closer and whispered the story of the Crillon Hotel and Suite de Napoleon. She had giggled about how during the war she had stayed there for a night. An officer of the occupying force had taken her for dinner. In return she had gone back to his room.

'It was quite a surprise when he found out I was a Vampyre,' she had joked in a way that sounded as if she was talking about finding a lost relative. 'The look in his eyes, and the tears were hard to understand. He begged and begged that I should not take his life, but hey, who cares, there was a war on . . .'

Lana laughed as she told Jago how she had taken the body and thrown it from the roof to the Place de la Concorde. 'Very fitting. In the Revolution, over thirteen hundred people met their death by the guillotine right outside the Hotel. I don't think anyone suspected. He was just another soldier driven mad by the war who jumped from the roof. The view was amazing – as he fell I could see the Eiffel Tower. It was so pretty.'

Jago had tried not to answer. In some way she was so unlike her sister – so unlike that he found he couldn't stop looking at her. Lana could see this and as the carriage rattled through France, she stared back at him, hoping he would speak. She was equally fascinated.

Eventually the train slowed down as it reached the outskirts of Paris. Throughout the journey, a tall companion with a slit moustache had sat opposite them with his face buried in the pages of a French newspaper. When not looking at Lana, Jago had tried to see what the photographs showed. They were mostly of troops returning home and people rebuilding after the devastation of the war. In the bottom corner of the front page was one picture that caught his attention. Lana saw him looking.

'What is it?' Jago asked.

Lana reached across and took the paper from the companion. She read the story as Jago looked at the photograph of a dead wolf being held up by two hunters.

'It says that there were two deaths in a forest. The men lived at an abbey and they were killed by a wolf.'

'I didn't know such creatures still existed,' Jago said as Lana rolled the paper and slipped it onto the seat next to her.

'In the war there was no one to kill the wolves so their number increased,' Lana answered.

'So you read French?' he asked, trying to make conversation.

'I am fluent in eleven languages. When you have lived as long as I have you have plenty of time. It helps when you have to move on,' Lana said, her voice reluctant as if she was remembering where she had been throughout her life.

'Do you miss your mother?' Jago asked.

'Why, out of everything you could have said, did you ask that?' Lana replied, as if it was the one question she did not want to answer.

'Mina told me about the doctor and the plague and your mother dying,' he answered.

'I miss her very much. She was too far gone to save. Mina was the first and then me. If it had not been for Doctor Salafia, the Black Death would have killed us all.'

'Are Vampyres safe from disease?' Jago asked her.

'The ravages of the body trouble us not,' Lana said. She

ran her finger across the back of his hand. 'Well, not the bad things.'

The steam engine lurched as it braked suddenly. The companion looked to the door and slipped his hand into his coat pocket.

'The guard told me there would be problems as we got to Paris. They found an unexploded bomb by the side of the track. The trains have to go slowly in case it explodes,' he said as he looked at Lana.

'We are not immune to explosions, Jago. As you well know.' Lana looked at him even more intensely. 'Tell me. What was it like to be there that night – when the bomb exploded?'

'I was frightened,' Jago answered truthfully. 'The sky burnt bright white . . . The air was on fire and then came the screaming.'

'I lost a good friend that night, Aldus Flood. Did you ever meet him?'

'He saved my life and then he gave it away again,' he answered as he thought of Medea.

'I heard that you were reluctant to become one of us,' she said as she linked her arm to his and rested back in the couchette.

'It was not something I had planned,' he said, enjoying being near to someone again.

Jago felt strange inside. He had forgotten what it was like. Lana smelt of spices and vanilla. She was warm and comfortable, easy to speak to and beautiful.

'But even things we have not planned can turn out for the good,' she said. She touched his hand softly, as if she were drawing the letters of a word on his skin. She turned and looked Jago in the face. 'This isn't a bad thing that we are do-ing. Taking you to Luna Negri was the last thing we wanted.'

'I am being put in prison. It doesn't seem a good thing to me,' Jago replied.

'It isn't like that. I spent many years there. I killed another Vampyre. We were hunting the same blood and he got in the way. It was just one of those things. The Maleficarum sent me to Luna Negri to think about what I had done. Imagine it to be a monastery and not a prison.'

'Are they not the same?' he asked. 'Don't both take away your freedom?'

'Were you free in Scotland? Stuck in a draughty castle for year after year pretending you were sick?' she asked.

Jago shrugged his shoulders and pulled up the collar of his coat.

'But I could come and go if I wanted,' he said.

'You would have been stopped before you got to the gate. At least at Luna Negri you will be amongst friends.'

'I have to find Hugh Morgan. Walpurgis has to be stopped,' Jago said.

'Perhaps Hugh will not be far away from you,' she whispered. 'Sometimes if you stop looking you often find that for which you search.' Lana smiled and squeezed his hand. 'I have been told to stay there with you until it is decided. They want me to get to know what you are like. The Maleficarum don't want to kill you, Jago. They would just like to solve the dilemma of your birth.'

As Lana spoke the train rattled along the track towards Paris. The companion stood by the locked door as the train drew into Gare du Nord. From inside, Jago could hear the shouting on the platform. The steam engine hissed and moaned as it pushed against the iron buffers.

'Gare du Nord,' shouted a man on the platform as the door opened.

Jago stepped outside, his arm gripped by the companion. Lana Karlstein held his hand as they walked towards the entrance.

A small, shrew-like fat man scurried towards them. He was dressed from toe to hat in priestly black. The tell-tale white collar fitted tightly around his triple chin. He eyed them through small round spectacles that perched on his long proboscis as if they could be of no use.

'It is this way – the car is waiting,' the man said as he clutched a thick black book in his hands. 'Exciting, exciting – nothing like this has ever happened since . . . since they chopped off the head of Robespierre.' The priest turned on his stacked heels and went ahead of them, pushing his way through the crowds to a small door at the far side of the station. 'If you can keep up with me. There are those who would not take kindly to you being here.'

'And who would that be?' Lana asked.

'I have heard that there are followers of the Cult of the Oracle within the city. Rumours are rife that the Oracle diamond has been found. I heard only the other day –'

Lana Karlstein pushed the priest in the back to bid him be silent.

'Then you should not speak of it so noisily, little man,' she said as he led them through the door and out of the station into the busy street.

The companion dragged Jago to the waiting car that was

parked on the pavement, its engine running. He glanced at the buildings and saw no sign of the war. It looked so different to London, with its bombed-out buildings. Here, everything looked neat and in order, as if it had been untouched.

The priest got in the front seat of the car. Jago was pushed in the back. He slid across the red leather to the far door. The companion got in next to him as Lana closed the door. As they drove through the streets, Jago looked out of the window. He watched men drinking coffee in street-front bars. Packs of dogs ran down the alleyways, and on the busy pavements people pushed past each other without speaking.

'Was Paris ever bombed?' Jago asked, wondering why the city looked so untouched.

'Just the car factory and some of the areas to the south of the city. Paris is too beautiful to be destroyed, even by the most wicked-hearted people,' the priest answered without turning around. 'The Resistance blew up a bridge, but it did no damage.'

Jago slipped back into the seat of the car. He stared blankly at all that passed his eyes. He could soon smell the river. The car pulled up outside a large stone building that looked like a museum. It was emblazoned with lights that shone upwards against the stone and cast shadows from the Corinthian pillars. A man in a top hat, a long red coat and dazzling black shoes strode across a red carpet and opened the sedan door. Lana Karlstein got out and looked around as if she was checking to see if they had been followed.

'It's fine,' she muttered to her companion, who slipped from the car and pulled Jago along with him. 'Welcome to the Crillon Hotel, Jago.'

'We're staying here?' he asked, looking up at what he thought was a palace.

'Sadly, the George was full and the Ritz is not safe for us. We are only here for the night,' she said as she walked towards the entrance, followed by the priest. 'We will be fine,' she said.

She suddenly realised that the priest was behind her like a little lap dog. 'There are things that I need to tell you. Things that have changed,' he muttered as he handed her a cross on a chain with black beads.

Jago did not hear what Lana said in reply. All he could see was that the priest bowed, doffed his stupid hat and walked away still clutching the black book.

Lana Karlstein didn't check in at the desk. She walked straight to the stairs. They were soon on the third floor. Pulling a key from her jacket she opened a door that looked like an old broom cupboard.

'This will have to do. The Suite de Napoleon is busy.'

Flicking on the light switch she walked inside.

Jago stared. The room was remarkably similar to Lucca's at the Bank Perazzi. Even the red velvet couch, the leather chairs and the expensive-looking drapes over the windows were all the same.

'It's –' Jago said.

'What we have in taste we sometimes lack in originality,' Lana answered.

Slumping to the sofa, Jago looked around the room. It was oppressively opulent. The walls shone with gold, and everything was outlined in silver. He realised it was even more intricate, even more ornate than the Bank Perazzi.

133

'How did you just have the key?' he asked.

'We own a room in several hotels and in some cities we own the hotel. It became necessary during the Inquisition. Vampyres were often thought to be witches and we were burnt and tortured. There was once a whole legion of Vampyre knights. They were all put to death on 13 October 1307. The Emperor thought that it would be a good way to get his hands on our money. That has always been the same. People find out about us and our wealth and then want to steal it from us. When the Maleficarum first met, it was decided to provide a place of safety for a Vampyre in every town.'

'And in every town a companion?' Jago asked.

'It is better than working for a living,' she answered. 'Good food, good company and more money than most people could ever spend. In many lifetimes it is amazing what can be made.'

'And now – what will happen now?' Jago asked. 'Why are you at war?'

'Because we are vain,' she said politely as she unpinned her hat and slipped the coat from her shoulders. 'There is something about our condition that makes us preen ourselves like beautiful birds and think we are better than anyone else. No different to humans.'

Her companion laughed. In the entire journey, Jago had not been told his name. The man appeared to be surly and arrogant. He bit his fingernails and picked his teeth. Jago could see that his clothes were threadbare. The man smiled at him as he pulled a chair close to the door.

'The priest spoke about a Cult of the Oracle. Is that to do

with the diamond?' asked Jago as he looked to see if there was another way from the room.

'It's not for talking about, not here,' she answered brusquely. 'The priest is not one of us. He is another companion.'

'Didn't think it would leave much room for what he believed in,' Jago answered.

'In all my years I have met many unbelievers who garland their necks with the collar of a priest.' Lana looked quickly at her watch. 'There is something I have to do before it is late. I have an appointment.' She looked at Jago and then to the companion. 'Look after him and make sure he is still here when I get back.'

Lana Karlstein picked up her coat and left the room. She took the stairs, pressing the button of the elevator on every floor that she walked through. She listened like a child as it stopped on every landing, following her to the lobby.

In the street she turned right and walked across the Place de la Concorde. From the Champs Elysées she crossed the bridge and took the steps from the Quai d'Orsay to the footpath that ran along the river. She waited in the shadows and watched the night boats chug up river. There was no meeting, no appointment. Lana twisted the cross and beads in her pocket and fumbled with her fingers over the rosary. It felt uncomfortable to the touch; each bead snagged in her fingers as if it didn't want to be handled. She thought of the man who had once tried to stop her by holding a crucifix to her face. She could still see his frightened eyes as she snatched it from him and cursed the old wives' tales.

She did not have to wait for long. Soon came the sound of anxious footsteps walking the towpath. They came from the direction of Notre Dame. Lana hid in the darkness under the bridge of Pont Royal. She could hardly hold her breath for the excitement that bubbled within her.

'Going far?' she asked as she stepped into the light. 'I am lost, not a native of Paris – a tourist,' she said in the impeccable French of an aristocrat.

'Not far,' the woman answered suspiciously. 'Where do you want to be?'

'Notre Dame,' Lana answered as she smiled.

The woman looked at her. It was as if she had seen her before.

'Do I know you?' she asked. A sudden and sharp churning of fear swelled inside her as if her stomach would burst. 'I know your face.'

'My name is Lana.' She said no more. The woman didn't have time to run or cry out. Lana fell upon her with such force that it knocked the woman to the ground. Her red shoes fell from her feet and rolled into the river, and her skirt ripped as she hit the wall. It was probable that she was dead before Lana bit into her neck. She was already limp, her arms flattened on the cold stones, her head to one side. Lana drank until she heard a car stop on the bridge. Doors slammed and the shadow of a man was cast across the towpath. Taking the rosary from her pocket, she placed it into the woman's hand, taking time to curl the dead fingers around it. 'Should be easy to find him from that,' she said as she slipped off her coat, smoothed the lines of her trousers and walked along the bank of the Seine like a courtesan.

13

Curzon Street

THE ALLEYWAY AT THE BACK of Curzon Street that led from Market Mews was littered with broken slates and smashed wood. Nothing had been cleared away since the end of the war. A bombed wall had fallen across and blocked the alley and Walpurgis found the broken bricks hard to climb. The wound to his leg burnt. His body shuddered in pain, even though Julia had brought a doctor who had given Walpurgis morphine. As he walked, he felt the tight bandage and the wadding that had been pressed against the deep incision and he cursed Jago Harker, vowing to seek his revenge on him.

'Ruined a good suit,' Walpurgis said as he climbed the rubble. 'Got her killed.'

Pulling himself up on the capstone of the wall he looked along the alley. It was dark, empty and foreboding. He waited to see if he could hear anyone. The kitchen door of Crockford's Casino was open. A man in a small white hat and apron leant against the wall drinking coffee and looking up into the clear night sky. Walpurgis waited. The man threw the dregs of his coffee against the wall and then went inside, the slam of the door echoing in the alleyway.

Beyond the door was the fire escape. It clung to the back of the building like a spider's web cut from rusted iron. The steps slanted back and forth up the building to the terrace on the roof.

Walpurgis looked up. He knew that this was where Ozymandias was staying. It was where they had first met to do business. This was 30 Curzon Street, with rooms that had been rented on the top floor of the Crockford's Casino. It had been some years ago when Ozymandias had asked him to search for the Hand of Glory. It was believed that this had the power to keep people asleep when the waxed fingers of the severed hand were lit. To Walpurgis it was just a superstitious trinket, and when he promptly discovered and sold the artifact to Ozymandias he couldn't believe how anyone could get so excited over a dried-out hand with tanned leather skin stretched over old bones.

'If only you knew what it meant to me,' Ozymandias had said on the evening when Walpurgis had presented the Hand of Glory to him in a wooden box. 'This is the hand of my dearest companion, Lucinda Grijak. She was hanged for murder in Whitby many years ago. It was a crime she did not commit, for the victim was already dead,' Ozymandias had insisted.

Walpurgis knew that he was wrong. He had bought the hand from a butcher and blood-seller in Kensal Green only two weeks before. He took it back to his rooms in Corpus Christi College wrapped in a hessian sack and there had transformed the recently dead hand to that of an ancient artifact. This he had done by dry-roasting it in the college oven whilst the cook slept, tanning with alum and then scrubbing with boot polish. Walpurgis had then covered the hand in wax and used it to illuminate his room for the following week. By the time he had sold it to Ozymandias it looked as though it was a thousand years old. What made him even more merry was that Ozymandias was so blinded by his desire for the ancient and mystical that he could not see that the hand was that of a man. A man who was obviously large, brutal and at some time in his life had had a finger bitten off by a dog. This was not the fair hand of Ozymandias's favourite companion, Lucinda Grijak.

As he stood in the alleyway and looked up, Walpurgis wondered how he would ever climb the fire escape. He had thought of going into the building through the front door, but was unsure of his reception. Walpurgis had the look of a rogue. This had been his handicap since birth. Even though he had lectured at Cambridge he could not escape the demeanour of a ruffian.

Forcing himself onto the iron steps, he made his way up the staircase. On every landing he stopped and looked back. He was sure that blood was seeping from the wound. Finally he stepped onto the veranda. He looked up and counted the stars of Ursa Major. They were bright and even in the city could be seen clearly. His eyes followed the stars that pointed to Polaris.

Walpurgis swallowed hard. He found freedom a strange friend. Throughout the war, since being captured by the Gestapo he had been kept in a small room. He was never allowed to see the world outside. His daily life consisted of eating lice-filled food, scrubbing his cell and counting the stones in the wall. Now he stood under the canopy of heaven and felt as if he would be consumed by its capaciousness. He trembled at the heavens above him, knowing he was feeble and frail. The blackness stretched out endlessly into space. Time was meaningless, life useless.

'We are but a flower of the field; when the wind blows over it the flower is gone and the ground knows it no more,' Ozymandias said as he stepped from the double doors of the apartment that overlooked the veranda. 'I wondered if you would call on me. I was informed by the Hotel Julius that Madame Arantez was no more.'

'Did you kill her?' Walpurgis asked, thankful that he was no longer alone under the weight of the stars that he could feel pressing down from space.

'She was a good friend. More of a friend to me than she was to you.' Ozymandias paused and sighed. He rolled the hazard dice in his hand and looked at Walpurgis. 'A strange game, hazard . . . The rules are complicated, the betting difficult, and yet I am addicted. With a throw of the dice I believe I can change fate. I only wish I could throw them and win her back.'

'Did you send the assassin?' Walpurgis asked.

'To kill my own friend?' he sighed in disbelief.

'Then who did?' Walpurgis replied as he walked into the room that lay beyond the doors to the veranda.

'I have enemies and you have enemies. Any one of them could have planned this. It is not a secret that you are back in London. In fact, I was speaking to a man this very evening who was worried you would kill him.' Ozymandias lounged in a high-backed leather chair that stood in the middle of the spotlessly neat room, void of any character.

'But they knew where I was. The assassin even gave me a message.' Walpurgis picked up a folded copy of *The Times* newspaper from the table by the door and read the headline.

'Was it pertinent?' he asked.

'He said that I was a cheat and a liar and that he had come on behalf of the Oracle,' Walpurgis answered as he placed the newspaper back on the desk and rubbed the smudged ink from his fingers.

'The Oracle . . . I wondered if that name would ever be mentioned,' Ozymandias said earnestly. 'We are living in troubled times. I find that when there are external forces at work, people often turn to religion.'

'Even Vampyres?'

'We are not immune from fantastical thoughts. It is not only true-blood humans who find they have to invent a supreme being to fulfil their fearful lives. The Cult of the Oracle has come and gone throughout the centuries. There have been times when it was almost forgotten. Now, my dear Heston, we are in the midst of a crisis. People once again turn to what they cannot see in the hope it will help them.'

Ozymandias looked worried. His brow wrinkled as he rubbed his drawn face.

'I take it that the Oracle diamond has an importance in all this?' Walpurgis asked.

'That is why Ezra Morgan wanted the diamond so badly,' he said as he watched Walpurgis limp to the door. 'He too had begun to believe in the Oracle. Rumours had spread amongst the Maleficarum and even Strackan feared what was to come.'

'And what do you get for believing?' he asked.

141

'The Cult believes that the Oracle was the first-ever Vampyre. It goes back beyond the time anyone can remember and suggests that the creator of us all is still alive. No one knows who or where it is. Some thought that it was Strackan, but many know that he was born a man. The Oracle – if it exists – is far older and far wiser. When you found the diamond, this was a sign that what was spoken of would come true.'

'It is poppycock and we know it,' Walpurgis replied. 'If there was such a Vampyre they would have been discovered long ago.'

'At the centre of the faith is the belief that the Oracle lived amongst us and we didn't know it. The creature secretly touched all of our lives. Now that conviction grows and grows. Whoever has the diamond can control the Cult of the Oracle.'

'So I take it you don't believe?' Walpurgis asked as the wound in his leg throbbed.

'I was an atheist in life and I am still the same in death. I believe in that which I can see, and I have never seen a god – or an Oracle. With each day that passes more of our kind will be added. Soon we will be strong again. I intend to be in control and I would like you to help me.'

'I would never be a companion,' Walpurgis said.

'I would not want your blood, just your able assistance in eliminating any *problems* . . .'

Walpurgis stared at the man. Ozymandias looked younger than he had before. With each hunt for blood he had been transformed. The blood of the chase apeared to be more efficacious than that freely given or bought from the blood-traders who lived in the back streets of London. They diluted that taken from people with animal blood, water and red dye. It did not have the same effect as blood taken from a frightened life chased through the night and then snuffed out.

'I see you are hunting more?' he asked Ozymandias.

Ozymandias got to his feet and looked in the mirror that hung on the hide-covered walls.

'I didn't think it could be noticed, Heston,' he answered as he smiled at the reflection of himself in the looking glass. 'I was only thinking the other day how wonderful I felt. So old and yet so young . . .'

'Surely hunting attracts attention?' Walpurgis enquired.

'Now that we have Bloomsbury House things are kept secret.' Ozymandias offered the words like a baited hook, knowing that Walpurgis would not be able to resist. 'It is a better game than hazard.'

'I think I know what you are doing,' Walpurgis said as Ozymandias took out an ivory comb and ran it through his hair.

'It is not as wicked as it seems. We offer a thousand pounds to anyone who can get from the attic of the house to the front door. One Vampyre waits and as the victim makes their way from the building we give chase. All they know is that it is a matter of life and death.'

'They don't know that you chase them for their blood?' he asked.

'No. That we keep to ourselves. You would be surprised what people will do for a thousand pounds.'

'Does anyone ever win?' Walpurgis asked.

'There was a woman who managed to escape. She was a

tramp. I had found her under the arches at Charing Cross. I thought that she would be caught within the first five yards. Sadly, I was wrong. She outwitted an old friend and got to the door.'

'And did she get the money?' Walpurgis asked, thinking that Ozymandias would never let fresh blood walk from the building.

'Indeed she did. In fact we gave her more than she expected. A fair price for a game of hide and seek.'

'And you let her go?'

'Of course – do you think I am a monster?' Ozymandias laughed. 'She even came back a week later, having spent all the money on Gin and Wheel.'

'And she escaped again and you paid her?'

'No.' Ozymandias laughed. 'I found her hiding in the dining room and ripped out her throat. It was the only door that I had left unlocked. I thought it quite fair.'

'You cheated,' Walpurgis said. 'You locked all the doors so she couldn't escape.'

'Hide and seek is such fun – perhaps you should try it one night.'

'Running around your charnel house? Do you think I am mad?'

'I know you are mad, Heston. I can hear the garbled thoughts that jump in and out of your mind. But then again, I suppose you are never alone with a head full of voices . . .'

Walpurgis didn't answer. He paced the room and stood by the door to the veranda, looking out across the London skyline. Far away he could see the dome of St Paul's. It appeared to fill half the sky. The white columns that surrounded it

144

glowed brightly in the light from the street below.

The two men stood silently. Ozymandias knew he had offended him. The words were true but harsh and regrettable. 'I should have thought before I spoke,' he said as he went and stood by Walpurgis, putting a hand on his shoulder. 'Not many people have seen the monstrosities upon which your eyes have stared. They would drive even the most callous person completely mad.'

'It is of my own doing, Ozymandias. I have the free will to decide. Sometimes I just cannot stop myself,' he answered, his voice choked.

'If it is too much for you I could always ask someone else.'

'The only other man would be Toran Blaine. I was told that he was dead.'

'Regrettably . . . A fine man and a wasted life,' Ozymandias said as he stepped on to the veranda and looked at the bay trees that lined the wall in fat terracotta pots. 'I hope you will continue. I know a doctor in Strasbourg who I can recommend.'

'I am well,' Walpurgis said. 'The voices come and go. Now, I don't listen to them.'

'Would you ever consider becoming one with us?' Ozymandias asked, already knowing the answer to his question. 'It would be such a shame to allow age to corrupt such beauty. The years are already stripping you of your looks. It would be a shame for them to go to waste.'

Walpurgis instinctively touched his face. He coughed to clear his tightening throat. 'I don't think you would want me as one of your number,' he answered.

'Like me you have a thirst for . . . excitement,' Ozymandias said. 'You would enjoy Bloomsbury House. I have never been disappointed.'

'I loved her, did you know that?' Walpurgis asked suddenly as he turned and faced Ozymandias.

'Arantez did say you were very close.'

'It was more than that. I would have married her,' he answered.

'Even though she had become a Vampyre?' Ozymandias asked.

'That made no difference to me. She was still beautiful.'

'But you would have aged and she would have stayed the same. A relationship of mixed blood will never work. She would have watched you decay and the love would fade. I have seen it so many times before.'

'That possibility has been taken from me. I need to find the one who sent the assassin. I ask you again, was it you?'

It was as if the question had stayed with Walpurgis throughout their conversation, bubbling in his mind as he waited for the time to ask it again. He watched Ozymandias for the slightest hint of a lie.

'I do not want you dead,' he said softly. 'In fact Heston, I hold a special place in my heart for you.'

'Then who tried to kill me?'

'You will have to discover that for yourself,' he answered reluctantly. 'The Cult of the Oracle will be hard to pin down.'

'I need a name. Somewhere to start. You must know something,' he insisted, his voice raised in concern. The lights of the room flickered and then burnt even brighter.

Ozymandias looked away as he thought. 'Even when we are at war with each other there is a certain loyalty amongst us,' he said slowly.

'I need a name,' Walpurgis repeated, knowing Ozymandias could give him at least one clue.

'Find Jago Harker and his friend and kill them. Then I will tell you what you need to know. It has to be that way.'

'Would you keep that from me? You must know something about who could have sent the assassin,' Walpurgis said adamantly.

'Very well. There is one name that has been mentioned. But under no circumstances should it ever be said that I was the one to inform you.'

'Who is it?' Walpurgis asked.

'Within the Lodge Maleficarum there is a traitor. A follower of the Cult of the Oracle all their life. I once spoke to them of their *habit* and they would not deny it. Last week I was told that they would do anything for the diamond.'

Walpurgis stared at him as he spoke, the sudden realisation of whom he thought it could be written across his face.

'Mina Karlstein?' Walpurgis asked.

'How did you guess?' Ozymandias replied with a shrug. 'I never said her name.'

'She once came to Cambridge and asked me about the diamond. It was she who introduced me to Ezra Morgan.'

'You see,' Ozymandias said as he pointed to the sky. 'The clouds are clearing . . . Find her and she will give you the answer. And take this,' he said, handing him a small green bottle of viscous liquid. 'It will take away the pain.'

'I will kill her.'

'Make sure she speaks to you first and remember that if she is killed her sister will come for you.'

147

'Then they will both die.'

14

Cupcakes

JAGO STARED at the breakfast plate and wondered if he dare eat. Every inch of a large dish decorated with ivy leaves was covered with iced cakes. They had been left there whilst he had slept. Fourteen red, creamed cupcakes in crimped paper cases, each one topped with a small piece of sugared fruit. Next to the cakes was a pot of steaming chocolate. He could never forget the smell – it reminded him of Julius Cresco, the man who had looked after him when he was younger, the man who had turned out to be a Vampyre. Every Saturday morning, Cresco would make hot chocolate and cupcakes. He would invite Jago to his apartment and together they would read newspapers, listen to the radio and dip the cakes into the steaming chocolate. The man defied any attempt at rationing.

'You never know when your time is up,' Cresco had always said. 'Best to eat as much as you can each day as a meal on the plate is the only certainty we know.'

Jago remembered the words as he sat up on the velvet couch and wondered why he was alone. The room was empty. There was no sign of Lana Karlstein or her companion. In the square below, he could hear the sound of a street musician playing the violin. The drapes on the window blew and twisted in the fresh morning breeze. The scent of Paris crept over the window ledge and spilled across the room. It was so unlike London. The air was warm, even for that time of year. Car horns, cycle bells and shouts drowned out the hum of the Metro railway beneath the road.

In the morning light, the room appeared much larger and far shabbier than the night before. He could see the fine cracks that criss-crossed the plastered ceiling. The carpet had faded and everything was coated in a thin layer of dust. Picking a cake from the plate, Jago sniffed the cream. It smelt like nothing he had known before. He put it to his lips and tasted it with the tip of his tongue.

'Blood . . .' he said as his thoughts escaped.

'What do you expect?' Lana Karlstein asked. 'I am a Vampyre.'

Jago had no idea how she had got into the room. She sat on the leather chair by the fire as if she had been there all along. He didn't want to ask her how she had done it for fear he had been mistaken.

'But it's sweet,' he replied licking the icing from the cake and for a moment not caring what he was doing.

'It is the speciality of a small restaurant nearby. I ordered them last night.' Lana got up from the chair and sat uncomfortably close to him on the sofa.

Not moving from his place, he leant against her and laughed. 'Never thought I would be eating bloody cream cakes in Paris,' he said.

'And I never thought that I would be with someone like you,' Lana answered as she wiped a fleck of cream from the

150

tip of his nose. 'I am so glad that I was asked to do this. I thought that you would be a petulant brat. I was so very mistaken . . .'

Lana glanced at him, as their faces drew closer. She thought he looked much older than she had been told. It was something that she had seen time and time again. It was as if the venom of the bite stopped the process of ageing. A Vampyre always looked as they did on the day when the venom first took hold – the victim was frozen in time. Yet even with Jago, she saw the tell-tale signs. The skin of his face was thinning so that it had become opaque. The veins within were near to the surface and tinged his cheeks with a turquoise glow. The bones of his fingers were more pronounced, as were the knuckles and joints of his hand. There were slight signs, easily visible if you knew what to look for. The most obvious and visible change was that of the eyes. Around the iris, the eye was always reddened. It was even more so when the Vampyre had recently eaten. Lana Karlstein could tell that Jago was hungry.

'So what will happen today?' he asked. He moved away as the companion opened the door.

'Will you try to escape?' she asked.

'Is it worth it?' he answered. 'How far would I get?'

'All depends how far I wanted you to go before I swooped down and bit you,' she joked, opening her mouth and making as if she would bite him.

Jago lounged back into the soft cushions that were scattered on the couch. He had not felt this way for many years. He was happier than he had been for longer than he could remember.

'You said something about giving up the search and then finding what you want,' he said as he looked at her.

'Yes?' she answered.

'Would it be wrong of me not to look for Hugh Morgan?'

Lana Karlstein leant forward and whispered in his ear. 'I think you would surely find him that way,' she said softly, as if she wanted only him to hear the words.

'Luna Negri?' he whispered in reply as the companion fussed with a small bowl of flowers by the window.

'A place of beauty where we often find what we are looking for,' she answered as she looked over his shoulder to the companion, telling him with her eyes to leave the room. The man tutted as he walked across the room and pulled the white doors tightly shut. 'If I were to tell you something could you be trusted?'

Jago answered immediately. 'Of course, whatever you tell me will be a secret.'

She looked at him as if she was searching for the truth. He tried not to show how he was feeling, as if in some way he would betray her.

'The priest who brought us here yesterday is a traitor. There is a gathering of Vampyres who want you dead. They say that your birth was predicted and that the Lyrid of Saturn was a sign that you will be the destruction of our race. The priest is their spy.'

'How did you know?' he asked.

'He was planning to meet a woman by the Seine and tell her all that he knew. I managed to meet her before him and left a sign that would implicate him,' Lana answered with a slight laugh.

'You killed her,' Jago replied. He glimpsed her thoughts as if he had been allowed to see into her mind.

'Of course – she was working for the enemy. Your life would have been in danger.'

'And the priest?'

'I had asked for his rosary. I told him that I would like to follow the Cult of the Oracle. He kindly obliged. I noticed that it was engraved with his name. I left it in her hands. The police will think he is the murderer.' Lana crossed her legs and looked at her reflection in the toes of her polished boots.

'Why didn't you just kill him?' he asked.

'It had to appear that we do not know what he had planned. The priest will be arrested and taken away. We can then continue our journey,' she said complacently. She reached into the bag that hung from her shoulder and picked an almond-shaped mint imperial and ate it quickly. 'For some reason, the Cult of the Oracle want you dead. Since the Lyrid of Saturn, the only thing that Vampyres want to talk about is Jago Harker.'

'I wish all this had never started,' he answered as he got up from the couch and walked to the window. Lana followed, staying close as a shadow.

'There are things in life that are meant to be,' she said before she turned him towards her. 'How old are you in earth years?'

'I will be twenty-one,' he replied realising for the first time that putting a number to his age did not make sense. Jago felt just as he had done all those years before. His appearance had changed so little that he had forgotten that he should look much older.

153

'That doesn't make it so bad,' she said in reply, knowing she could say no more. 'I will get Clover to take away the breakfast,' she added as she stepped away from him.

'Clover?' he asked.

'The companion – his name is Clover. He was once an actor. Clover has been with me for ten years. I could not be without him,' she said, as if he were a pet dog.

'Strange name for a man. He is so tatty. I noticed his clothes are threadbare,' Jago said. He heard a busker stop playing outside the window.

'That is only how he dresses when we are away from London. He is very elegant. I should know, I pay his bills. That is the benefit of being a companion.' Lana edged closer to Jago and brushed the dust from the shoulder of his leather coat. 'And if any one is tatty then it is you – have you seen . . .'

He did not have time to answer. There was a sudden thud and the double doors to the room swung open. Clover hung from the door, pinned by his hands, crucified with two long-bladed knives. He screamed in agony as four dark figures walked slowly towards Lana and Jago. Each was masked. They wore black gloves and long coats. The tallest wore a black shirt with a red necktie.

'Jago Harker? We have come to take you back to where you really belong,' he said as he pushed Lana out of the way with a sudden blow.

'Leave him,' Lana shouted as she got to her feet.

'You have done enough damage, Lana Karlstein. Stay out of this,' the man shouted as he grabbed hold of Jago by the wrist and pulled him towards him.

'Who are you?' Lana asked as she lurched forward and tried to grab the mask from the man.

As she struck out, the man pushed her away. 'Don't hurt her,' he said to the man behind him.

The other man stepped forward quickly and just as Lana went to strike him with her fist, he grabbed her by the hands. With one fluid movement he twisted her round, and before she could fight back another man close behind struck her across the head. Lana Karlstein fell to the ground.

'She won't bother us now,' the man said as he took hold of Jago by his other arm and with his companion walked him from the room.

'Good,' the other replied as he put a hand across Jago's mouth. 'Let's get him to the car.'

Lana could hear every word as they dragged Jago from the room. Her companion screamed as the knife cut through the skin of his hands, the weight of his body pulling him to the ground. She tried to get to her feet but the blow to her head held her to the floor. Fighting against herself, she struggled to the sofa and got to her knees. Lana looked about the room. In her befuddled mind she tried to work out which way they would have gone.

As the spinning in her mind calmed to a faint dizziness, she got to her feet and made her way across the room.

'I have to stop them, Clover. I will be back for you,' she said as she stood by the open window and looked down to the square below.

A car was waiting on the cobbles under the canopy of the hotel. Four men walked towards it. There was Jago. Instinctively he turned and looked up, and she saw his face.

'In the car,' one of the men shouted. 'Police – get out of the way!'

The crowd stood back as Jago was bundled into the car. No one in the street seemed to care. He looked as if he were just someone else being arrested. It had become a common sight. The last man looked back to the hotel and then got into the car and slammed the door.

It sped across the square towards the river. Lana jumped from the window and slid across the canopy. She landed on the ground as if she were a large black cat. Then, without taking a breath, she began to run through the crowd of people.

The car was always ahead of her. It followed the roadway around the Place de la Concorde and headed towards the Avenue des Champs Elysées. Jago looked back from the rear seat of the car. Two guards, their masks still in place, pressed him in. Silent and sweaty, they smelt like over-worked horses. He was sure that he saw Lana running through the crowds, but then she was gone.

'Turn around,' one of them commanded as he pushed Jago in the ribs with a sharp fist. 'Keep your face down in the car. Don't want you to be seen.'

The car turned away from the river and was soon in the narrow streets around Saint Lazare. It crawled through the traffic, the horn sounding at the small motorcycles that cut in from all sides.

'Get them out of the way,' the man in the front seat shouted. 'Knock them down if you have to.'

Jago could hear desperation in his voice.

'Who are you? Where are you taking me?' he shouted at the man.

'Keep quiet, you fool,' the man next to him shouted as the car swerved, knocking an old man on a bicycle to the ground.

Jago looked for the moment, and without warning he reached out to the door handle at the far side of the car.

'What do you think you are doing?' the man said, twisting his wrist as the car drove off leaving the old man in the road.

'Let me go!' Jago shouted, hoping someone outside the car in the crowded street would hear him.

'Stay where you are and shut up,' the man on the front seat commanded.

The car screeched around the corner of Rue Moncey, narrowly missing the street-front coffee shop with old men playing cards at small tables. Jago looked out of the back window. He knew that Lana would never find him. The car drove quickly down the road and then stopped in traffic.

'It will be like this all the way to Montmagny,' the driver said as he turned the wheel of the car, slipped the gearshift and accelerated away across the pavement, scattering the pedestrians. 'If I can just get out of this street . . .'

There was a sudden shadow as a body landed and thudded on the windshield. The car skidded and crashed into the wall of the Bank Montmartre, smashing stones from the doorway. Steam billowed from the engine and the body of a woman was slumped on the bonnet.

'Look, you fool!' the man in the front seat shouted at the driver.

The woman outside got to her feet. Jago saw her face. 'Lana Karlstein,' he whispered.

In one movement she smashed her fist through the glass and grabbed the passenger. She pulled him through the broken windshield and onto the bonnet.

The guard in the back tried to get from the car, but his door was jammed against the wall of the bank. Jago lashed out at the man next to him and then grabbed the door handle. A fist came through the glass and punched the man in the face. He slumped back, his nose broken.

'Jago, watch out!' Lana shouted as the other man grabbed him by the throat.

'Stay where you are!' the man shouted as he tried to strangle him.

Footsteps crashed over the roof of the car. The door was pulled open. The man was dragged from the leather seat. He hung in the air, his feet off the ground. Jago could hear him gasping for breath, and then his body fell to the ground as if dumped from the gallows.

'Quickly, Jago,' Lana shouted. 'We have to get away.'

A screaming crowd gathered around the car. In the steam and smoke that poured from the engine, they all stared at the tall blond woman with her hands covered in blood.

'Get her,' a man shouted.

'They are Gestapo, they have been hiding in the city,' Lana said as the mob came close. 'They were kidnapping him.'

'Gestapo?' he answered, his face turning red with anger as he saw that the men were masked and a Luger pistol lay on the floor. 'Gestapo?'

The man pulled on the door and dragged the unconscious guard from the car. Jago slid free as Lana jumped from the roof and took him by the hand.

No one saw them escape through the howling mob that descended on the black sedan like a swarm of ants. As they slipped away, Jago could hear smashing glass and faint screams echoing through the narrow streets as the car was pulled to pieces. The crowd roared as an old blacksmith in a leather apron smashed the petrol tank. They stepped back as the first flames took hold and the car began to burn. Thick acrid smoke plumed into the air and wafted between the tall buildings.

'Don't look back, Jago. You don't want to ever see what they are doing,' Lana said as they turned from the road with the old buildings and onto a wide tree-lined boulevard that led back to the river. 'We will get a taxi and leave the city. They know where we are.'

'What about Clover?' Jago asked. He could see from the grimace on her face that he should ask no more.

'I think we will be going alone,' she answered as she took a handkerchief from the coat of her pocket and tried to wipe the blood from her hands. She waved the bloodied handkerchief at the stream of cars that crowded the boulevard. 'We are not safe. We have to go now,' Lana said as a taxi pulled over and the door opened.

'Who were they?' he asked.

'The Cult of the Oracle. They were going to sacrifice you,' she said casually as she pushed him into the back of the taxi and pulled the door behind them. 'It is the prophecy.'

15

Mina ... Mina ... Mina ...

THE MORNING WAS grey and cloudy with little chance of the sun ever breaking through the clouds. The gloom stretched over Whitby like a funeral pall, mixed with the smoke from a thousand chimney pots on the old cottages beneath the Abbey. As Walpurgis walked down the five steps from the shabby railway station he looked across the river to the far side. The banks of the cliff were lined with old houses painted in bright colours like nothing he had ever seen. High above was the old church and the ruins of the Abbey that stood next to a vast house made of dulled sandstone and covered in coal grime.

He walked across the street to the tobacconist's, where three taxi cabs stood in a row waiting for passengers.

'Hawks Moor?' he asked. Each driver politely refused and then drove away.

'Won't take you there,' a woman said, listening from a doorway of a disused shop. 'Not since all that has been happening. People around here are quite suspicious.' The woman sucked on an old pipe and blew white smoke into the morning air.

'What would put people off going to Hawks Moor?' he

160

asked as if he didn't care, so she wouldn't be put off her answer. 'It is a fine house.'

'Police inspector was killed during the war. There were rumours of things happening in the old maze they had there. Trouble with . . .' The woman paused and looked around to see if anyone else was listening. 'Vampyres.'

'So how will I get there if no one will take me?' Walpurgis asked as he hitched up the leather bag on his shoulder.

'Walk,' she answered, pointing to the pathway that led up to the church and beyond. 'That will take you all the way to Hawks Moor. Not many miles, just keep the sea to the port side of you and it'll be fine.' The woman waved her left hand as if to show him which way to go.

'You could always come with me – keep me company,' Walpurgis joked as he raised his eyebrows in surprise.

The woman didn't laugh. She tapped the cup of the pipe against the wall and knocked out all the burning ash before she spoke.

'Would rather dine in hell than take my chances outside the town. I have lived here for fifty-five years and never set foot outside of the place,' she said smugly, as if this self-imposed incarceration was something of which she was exceedingly proud.

Walpurgis touched the brim of his fedora and walked on. Every now and then he stopped and took the small green bottle from his pocket and sipped the linctus. It took away the pain and numbed the wound to his leg. Ozymandias was right when he had said it was an elixir to die for. He could feel nothing – no pain, no sensation, no life.

Soon he was across the bridge and through the narrow

streets crowded with fishermen and groups of soldiers emptying sandbags on the beach. Within an hour, Walpurgis could see the tall chimneys of Hawks Moor in the distance. Heather and bracken gave way to small fields of rough grass. Covens of tattered sheep stared suspiciously at him as he walked by. The sky was still laden with cloud that blocked out the horizon, though every now and then it broke into open blue. There was not a hint of breeze. The world stood still, as if it were dying and unable to draw breath.

By the time he had crossed the moor and stood on the high bank looking down on the house, the fog had thickened. It moved slowly, like fumbling party balloons or swirling candyfloss. The house vanished under a blanket of mist only to reappear suddenly as if the ground had swallowed up the clouds. A fire burnt in the house and a spiral of smoke welled up from one of the chimneys. Walpurgis reached into his shoulder bag and took out a pair of brass binoculars.

A car rattled down the lane behind him. Walpurgis hid in the long wet grass and waited until it had gone. It chugged on, clunking through the potholes, and within minutes it was outside the house. Through his binoculars Walpurgis saw the driver get out, leaving a passenger reading a newspaper in the front seat. He could not see the face, but by the fingers that clutched the newspapers Walpurgis knew this was a man.

A group of people walked to the car. An older man with grey hair and a straggly beard held the arm of a younger girl with red hair and a frightened look on her face. Walpurgis could see they were manacled together. He could hear the man protest as he was pushed towards the car. A tall woman in a rugged black suit followed them. Her black curled hair was piled on her head and shaved at the sides. Walpurgis focused the binoculars on her face. She was giving out orders and, not content with shouting, pointed her long fingers at the older man with the beard.

Walpurgis tried to read her red lips. They moved quickly, slipping from English to German and then to French. He could make out the occasional word. Most were spoken harshly in her staccato voice.

'Mina Karlstein, you never change,' he whispered under his breath.

Before she slammed the car door, Walpurgis had taken the path down the bank side to the back of the house.

Mina Karlstein waited as the car turned on the gravel and drove back towards the gate. Biatra looked out of the side window as she was driven away, wondering why Mina had broken her promise. The woman smiled at her as if she was saying goodbye to an old friend. The smile cracked the face powder that was daubed thickly on her cheeks. She stopped for a moment, sniffing the air like a dog taking in the scent. She looked up to the hill as if she could sense something was there that she couldn't see.

Closing the door to Hawks Moor behind her, Mina crossed the hallway. The painting of Ezra Morgan stared down at her. His face frowned in discontent as if he knew what filled her thoughts.

Then she stopped suddenly. On the floor, outlined in the dust, was a large footprint. From the drawing room came the sound of the fire being griddled with the iron rod. The coals scraped against the firedogs as the embers crackled. Mina listened, and as the poker was dropped on the stone fireplace she walked slowly to the door. Taking the handle she pushed gently, listening to every sound as she did so.

'I am quite comfortable, if you want to come in, Mina,' Walpurgis said as he settled back in the armchair by the window with his leather bag on his lap.

Mina Karlstein looked around the door. A flop of curls fell across her face. She wiped them back quickly as she stepped into the room and held the door.

'Heston Walpurgis. Have you taken up burglary as a pastime?' she asked sarcastically.

'Your name came up in conversation so I thought I would come and see you,' he answered. 'It is a long time since that afternoon in Cambridge. If my memory serves me well it was enjoyable for us both.'

'My tastes have changed since then, Walpurgis. In fact it was meeting you that set my mind once and for all.' Mina eyed him warily, wondering why he was there.

'I am so glad I was of service. Perhaps you will be able to help me?' Walpurgis asked as he reached into the bag and concealed his hand within.

'How did you know I was here? It was a secret,' she answered.

'That is the world of the Vampyres. No one can keep anything to themselves. I think that your venom addles the mind and you all chirp gibberish and we mortals are led to believe it is supernatural truth.' Walpurgis crossed his dirty brown boots and relaxed back into the chair and yawned.

'Then tell me what you want?' she asked. 'Was it you on the hillside when I was out with the car?'

'Did you see me?' he replied in a half laugh.

'I could feel your presence. Another skill we Vampyres have over you mortals,' she joked as she walked to the fireplace and warmed herself. 'I would be glad of the company. This is a lonely house and filled with death. Sibilia Trevellas and Julius Cresco both died out there. Did you know them?'

'I knew Sibilia by her reputation. Did she teach piano or was it French?' he asked, not caring what the answer was. 'How did they die?'

'There is a Vampyre who does not know the reason for loyalty and why he is truly here,' she answered as she reached for the fire poker and set it neatly on the iron rest.

'Jago Harker?' he asked, his voice unsurprised. He waited to see her response.

She swallowed deeply. Her throat churned as she sucked in the breath. 'You have heard of him?'

'His name has been spoken by everyone I have met since returning to England. It seems he has caused much pain to many people. Where is he now?' he asked calmly, knowing she was trying to see what he was thinking.

'It would all depend on why you want to find him.' She was unable to see behind the junket of thoughts that blocked out what he was really thinking.

'I want to kill him – why else should I seek out a Vampyre?' Walpurgis said as he moved uncomfortably in the chair. 'I believe he caused the death of Madame Arantez.'

Mina Karlstein looked surprised. Her eyes widened as she looked at him.

'When?' she asked.

'Not long ago . . . On the night I first got back to England.' He looked at her and thought how much she reminded him of his mother. 'Someone came to our room in the Hotel Julius and there they stabbed her to death.'

'I knew her well. She was the companion of Ozymandias. They lived not far from here.' Walpurgis could see her eyes as they flickered around the room search for something on which to anchor her thoughts. 'I can't understand . . .'

It was as if they had been close and Mina had lost someone that she cared for. Walpurgis could hear it in her voice and see the shock on her face.

'I am sorry to bring you such news,' he said. 'She and I were going to be married,' he said, his voice insistent.

'Married? Arantez? Married?' she asked quickly, not sure she had heard him correctly. 'But you hardly knew her. She told me.'

'I was going to ask her on my return. She was in my mind all the time I was locked away. Ezra Morgan saw to that. He had me arrested by the Gestapo. All over the matter of a diamond.'

Mina ignored what he said. Walpurgis could tell that this was the case. She tightened her lips across her teeth and she breathed deeply and looked out of the window. 'I think it was the diamond that you asked me about in Cambridge. I regret the day you introduced me to him.'

'It was business,' she said as she snapped from her daydream. 'It was what I did before the war. He paid me well for the information and didn't he get the diamond?'

'Morgan got the diamond but didn't pay me the money. I left England and was then conveniently arrested by the Gestapo before the payment could be made. He told them where I was and how I could be found.' Walpurgis got up

166

from the chair and walked across the room. He put a hand on her shoulder and squeezed it tightly. 'Did you know anything about that?'

She looked at him and then turned away.

'I think you should come with me. I could have the answer you are looking for,' Mina said as she walked away from him.

Walpurgis followed. They took the broad stairs that led to the upper floors that were lined with paintings. Mina told him who each one was as they walked by. They soon came to a narrow door at the end of the dark passageway. It smelt musky, as if the place had never seen the light of day. 'That is Jago Harker,' she said as she pointed to a small portrait of a young boy in a school cap. 'It was painted by Julius Cresco. We found it in his apartment after he had been killed. Strange to be murdered by someone you have taken care of all their life.'

'Is that what you brought me to see?' he asked, unsure why she should show him someone he already knew.

'No. Sorry – you asked about the diamond. This room is where Ezra Morgan kept all of his papers. There may be something that could help you in there,' Mina said apologetically. 'You go in and I will make coffee. Milk?'

Walpurgis nodded as he turned the miniature brass handle of the door and pushed it open with a creak. Mina walked back down the passageway, her boots clattering on the wooden boards. 'I think we have some food – I will bring what we have,' she shouted as she went down the stairs.

Walpurgis stepped into the room. It was like a large cupboard stacked with shelves. A slit window with thick glass was in the far wall. He flicked the switch to the electric light.

A single glass bulb burnt dimly and cast his shadow across the room and the wall. He stared at cases of papers. Some were written on vellum, others on old parchment. Each box was labelled with the years. Closing the door, he took off his hat and hung it on the hook, then he brushed back his hair and instinctively licked his teeth.

From outside, he heard Mina walking back along the corridor more slowly than before. She must be carrying coffee on a tray, he thought. There was a click of a lock. The door was shut fast.

'What are you doing?' he shouted.

'Stand back from the door,' she answered coldly.

Before he could speak, an iron gate dropped from the ceiling to the floor. It slid into place on two steel beams that dropped from the ceiling and stuck into the floorboards at each side of the door.

'What are you doing?' he demanded.

'I know why you are here. It has nothing to do with the diamond,' she shouted.

'Let me out,' he said.

'You'll be dead in the week. You could always eat the papers – perhaps that would help you live longer.' She laughed as she walked away.

'One thing,' Walpurgis shouted through the door, hoping she would hear him. 'Did you send the assassin?'

'Not I,' she replied. 'But I know who did. You are dealing with forces beyond your control and they are not frightened of you, Heston Walpurgis.'

Her footsteps trailed off into the distance. Walpurgis reached into his bag and took out a long-bladed knife. Pressing it between the boards, he had soon lifted the end of an oak plank. He dug his hands under the board. The nails lifted easily from the old wood. One by one he lifted the planks and then stared into the dark void beneath the room. He could see the ceiling of the room below. Taking his fedora hat and pulling it tightly on his head, he looked down. Then, like a man leaping from an airplane, Walpurgis jumped into the void.

His feet crashed through the ceiling plaster. Walpurgis hung momentarily, caught by the strap of his bag on a rusted nail. He looked down at the drawing room where he had talked with Mina. She stared up disbelievingly as she gripped the door.

'What a surprise,' he said as he fell suddenly to the floor, smashing the table beneath him. Mina Karlstein ran from the room as Walpurgis got to his feet, clutching the knife in his hand. From the look on his face she knew he would kill her. 'Come back, you bitch,' he snarled, eyes glazed with anger.

By the time she had got to the fourth step of the stairs he had caught her. Grabbing Mina by the ankle, he dragged her back.

'It wasn't me. I loved her as much as you,' she screamed as Walpurgis grabbed her throat.

'Then who sent the assassin?' he demanded as she twisted and fought like a strangled cat in his grip.

Mina Karlstein kicked out. She pushed him back with her foot and Walpurgis fell against the wall. Breaking free, she ran up the stairs. He chased after her. Again Walpurgis caught her by the hem of her jacket and pulled her back. She fell down the stairs, hitting each tread as she bounced from step to step.

'Leave me be!' she screamed as she got to her feet and made ready to fight.

Walpurgis smiled as he walked towards her. He held out the knife knowingly, the blade glinting in the light.

'Then you will know what death tastes like – silver-bladed and sharp as glass,' he said as she backed away. 'I am faster and stronger than you, Mina Karlstein. I can get to the door before you do.'

She looked at Walpurgis and then to the door as she measured her chances of escape.

'Then you have me at a disadvantage. Will you let me live?' she asked.

'No,' he answered slowly. 'You have walked the earth for too long. Now is your time.'

'Then I have nothing to lose.' She set off at a pace, running through the door of the dining room and slamming the door behind her.

Walpurgis kicked the door. The room was empty. The door to the garden was open. Standing his ground, he waited. It didn't seem right.

Mina Karlstein fell from above him. She kicked Walpurgis out of the way and the knife dropped from his fingers as she ran to the door. Picking it up from the carpet, he gave chase. They were soon across the drive and into the garden.

Mina ran faster than she had ever done before. Walpurgis could feel his wound burning as he tried to keep pace. The mist swirled about them as she ran towards the cliff.

Then she stopped. Mina could go no further – the high

cliff fell away to the sea. She had nowhere to run.

'Looks as if this is it, Mina,' Walpurgis said as he rolled the knife in the palm of his hand. Seagulls and gannets soared and swooped through the mist to the sea far below. 'You wouldn't want to take the chance of this knife cutting you and the sea is two hundred feet below – what shall it be?' he asked.

'Why do you want to know?' she said, hearing waves slap against the cliff like the sarcastic laughter of old wives.

'Are you in the Cult of the Oracle?' he asked.

'I would not tell you if I was,' she said as she turned her face from him.

'It would help you at a time like this. An afterlife for the Vampyres, a heaven, a land of milk and honey. I hear they believe in an Oracle that will tell the future, a Vampyre that is really God. That you were made in its image and every Vampyre would live for ever even if they were killed – as long as they believed.'

'Do you enjoy this, Heston? Is there no way we could make this right?' she pleaded as she looked at the drop be-low her feet.

'I don't think you would ever want me again,' he answered sheepishly. 'And I would certainly never want you.'

'Then I would like the right to choose my own way to leave this world,' she answered. She looked at him and then the drop to the sea. 'You will never stop us. There will be one who can come against you. Vampyre-hunters are all the same. You are fascinated by who and what we are but don't have the guts to live our lives.'

'Shut up, Mina. You preach like a harpy. What's it going to

171

be? Blade or sea?'

Mina Karlstein didn't answer. She looked at Walpurgis – a monster, hated by all her kind, but there was something of him that she found mesmerising. She thought how beautiful he was. The lines of his face, his sun-darkened skin, his bright eyes.

'I am glad you will be the last thing I see before I die,' she said as she smiled. 'Arantez tasted as sweet as you and never preened herself in the mirror. She told me that you were the vainest man she had ever known.'

Taking a final glance, she stepped from the cliff.

Walpurgis rushed forward and watched as she fell to the water below. Mina Karlstein dropped like an arrow, her body spiralling and twisting as she went down and down. She never made a sound.

Walpurgis watched and silently counted the seconds as she plummeted towards the lapping waves and then crashed into the dull grey sea. The water consumed her, the waves took her, and all was again silent. Walpurgis waited. He looked down from the high cliff, hoping he would see her body. There was no sign, no fragment from of her clothes, nothing to be a memory of her. The seabirds fell silent as he called her name.

'Mina . . . Mina . . . Mina . . .'

16

Chateau Cardonne

THE TRAIN FROM PARIS had taken three hours to get out of the city. It had steamed through the countryside as far as Avignon. Then Jago had sat in the back seat of an old taxi next to a wooden crate filled with chickens. Lana Karlstein had laughed as she looked back and saw him huddled on the tattered seats, a chicken pecking at the sleeve of his coat. The car drove slowly on the wide avenues as it left the town. Everywhere were the abandoned tanks of a retreating army, rusted and bullet-ridden. Some were stained with blood; others had cut flowers placed against them like shrines to unnamed heroes.

They drove through the village of Sarrians and turned onto the long road that led to Chateau Cardonne. Jago looked out of the window of the car and saw the Chateau shining in the sun of the late afternoon. Twenty windows hung against the white walls like silver plates reflecting the light. Surrounded by tall, graceful trees, it looked like it had been there since the beginning of time. He saw two holes cut into the ground at the beginning of the avenue of trees that led to the house, and next to each hole was a new tree, a sapling not more than four years old in a gigantic terracotta pot. But he thought nothing of it as Lana Karlstein spoke to the driver in fluent French. He pulled embarrassingly on his black moustache and muttered a reply into his nicotine-stained hand.

'He thinks we are lovers,' she said as she translated what the man said. 'He wanted to know if we had run away together.'

Jago couldn't understand a word of what he said. Lana nodded and laughed, touching the man on the arm several times as the car drove along the avenue of trees to the front of the Chateau. She seemed to have forgotten what had happened in Paris, but Jago couldn't get the thoughts of the lynch mob from his mind; he could still smell the acrid smoke and hear the cries of the men in the car.

'War finished,' the man said in broken English as he turned and shook Jago by the hand. 'Your people helped us against the Gestapo. We all know that.'

The man stopped the car at the doors of the Chateau. A woman stood on the steps in a long dress and knitted coat. She looked homely, kind, with an open face and soft smile. Her silver hair looked out of place on such a young face. It was roughly tied back in a small knot at the back of her head and held in place by several pins.

'Good to see you,' she said as the door opened. 'I am so glad that you can stay with us.'

'Madame Camargue, it has been such a long time since we last met,' Lana said as she greeted her with an embrace.

'Fifty years I think,' the woman answered. 'That was when Chateau Cardonne was just a house. Since the war we have had to take in paying guests.'

'People?' Lana asked abruptly, like a dog whose hackles were raised.

'Tourists, travellers , . . and of course old friends,' the Madame answered apologetically. 'There are not so many old friends as there used to be. I am sure you will understand.'

Lana looked at Jago, and he held out his hand to introduce himself. 'Jago Harker,' he said, his voice optimistic.

'So there really is such a one as you,' Madame Camargue answered, holding back her hand and keeping it close to her side. 'I never thought I would ever see the day when it would happen,' she said as she turned to Lana. 'So it is true, he really exists.'

Lana gave him an uncomfortable stare, knowing she would have to explain what the woman had meant.

'It has been a long day. Could we have coffee?' Lana asked.

'I forget myself. Of course. It is already in your room. Just as arranged. One room overlooking the avenue with a full window,' the woman said as she took them into the Chateau.

There was no reception, just an old table with gilt legs and carvings of pigs. Everything in the chateau smelt of flowers. Vases stood at the entrance to every doorway; they were filled with roses and other flowers that Jago couldn't recognise. He knew the names of roses; Julius Cresco had always bought them for his mother. Every Friday when he came home from school there would be a bunch on the table. They were always blood-red and tied together with silk. Each type had a name and although at first they looked the same there was always something different about them. Even the colour of red petals was never identical. Cresco would tell him what they were and where they had come from.

'Beautiful and yet dangerous,' he often said as he cut off the thorns with a pair of silver scissors, leaving only one thorn on every stem. 'I do that to remind myself that there cannot be beauty without pain.'

Madame Camargue took them through the house, up the stone staircase and along the landing to their room. She handed Lana a long iron key.

'Keep it locked,' she whispered as she gave a slight bow. 'I will bring you some fresh clothes. I believe we have some from your last visit. Fashions never change so they will do.'

Then she spoke in French, her words quick and direct and spoken eye to eye. Lana Karlstein stepped back as if she needed to space herself from the onslaught. She answered quickly, her hands moving to emphasise each word.

'Typical, they always worry about being paid,' she said when they had got into the room and locked the door. 'I haven't seen her in all those years and now she complains.'

'I think you are lying. It was about me. I know it,' Jago said as he sat on the window seat and looked down the long avenue of trees back to the road. 'What did she mean about me when we were at the car – she said I really exist . . .'

'She was confused,' Lana answered as she took her hairbrush and dragged it through her tangled hair.

'Every time you lie, you close your eyes.' Jago looked at her reflection in the mirror of the dressing table.

'Then I shall always keep them open,' she answered, and she put the brush down.

'So, I exist?' he pressed her again, no longer feeling like her prisoner.

Lana Karlstein walked two paces and sat next to him. She

snuggled close as she leant back against the window ledge.

'There is a prophecy about the Lyrid of Saturn, written over two thousand years ago. It talks of a boy called Iago who would try to destroy the world of Vampyres. He would wreak havoc upon us just for the sake of it. There would be no reason why he should do this, just that he hates us.'

'Iago?' he asked.

'Iago, Jago – it is the same name. The prophecy says he will raise up a standard against us and that even the Oracle will not be able to stand against him. He will be a monster of motiveless malignity.'

'So she thought it was me?' Jago asked as he slipped his arm around Lana and pulled her closer to him.

She did not resist. Lana slipped her hand into his and entwined her fingers.

'I hoped it wasn't you, Jago. But after all that has happened it has to be. The Maleficarum told me about you surviving Strackan on the night of the Lyrid. Then you became one of us through the bite of Medea. It had to be her. She is mentioned in the prophecy.'

He thought before he spoke, remembering that night in the old temple.

'They could have called me Jago just to fit in with what had been said. Medea could have just been used to fulfil it.'

'And surviving the Lyrid, killing the Quartet, beating Strackan? All these things are mentioned in the prophecy,' Lana said as she held his hand tightly. 'That is why you have to go to the Luna Negri. We have to be sure.'

'Kept there out of the way so I can do no harm?' he asked.

'To protect you from the Cult of the Oracle. They would

have you killed to stop it all coming to pass. That is why they want you dead. Ezra Morgan was a follower of the cult. Morgan had agreed to come back to the Maleficarum in return for his life. He had the Oracle diamond and now it is missing. I have to take you to the Cave of the Moon.'

'And when I am there, you will stay with me?' he asked, not wanting to let her go.

'I never thought I would be able to say yes, but now I would want it no other way,' Lana said. She turned her head and kissed him on the lips.

Jago held her close. It felt so strange. Guilt, fear, rage – all came to him at once. His heart pounded as they lay together. The breeze pushed the drapes back and forth and chimed the crystals of the large chandelier above the bed. He gasped for his breath as they broke away. She reached out for him and pulled Jago back to her as if she would take all of his blood.

'There is someone else,' he said as they lay together, each reluctant to let go. 'Biatra . . . a girl from Whitby. I feel the same for her.'

'It doesn't matter,' she answered as she smoothed back the long strands of hair from his face. 'That was another life and this is now. One thing I have learnt in all my years is the sacrament of the present moment. I care nothing for tomorrow and the past is a place we cannot belong to. It's here, Jago – here and now . . .'

'Mina – your sister – said you were born in 1698. I never thought I would ever kiss someone so old.' He laughed as he kissed her again, forgetting Biatra and the world he had left behind.

'And I never thought I would ever kiss someone as dangerous,' she said as they parted to look at each other before they kissed again.

It was three hours later that they walked together down the majestic staircase to the dining room of the chateau. Jago held the carved iron banister and slipped his finger along the smooth rail. It was as if the chateau had become another place. Where there had once been silence, now the rooms were filled with conversation.

To the left of the hall was an elegant room with panelled walls. The alcoves of the salon were filled with books and lit with electric lights shielded from view by onyx covers shaped like small swans. Three sofas were arranged around the fireplace with a low table in between. A fat American and his peacock wife sat together in conversation with an Italian businessman in a floral shirt. The American talked about the Grand Tour and how he had found Rome lacking in character.

'Only thing about the place I liked was when there was an earthquake. I was using the bathroom,' he had said as they passed by. 'Rattled the building and threw me to the floor. Thought the world was going to end and Mamie said it was me all along . . .'

The man laughed at his own joke and nudged his wife in the ribs to encourage her to laugh too. By the look of her prune-like face, Jago thought this would be impossible. The Italian smiled a bemused smile while trying to see if he could escape without being discourteous.

All around, groups of men and women stood drinking cocktails, taking the drinks freely from the tray of the waitress as she walked by. Jago held Lana by the arm. She led him like a blind man through the night, nodding and smiling, never showing her teeth and looking to see if any of those gathered were of her kind.

Madame Camargue stood by the door to the dining room. She had changed into a long black dress with a fascinator tied to the side of her head. It looked like an elaborate trap for an exotic bird. Jago tried not to laugh. He guarded his thoughts.

'I have a table by the doors to the patio,' she said as if they were strangers. 'It will be cooler there. The dress looks beautiful,' she whispered to Lana. 'I am so glad it fits after all these years.'

They followed her to the table. It was set for two. Jago took the chair by the door, guided by Lana so she could see the rest of the room. The food was served quickly and they ate very little. Madame Camargue brought drinks between each course. It was fresh blood and blackberry juice.

'She thinks of everything,' Lana said as she wiped the corners of her mouth with the starched napkin. Then she stopped and, with her lips still covered, whispered to Jago. 'Don't look, but there is a man over there who keeps glaring at us.'

Jago laughed as at a distraction and then looked. The man was middle-aged and well-built with a small moustache. His face was tanned, as if he worked in the fields.

'Vampyre?' Jago asked, turning his head so his words could not be heard.

As she was about to speak, the waitress came to the table.

'From the man over there – he would like you to have some champagne. He thinks you are just married.'

Lana looked across, and the man lifted his glass and smiled. She nodded in appreciation as the waitress put the ice bucket on the stand and let the smoking bottle fizz by their side.

'I thought it would be the right thing,' the man said as he crossed the room, pulled a chair from an empty table and sat with them. 'I am Olricus Gisler, from Switzerland . . .'

Lana answered for them. 'We are travelling to Cannes. Côte d'Azur,' she said after she had told him their names.

'What a coincidence,' he answered as he sat back in the chair and folded his arms. 'I have just been there myself. It has not changed since before the war. I took coffee every morning at the Café Poet by the market and walked on the Croisette.'

'Then we will remember you when we are there,' Lana said hoping the man would go away.

'I was intrigued when I saw you. I said to myself that you both looked so different, other-worldly, not of this time.' He yawned as he spoke, his eyes fixed on Lana and the pearl necklace around her neck. 'I would say that you could be mistaken for creatures of myths and legends – children of gods, from ancient Greece.'

'That is what my father said on the day I was born,' Lana answered.

The man sat comfortably in the chair, his arms folded across his silk waistcoat, a silver pin through a yellow tie that didn't match his shirt, but Jago could sense he was dangerous. There was something about Gisler that made Jago feel anxious.

'I am sure I have met you somewhere before,' he said as he stared at Lana. 'But that could not be possible as it was a long time ago and you look so young.'

'She often gets mistaken for other people,' Jago said as he felt the foot of the man propped against his.

'It is late, Mr Gisler, and we have far to go in the morning,' Lana said.

Gisler could tell that he had outstayed his welcome. He thought that it was because they were in love. He looked at Jago and poured the champagne into two glasses.

'Then let us drink a toast to your new life – prosperity, love and happiness,' he said as he handed Lana her glass and clinked his against it. They sipped the champagne. 'It is not a toast unless you drink it all up,' he said as he swigged from his glass and slammed it down empty on the table. They both finished the drinks. Jago could feel it numb his lips. 'You better get to bed, you have a long way to go in the morning,' the man said as he got from the chair, bowed to them both and walked from the room.

'I don't trust him,' Lana said when he had gone. 'He wasn't one of us.'

As they climbed the stairs back to the room, Jago trudged from step to step. His feet felt heavy, tired by all that he had done. Lana walked ahead, took the key from her bag and opened the door. She lay on the bed and snored. Jago locked the door and looked out of the window. Lana slept deeply, the strands of her white hair falling across her face.

Looking out of the open window, Jago watched the wind blow through the avenue of trees. The leaves of the eucalyptus rattled as the branches swayed. The moon seemed bigger than he had seen before, creeping up from the far horizon like a crimson disc. Jago sat in the chair by the door and watched Lana as she slept. He could easily escape, run away and never see her again. He could take all the money from her bag and make it back to England and find Biatra.

Lana curled up and rubbed her face with her fingers. She looked like a sleeping child. Jago took the blanket from the wardrobe and covered her. He sat back in the chair, unable to keep his eyes open. He thought he could hear footsteps in the corridor, someone coming closer. He tried to wake, but sleep gripped him as if it were death. His legs grew numb and his arms sagged at his sides, unable to move. Jago watched helplessly as the door opened.

Gisler stood in the light of the hallway in razor-pressed trousers, waistcoat and shirt sleeves rolled neatly back to the elbows.

'I thought you would be unconscious by now. The champagne had enough sedative to make an elephant sleep – perhaps Vampyres are a little different.'

Jago could no longer keep his eyes open. He slumped in the chair, unable to focus and dead to the world. All he could hear was Gisler dragging Lana from the room. Jago could do nothing.

17

Museum of an Extinct Race

T HERE WAS A SUDDEN, shrill scream and Jago was thrown to the floor of the room. He landed by the bed, far away from the chair where he had been sleeping. He looked at his hands. The veins almost broke through the skin and burnt deep purple, and his fingers trembled as the sedative was consumed from him as if it were being burnt away. His throat was dry and he was convulsed in hot sweats .

As Jago got to his feet his legs buckled beneath him. His memory of Gisler was like a dream. Looking to the bed, Jago saw that Lana was gone. The impression of her sleeping body was imprinted on the eiderdown and the blanket, which had covered her, was discarded and cast by the window. Staggering to the door, Jago tried the handle. The door was locked from the outside. He pulled hard. It refused to move.

Running to the window as the life came back to him, he looked out. All the cars were still parked just as they were before. There was no sign of any movement and all was quiet. He looked up and saw that the room above had the shutters open. He was sure he could hear Madame Camargue speaking. Her words were carried out and into the night as she stood by the window.

Climbing through the window, Jago gripped the deep joints between the stones and moved across the ledge from window to window until he reached a small balcony. He was soon through the open window and into the hallway. Jago followed the stairs higher until he was in the eaves of the house, where a long corridor led to the room at the end. He walked along, keeping to the side and remaining as quiet as he could. Jago slipped his hand into the lining of his coat and pulled out the flick knife that he had hidden within. He held it firmly in the palm of his hand, ready to squeeze the blade open.

At the door, Jago listened. He could hear a grumbled conversation. Holding his breath, Jago looked through the large keyhole. Inside, he could see Madame Camargue. She was still wearing the same dress she had worn at dinner. Gisler was stood with his back to the door, next to the bed. Lana lay tied to the four-poster bed, he wrists tethered. Gisler was rummaging through a selection of medical equipment. Every now and then he would hold up a scalpel or a pair of surgical scissors to the chandelier as if to see how sharp was the blade.

'You should have given me more time,' Jago heard him say to the Madame as he looked at the blade of a long scalpel and glinted it before his face. 'I need time to prepare.'

'What about Jago Harker – what will you do with him?' she asked.

'When I have finished with this one, I shall go downstairs and poison him. Then we can tell the police that he murdered her savagely and then killed himself.' Gisler spoke calmly, as if he had done this many times before. 'This should not take long, but has to be done whilst she is still alive.'

Jago saw the look on the face of Madame Camargue. She

held her old fingers across her mouth.

'Is it really necessary?' she asked.

'You were the one who told me they were coming here. You knew what I wanted to do and agreed. Is it not enough that I have given you ten thousand dollars?' he answered angrily, his whispered words cutting through his teeth.

'I feel as if I have betrayed her,' the woman replied.

'But you have, Madame Camargue. Your need for money took precedence over your friendship,' Gisler said. 'And then you contacted me . . .'

'Do you have to kill her?' she asked.

'Of course, how else do you think I can remove the venom? Under the jaw of every one of these beasts is a gland of poison. If I distil the poison I can save the lives of anyone bitten by such a creature,' Gisler said. Then he stepped away from the bed and looked at the door.

Jago froze, hoping he would not be heard. He held his breath.

'You told me you wanted the venom for business?' Madame Camargue asked, as if she suspected a lie.

'The man I work for has a son who fell in love with someone like this. She took his life and turned him into a beast like her. My employer has kept his son locked away from the world and fed on pig's blood until I can find a cure for him. When I do, I shall be a rich man, then I will build my museum to an extinct race. I have a collection of Vampyre heads that I bought from a man in England. That number of artifacts proves their existence. When the last of the beasts is dead I will open the doors of my museum and welcome the world.' Gisler held the scalpel in his hand. 'Now I need your assistance, Madame. Hold the woman down and I will make the first incision.'

'It doesn't feel right, Herr Gisler,' she said as she stepped towards the bed and moved the table lamp closer to Lana. 'Perhaps we could find another?'

'This is the one that I want. Now come and help me before the sedative wears off and she screams hell upon us,' Gisler answered as he wrapped a rubber apron around his waist and covered his expensive shoes in galoshes.

'Very well,' the Madame answered reluctantly. 'But please do not make me watch.'

Gisler reached forward, leaning over Lana with the knife in his hand as if he were was looking for the place to make the incision. Jago stepped back silently from the door and squeezed his fingers tightly together. The knife blade jumped from the handle with a loud click.

'What was that?' he heard Gisler say from the other side of the door.

Before he could find out, Jago kicked the door with as much force as he could. It separated from the wall, the hinges and boards still intact as it fell in to the room. Gisler was knocked beneath it. Jago heard his muffled cries as he walked on the door and into the room.

'You betrayed her,' he said as he stared at the Madame.

'I had to – he made me,' she answered, pointing at the arm that lay outstretched from under the door still clasping the scalpel. 'He was in the Gestapo, stationed here during the war when this was a house for the officers. He heard the stories of our *guests* and gave me his contact in Zurich. He said that he would tell the authorities I was a collaborator if

I refused.'

Jago opened the door from its frame and Gisler stared at him. The small bifocal glasses were smashed across his face. Blood was smeared over his silk shirt. He looked up at Jago and saw the knife in his hand.

'You are supposed to be asleep,' he said softly, as if he spoke to an unruly child. 'Then again, your kind have never met any of my expectations.'

'You were going to kill her,' Jago said as he waited for the man to stand up.

'It would have been a necessary waste of her life,' he said serenely, as if it were of no consequence. 'In the war I saw many people just like her, but I could never find enough venom to make an antidote. They all had their uses and in the end they can be boiled down to make the most luscious glue.'

Jago ignored him and cut the bands around Lana's wrists.

'Do you have a car?' he asked the woman.

'Herr Gisler has a car, a Rolls-Royce. He keeps it in the barn,' she said as Jago took the gag from Lana's mouth. 'It has a travel warrant. No one will stop you.'

'But you can't,' Gisler said as he got to his feet and turned his back on the woman. 'I need to get to Zurich.'

Gisler stopped speaking and held the front of his waist-coat. Jago saw the long steel instrument sticking from his back. Blood trickled through his fingers and across the palm of his hand. He turned back to Madame Camargue.

'You are a monster,' she said. 'The children that vanished . . . the Jewish woman from the farm by the bridge – it was you,' she said, her voice shaking. 'You experimented on them all.'

Herr Gisler shook uncontrollably. He tried to push the blade from within him and reached around to his back to take hold of the handle.

'Is that true?' Jago asked as Lana woke from her sleep and rubbed her face.

'It was my job. I am a doctor. Is that a crime? How many people do you kill in your quest for life?' Gisler laughed as he spoke. It was as if he no longer cared what happened to him. 'I am proud of what I have done and long would it have continued.'

Jago rushed towards him and, grabbing the man by the shoulders, pushed him to the wall. The blade pressed through his chest. Gisler hung against the wall like a discarded puppet. Blood seeped from his mouth as he coughed and choked and then slumped to the floor.

'You are a fool, Madame. You complain of him taking life and yet you gave Lana to him,' Jago said as he held the knife towards her.

Lana looked around her. 'Jago?' she said, not knowing how she had got there.

'It was Gisler. He drugged the champagne and wanted to kill us,' Jago answered.

'He has a companion, in the barn,' Madame Camargue said. 'He is a driver who was with Herr Gisler during the war. That man has the keys to the Rolls-Royce.'

'What?' Lana asked.

'We have to get away from here, Lana. It is not safe,' Jago said.

'Gisler wanted your venom. He worked for a man with a child who is a Vampyre,' Madame Camargue said apologetically.

'You told him about me,' Lana replied as she stared at the woman. 'That was why he was here. When I called you from London you must have told him.'

'It was blackmail . . .'

'And ten thousand dollars for your trouble,' Jago added as the woman tried to vindicate herself.

'Go to the barn and tell the man to come here. If you warn him, I will kill you,' Lana said to the Madame as she sat up on the bed and tried to shake the drowsiness from her. 'Tell him that Gisler has something for him.'

The woman left the room. Jago dragged the body of Gisler into the bathroom. Then he lifted the doorframe and slid it back into the wall. It looked loose and broken. Lana laughed at him.

'I thought he was going to kill you,' Jago said, trying to explain why the door was that way. 'I just kicked it and the door fell down.'

She touched his hand. 'I am so thankful for you. You had a chance to leave but –'

'It crossed my mind. I thought of it, but didn't want to leave you here – no matter what is to come,' Jago answered. 'What will we do with the man when he comes?'

'You will do nothing. Just stay in the bathroom and close the door,' Lana said.

It was not long before footsteps came along the landing. Jago had left the door open. Lana lay on the bed. The voice of the man carried along the passageway with his footsteps.

'Gisler,' he said in German, his accent strong and from the suburbs of Berlin. 'Why do you wake me at this time of night?' The man pushed the open door further and the wooden frame moved. He looked at Lana. 'Where is Gisler?'

'I am here for you instead. He left me as a present – he is with Madame Camargue.'

The man stood in the doorway and looked at Lana. He smiled to himself.

'I remember this place during the war. It was even better than it is now. Are you German?' he asked her.

'I am Flemish, but I know Berlin very well,' she said as she smiled and rolled her lipstick across her lips.

'Why waste it – when I will smudge it from your face?' the man said. 'I will never know Berlin again. There are too many Russians in the place. But Flemish women are another thing.'

The man stepped forward. Lana slipped her legs to the floor and stood before him. He reached out with a hand and placed it on her shoulder.

'You have a strong hand,' she said as she smoothed her fingers over his arm.

'Gisler brought me here for that reason. He was obsessed with Vampyres. Quite mad. He thought about them all the time. He said that they were everywhere in France and that he would find a cure for their poison,' the man answered as he touched her face and pushed her back towards the bed.

Jago listened from behind the bathroom door. He looked around at Gisler slumped in the bath with a towel over his head so that Jago could not see his dead, staring eyes. In the room, Lana pulled the man closer to her. He was tall and stocky, with a day's growth of beard and the smell of French beer. The veins in his neck stood out from his skin. She counted the beats and could see his heart pulse faster.

191

His thoughts were garbled, beer-soaked and concerned for only one thing. He held her tighter and tighter, as if he would never let go. Lana could feel herself being lifted from the floor. She kissed his neck, nuzzling the skin. The man smiled and sighed at the same time.

It was then that she bit him. At first he felt nothing. Then as she bit deeper he began to jerk. The venom seared instantly into his blood as if his veins were filled with acid. He began to scream and with all of his strength pushed Lana to the bed as the blood pumped from the wound. He stepped back and grabbed the table lamp.

'Where is Gisler?' he demanded.

'He is dead,' she answered.

'You are a –' he tried to say as he felt his legs fade beneath him.

'A Vampyre?' she asked, tormenting him as she got to her feet.

The man dropped the lamp. The bulb smashed and the room darkened, lit only by the crack of light that surrounded the bathroom door. He tried to turn and walk from the room. Lana stepped to him and, taking hold of his shirt collar, pulled him back into the room.

'Where are you going?' she asked as he staggered away from her again like a cat playing with a dying mouse. 'Jago, come and see . . .'

The bathroom door opened. The man caught a glimpse of Gisler, his arm hanging out over the bath. Then Jago stepped into the room.

'They would have killed us, Jago,' Lana said as if to justify what she was about to do.

192

'Please, no . . . you don't understand – I never . . .' the man said as he started to cry.

Jago pushed the man out of the way as he walked from the room. His stomach turned at the smell of the blood. He heard the body of the man slump to the floor as the lamp was smashed. There were footsteps and a sound like a cat lapping milk. He sat on the floor with his head in his hands and tried to get the image of Gisler out of his mind.

Madame Camargue was climbing the stairs.

'Back to the room. Get back there now,' she said. She was pointing an old Luger pistol with a long silencer at Jago. 'I want my money. I want all of it for me.'

Jago got to his feet and did what she had asked. She pushed the gun into his back and walked him to the door.

Entering the room, he saw Lana over the body of the man. She was wiping the blood from her face with the towel that had covered Gisler.

'Madame Camargue wants her money,' Jago said as he stepped inside.

'What are you doing?' she asked the woman.

'I telephoned the man in Zurich. He said if Gisler was dead I could have all the money for your venom. All I have to do is kill you and he has a chemist who can do what is needed. He is sending a butcher from Valence to take it from you.'

'How much did he promise to give you?' Lana asked as she got to her feet and stepped over the body, watching the Madame closely.

'Thirty thousand dollars.'

'I will give you sixty. Did you think we would ever give up on you? It was our money that built this house. Your family have always been our companions. I have stayed here many times and remember the day you were born.'

Madame Camargue hesitated. The gun trembled.

'Sixty thousand? I remember you when I was a child, you always brought me things from Paris,' she whispered as if speaking to herself.

'We are old friends. Just give me the pistol and I will make it safe. I have nearly that amount in my bag. We can go to Valence and get more in the morning,' Lana answered.

'But what about the butcher?' Madame Camargue asked, her mind changed.

'You can tell him we escaped. I will give you money to make him sweet.'

'And the man in Zurich?' she asked.

'Give me his name and telephone number and I will speak to him. I will help him with his own son.'

Madame Camargue reached into the pocket of her dress and handed a small gold card to Jago.

'That is the man,' she said. It was as if she could no longer think.

'And the gun?' Lana asked softly, her voice warm and as rich as her lipstick.

The Madame turned the pistol and handed it to Lana and stepped back.

'I am sorry, Miss Karlstein. It was the war. The things that happened have changed me so much,' she said, and she put her hands to her face as if they would catch her tears of regret.

The bullet crashed into the wall as Madame Camargue fell to her knees. She grabbed Jago's hand as if he could stop her death. He jumped back, seeing the puncture wound in her chest as she fell to the floor.

Madame Camargue was dead.

18

Five Gold Rings

THE STEAM TRAIN pulled into King's Cross Station, filling the cavernous building with white smoke. It reflected off the gas lamps and the opening doors of the carriages as Walpurgis stepped from the train and followed the line of bedraggled night-time travellers. As he looked up through the swirling smoke, the illuminated clock above Platform 9 crept towards the third hour of the morning.

He had slept on the train. His compartment had been empty since Doncaster. All he could dream of was Mina Karlstein. Again and again he re-lived her falling from the cliff, dropping like a stone and vanishing in the sea. Walpurgis had stayed for an hour above the water and waited to see if anything of her remained. Among the waves that ebbed back and forth and beat against the cliffs there had been no trace of her. He had gone back to Hawks Moor and searched the house, but like the sea it offered nothing.

There was no evidence, no sign of where he should go next, nothing concerning Ezra Morgan. Even the papers in the manuscript room had been searched through. It was as if any memory of Ezra Morgan had been erased from life. The only thing he had found, hidden in an envelope and wrapped in fine tissue paper, were five gold rings. They were identical in every way and the size of a ring finger of a man. The writing on the envelope gave the date as 29 December 1709. The envelope had been sealed with wax and signed by Morgan. On each ring, Walpurgis had found a word written in symbols he could not understand. Now, as he walked along the platform to the rank of black taxi cabs, he thought of where he might have seen the writing before.

In his travels, Walpurgis had heard that Vampyres had created their own language and disguised their writings in a coded text. But having never seen any of this writing, he could not be sure.

Leaving the station, he opened a cab door and sat in the back. The taxi driver threw the remnants of tea from his tin cup out of the window and looked in the rear-view mirror.

'Where to, mister?' he asked in a thick Bow accent.

Walpurgis thought. He didn't know where he was going.

'Two Bridges,' he said after a while and a raised eyebrow from the driver. 'Two Bridges, just by the Strand.' He had not been there for many years, but knew the bar would be open. It was discreet and hidden away from London life in a quiet side street. Walpurgis knew that it would be full at this time of the morning. Actors, dancers and radio announcers would be crowding the tables and fill the air with loud conversation.

When the taxi pulled up outside, Walpurgis looked at the door. 'I have changed my mind,' he said to the man's annoyance. 'Take me to Ludgate Hill.'

'And that will be the last place?' the driver asked.

'Unless I change my mind again,' Walpurgis said as he closed his eyes and settled back in the leather seat.

Stopping again on the corner of Old Bailey, the driver looked in his mirror.

'This good enough?' he asked expectantly, an unsmoked cigarette hanging from his lip. 'Would you like to go anywhere else?'

Walpurgis looked out of the window. The street was empty. 'This will be fine,' he said. He paid the man and opened the door.

He watched as the red tail-light of the taxi vanished in the London smog. Crossing the road to the small door, he checked the contents of his bag. Then, checking that the street was empty, he kicked the door of the Banco Perazzi as hard as he could. It smashed open. The locks splintered the wood and fell to the tiled floor of the entrance.

'Heston Walpurgis,' Lucca said as he came forward. 'Most people knock when they want to come in.'

'The last time I was here you tried to kill me,' Walpurgis answered.

'The last time you were here, you wanted to see the contents of every deposit box,' Lucca said.

'I was looking for something valuable,' Walpurgis replied as he looked suspiciously around the room. 'Where are your companions?'

'Sadly, I only have Carlo. His brother was murdered,' Lucca answered.

'Murdered? Here in the Banco Perazzi?' Walpurgis asked mordantly.

'By Jago Harker. He stabbed him with a silver knife. Just like he did to you,' Lucca said, pointing to Walpurgis with a long, bony finger.

Walpurgis laughed. 'What trouble the lad causes us all. I was talking to Ozymandias about him. It seems everyone wants him dead.'

'Even you . . . Harker told me of the debt and the money you want. He came here and asked me to pay him the money. I told Harker that unless Hugh Morgan gave his consent then I could not release any money,' Lucca said as he crossed the lobby and closed the door to keep out the smog that hung about Walpurgis as if it oozed from within him.

'Where is he now?' Walpurgis asked as he picked up the shackle of a broken lock and held it in his hand.

'Gone. Taken far away to another land,' Lucca said. 'I don't know where, only that it will be for a long time.'

'Who by?'

Lucca's brow wrinkled, and a small lined creased at the side of his mouth. He looked at the ceiling and then to Walpurgis. He knew he couldn't lie. The man would just kill him.

'I want you to leave and when you leave I would like to still be alive,' he said, his voice taut. 'For that I will help you as much as you want.' Lucca cupped his hands together and tried to look Walpurgis in the face.

There was the snap of a hand. Walpurgis grabbed him by the lapel of his cashmere suit and pulled him from his feet. 'I don't make any deals,' he said as he dragged Lucca across the room and threw the man across a table. Then, taking the knife from his bag, he held it to his throat. 'Who took him and where did they go?'

Without warning, a small door opened just below the ceiling. It smashed to the floor below as Carlo leapt from the dark void into the room. Instantly the monkey was on

199

Walpurgis. It held fast, biting into his shoulder as hard as it could. Walpurgis lurched back and staggered across the room. He twisted and turned as the monkey bit harder.

Lucca feverishly searched the desk drawer. Walpurgis fell back against the wall. The monkey screamed and dropped to the floor. Walpurgis kicked the creature as it grabbed his leg and held tight.

'Leave, or Carlo will kill you,' Lucca shouted, his voice in a panic.

'Get it from me,' Walpurgis answered as the claws of the beast dug into the sword wound in his leg.

Lucca pulled out a small Derringer pistol from the desk drawer and pointed it at Walpurgis.

'Leave now, or I will shoot you,' he shouted, his hand trembling as he pulled back the firing hammer. His face looked like that of a bearded Pierrot clown. A fearful tear trickled down his cheek. Fingers of thick smog crept into the room from under the door.

'Get the monkey off my back,' Walpurgis insisted.

'Carlo, leave,' Lucca shouted.

The monkey jumped to the floor. In two long strides it leapt across the lobby and onto the table. It sat by Lucca, bloodied mouth open, staring at Walpurgis.

'All I want to know is how to find Jago Harker. Tell me and I will leave you alone,' Walpurgis insisted as the monkey continued to snarl at him. 'And I have these five gold rings. They each have a word written on the outside in a language I do not know.'

'Rings? Five rings?' Lucca asked. 'Where did you get them from?'

'Hawks Moor, in an envelope signed by Morgan. It is dated 29 December 1709 and sealed with wax. Look.'

Walpurgis reached into his pocket and threw the envelope onto the table. Lucca put down the pistol and looked inside. Taking a magnifying glass from his coat, he held each ring up to the light from the chandelier.

'Varzik,' he said. 'An old dialect, but I am sure of it.'

'Beyond Constantinople?' Walpurgis asked. He had heard of a village of this name, far away from any other town or city in a desolate land.

'Beyond Babylon and the Garden of Eden. Varzik is a legend. A place where the history of the Vampyres started.' Lucca placed each ring back in the envelope and pushed it reluctantly across the table to Walpurgis.

'What does it say on each ring?' he asked.

'They are just names. Worthless names, of no consequence. It will do you no good to know of them.' Lucca hesitated, as if his mind suddenly thought of something. 'You say that you found them at Hawks Moor?'

'They were in a drawer in an old room where Morgan kept his papers,' Walpurgis said as he stepped closer to the table, keeping an eye on Carlo.

'And Mina Karlstein let you take them?' he asked.

'How did you know she was there?' Walpurgis replied.

'There are so few of us left, we all tend to know each other's business.'

'Mina Karlstein is dead.' Walpurgis put his hand on the table. 'Look at the rings again. Please, tell me what you know.'

'Dead?' Lucca asked, not distracted by Walpurgis. 'How did she die?'

'An accident. She was running on the cliffs and fell into the sea,' Walpurgis said, allowing the picture of her falling to flood his mind.

Lucca put his hand to his face as if to cover his eyes from what he could see. Walpurgis swept the table with his hand, picking up the gun like a magician picks up a card.

'What a pity,' Lucca said solemnly. 'She was always quite a favourite. We grow fewer every day.' His mind was occupied by many things at once. 'You do know that there are five rings for the five pillars of Vampyre wisdom? A ring for each finger and one for the thumb. That is all it says. Each word tells you of which pillar it is – superstition and hogwash, even I don't believe in all that.'

'Pillars of wisdom? I have never heard of such a thing,' Walpurgis said as he pulled the Derringer into his grasp.

'Breshovit – Shemot – Veyikra – Midvah – Devarim . . . They teach us the true meaning of what we are supposed to be. They were invented long ago when eternal life proved too much and some of my kind thought they had to have a god. I would rather have had a pillar of gold – in that can I trust. Secret societies and nonsense of new birth and life beyond death leave me cold.' Lucca laughed as he spoke, his voice cackling like an old witch's.

'So you don't follow the Cult of the Oracle?' Walpurgis asked. 'It would seem that the belief grows every day.'

'Only with those who have nothing else. Fear and isolation bring faith in such things. I may be a Vampyre but I am not a fool,' he answered.

'A supernatural creature that does not believe in the supernatural?' Walpurgis asked.

202

'Many years ago I met a man and we spent time together. We ate and talked and walked barefoot by the sea. I trusted him and he promised me a different life. He was a Vampyre and he took my blood. I am not a supernatural creature; I just live longer and need to be refreshed so that I can live. I am just a product of this world, a variation in species that will one day be proved by science. I just hope I live long enough to see that day.'

'What makes you think that would never come to pass?' Walpurgis asked.

'The man behind you with a gun pointed at your head,' Lucca answered. 'I pressed the alarm when you broke into the building. Since Jago Harker came here, the Maleficarum has placed me under guard. You have been outwitted, Heston Walpurgis – outwitted . . .'

Walpurgis slipped the envelope into his pocket as he felt the barrel of a gun press into the nape of his neck.

'Outwitted indeed,' he said. He smiled at Lucca. 'I have to say, I would have killed you. That was my plan when I came here. Yet in the last few minutes I had changed my mind. I saw in you something different, different and nearly human.'

The man holding the gun prodded Walpurgis with the barrel. 'There is a car outside. Someone wants to see you,' he said, his voice dark and gruff like a dishevelled bear's.

'But what if I don't want to see *them*?' he asked, knowing that he couldn't run away or grab the gun that was stuck in his neck.

'Aha.' Lucca laughed. 'I see you have not lost your sense of humour, Walpurgis. But I think that it is time for you to go.' The words ended abruptly as the monkey crawled on to

Lucca's back and hung over his shoulders like a fur cape. The eyes of the creature followed Walpurgis as if it knew what would happen.

There was a sudden and sharp cracking of bone as Walpurgis twisted the arm of the man behind him. Then, as the man dropped to his knees and the gun fell to the floor, Walpurgis kicked him as hard as he could. The body went limp and dangled like a puppet. Walpurgis lowered the man slowly to the floor.

'As you were saying, Lucca, it is time for me to leave,' Walpurgis said as he picked the gun from the tiles and slipped it into his pocket. 'Tell the Maleficarum that I am to be left alone. I work for Ozymandias.'

Lucca nodded nervously as Walpurgis looked about the room – it was as if he were trying to remember every detail for some future time.

'I trust you will not need to return to see me?' Lucca asked nervously as the monkey chattered on his back.

'There may be a time in the future when I need to speak to you again,' Walpurgis answered. Then he walked to the broken door, pulled the handle and looked into the street. 'For now I will say goodbye – and remember that I let you live.'

He slammed the door behind him and, taking two paces across the pavement, he pulled on the car door. It opened easily. Walpurgis reached in and grabbed the driver from the front seat and pulled him to the pavement. He hit him twice and dragged him into the shadows of a doorway, where he covered him with a pile of tattered old newspapers so he could not be seen.

The street was empty. There was no other car on the road.

In the distance a clock struck the half hour and even further away a steam train rattled through the night. Walpurgis got into the driver's seat of the car and turned the key.

Looking into the rear-view mirror, he saw two eyes staring at him.

'You took your time,' the man said as Walpurgis slowly revved the engine.

'I thought you were dead,' he answered.

'Sometimes it is better to be dead than alive. You can achieve much more,' the man answered as Walpurgis heard the slither of a metal blade shoot from the end of the walking stick in his hand. 'In the last six years I have learnt much about this world.'

'So have I. Every morning I walked around a walled cell. I could see the grey sky above me but nothing else. It gave me time to think,' Walpurgis said. He wondered if the man was going to stab him with the blade.

'That was a sad place, but it was necessary. If you had been free during the war I don't think you would be alive today. You should thank me for putting you in a place where you could come to no harm.'

'I was in a Gestapo prison. That wasn't fun,' Walpurgis said as he reached inside his bag.

'I wouldn't do that,' the man said. He put the blade to the back of Walpurgis's neck. 'I know that you will either have a knife or a gun or even some strange artifact to which I am allergic – so let me see your hands.'

'Are you going to kill me?'

'I think it is time to do a deal, my dear Walpurgis. I need information, information about people, and you are the man to get it for me,' the man said as he leant forward.

'I won't work for the Maleficarum,' Walpurgis answered.

'Neither will I. When you found the Oracle diamond for me it was the fulfilment of my life. It is in a very safe place and its purpose will soon be revealed.'

'Then what do you want me to do?' Walpurgis asked.

'I will pay you everything I owe you and give you the same again if you kill my son and Jago Harker.'

'It would seem that is what every Vampyre desires – but why does Ezra Morgan need them both dead?' Walpurgis turned and looked into the face of Ezra Morgan.

'It is a long story, my dear Heston. To cut it short, I should say that in both cases I was betrayed. I believe you have the rings that you found at Hawks Moor?' he asked.

'How did you know?' Walpurgis replied as he felt the envelope in his pocket.

'They are special to me. It is good that you have them and they were left for you to find. Breshovit, Shemot, Veyikra, Midvah, Devarim. They may mean little to you but to the Cult of the Oracle they are everything. Breshovit is the beginning; Shemot is the name; Veyikra is for the calling; Midvah is the desert and Devarim the word. It is only when we have passed through all of these things that we will know the real meaning of the world and the essence of the Oracle.'

'Why should I need them?' Walpurgis asked.

'Because there are people who want to kill you,' Morgan answered as he sat back in the leather seat and pulled up the fur collar of his coat.

'There have always been people who want to kill me,' Walpurgis answered as he felt the cold steel on the side of his neck. 'What makes this any different?'

'Ozymandias wants you dead. He is tricking you and you have fallen for him. The woman Arantez – she was going to murder you. That is why I sent the assassin. She had poison. You are a puppet. Ozymandias wants you dead. It is quite simple.'

Ezra Morgan grunted the words as if he were enjoying each breath. The car filled with smoke from the Havana cigar that he dragged upon. It burnt red and shone bright on his face.

'He too asked me to kill your son and Jago Harker. Why should he try to trick me?'

'You are being followed. Everywhere you go he has someone after you. When you find Jago Harker he will be rescued from your grasp and it's you who will end up dead. He thinks you will lead him to the diamond.'

'He has had every chance to kill me. Why should I trust you?' Walpurgis asked as his hand went to the handle of the car door to make ready for his escape.

'It is for you to decide who to trust. I will happily go inside the bank and get your money – but will it do you any good?' Morgan asked.

'At least I would be able to eat,' Walpurgis answered.

Morgan slipped a gold case from his pocket and unclipped the lid. Walpurgis could see it was a cover for an old chequebook. Taking a pen, Morgan scrawled on the cheque with thick black ink. He pulled it from the book, gripping his cigar between his teeth.

'I think you will find that is the money to cover the Oracle diamond. It will be accepted by any bank.' Morgan scribbled another cheque. 'I will sign this when you have killed Jago

207

Harker and my son.'

'I need to know why you want them dead,' Walpurgis said as he took the cheques from Morgan.

'It was what the diamond inculcated. It has to be obeyed. Your life depends on it.' Ezra Morgan sighed smoke from his cigar and smiled benignly. 'In one hour all of the council of the Lodge Maleficarum will be dead. As we speak, I have people ready to kill them. In New York, Paris, Rio de Janero and even London there will be much blood given. How does that make you feel, Heston Walpurgis?'

19

Slattern

'SHE WOULD HAVE helped us,' Jago said as he wiped the flecks of blood from the shoulder of his coat.

'Madame Camargue was a slattern. She worked for the Gestapo throughout the war. Now she was going to sell us to the highest bidder,' Lana said as she drove the Rolls-Royce around a narrow bend on the road through the mountains.

'But they will be discovered – three murders and people will know we have been there,' Jago said as he watched the winged angel on the bonnet of the car glint in the morning light.

'Two dead Gestapo officers and a traitor? It will go unnoticed and uncared for. She made so much money from them during the war that she was resented. I have never trusted her since she was a child. There was always something about her that made me nervous.' Lana pulled up by the side of the road that overlooked a narrow mountain pass. 'There was something that Gisler said that intrigued me. When I searched his jacket I found a key to a hotel room in Cannes.'

'It's where he was staying?' Jago asked, wondering about the significance.

'It was for Room 213 at the Carlton Hotel.'

'And?' he asked, looking out of the side window at the drop to the river below.

'That room belongs to the Lodge Maleficarum. No one else should have access to it. Gisler must have been working for someone in the Lodge.'

Lana started the engine of the car and drove away, following the road down the side of the mountain. They didn't speak for the rest of the hour. The old Rolls-Royce was as gentle as a feather bed and Jago slept fitfully, waking every other mile to check Lana was still awake. The sky grew brighter; the covering of cloud broke with the morning sun. He could soon smell the sea.

The car turned on to a long promenade with an avenue of palm trees.

'Have you been here before?' Jago asked as he saw the towers of the Carlton Hotel appear before him.

'In 1910, just after it was opened – or was it 1911? I can't remember. It is a good place to spend the winter,' Lana said as she geared down and pulled the car into a small and littered side street.

'What are you doing?' Jago asked as she turned again.

'Getting rid of the car, it is too obvious, even for Cannes. You get out and go back to the corner. I will be with you soon.'

Jago got out of the car and walked back down the road. Lana was soon with him, just as she had said. In her hand was the hotel key.

'Later I need to see a man who lives here,' she said.

'Another companion?' he asked.

'An old friend. He is one of us – a Vampyre of great distinction. He was once a famous artist and now mends motor cars.'

'Can he be trusted?' he asked, trying to keep pace with her long, quick strides.

'I don't know,' she said as they turned the corner back on to the long promenade. 'When we go into the hotel, act as if you own the place and remind me to buy you some new clothes.'

Jago looked at his leather coat. It was torn at the shoulder, the cuffs were stained and traces of blood covered each lapel. He could feel the grime of his shirt collar.

Lana took the steps of the hotel two at a time. A man in a long red coat and top hat opened the door. Lana flashed the brass Carlton key fob to him and then looked back at Jago and sighed as if he were a servant. The doorman smiled and doffed his hat, allowing the door to close as soon as Jago had walked through.

Jago followed Lana through the marble lobby with its glittering myriad of crystal lights and up the first flight of stairs. She walked purposefully, knowing where she was going. Turning the landing, she opened the door on a long gold-lined corridor. It had several doorways, each daubed in gilt that stood out against the red carpet. Jago heard her muttering the door numbers as she counted each door.

'Room 213,' she said as she slipped the key in the lock. 'Hope it's empty.'

The door opened slowly and she stepped in. Jago followed, not knowing what to expect. A large gold-framed bed with silk sheets was by the window. A suitcase was by the bed and papers were strewn on the dressing table.

'Looks like Gisler was coming back,' Jago said, as he read a letter on the desk by the window and ran his fingers across the Gestapo imperial seal embossed on the paper.

Lana took it from him and read the first few lines.

'He was a scientist. The Gestapo knew all about our existence and they were trying to see if there was anything in us that could help them win the war. I heard of some of the things they did.' Lana looked away as she screwed the paper defiantly in her hand. 'They thought we were monsters – what a joke . . .'

She stopped and picked up a discarded photograph from the desk and stared at it. Jago could see her eyes searching every detail. He looked over her shoulder at the sepia image. Gisler was standing by an old fountain, his arms around a man and a woman who looked liked Mina. Behind them stood another man. He was taller, handsome, and his long fingers rested on the shoulder of the woman as if he loved her. In his other arm, cradled as if by a caring father, was a small boy.

'It has to be a fake,' he said, unable to even dare think the truth. 'They couldn't know him.'

'It isn't a fake,' Lana said as she read the writing on the back of the photograph. 'This was taken in 1939. It *is* my sister, Mina, and Ezra Morgan. They knew Gisler, they knew what kind of a man he was. The other man – the other man is . . .'

'You think Gisler worked for the Lodge?' Jago asked.

'What was the name of the man in Zurich?' she asked urgently, holding out her hand as if she wanted the card she took from Madame Camargue. Jago searched his pocket and brought out the card. It was dirty and creased, with a smear of blood across the front. He gave it to her. 'Erik Leonhardt,' she said as she read the name.

'Does it mean anything to you?' Jago asked.

'That is the name often used by my blood-father. He was the doctor who saved Mina and me from the plague. He was a Vampyre. That is the man in the photograph.'

Lana searched the room until it was late afternoon. She took apart the luggage she found in the wardrobe and cut up Gisler's wash bag with nail scissors. Even the collars of the neatly folded shirts were ripped open as she searched for any clue or sign that she could find. She didn't tell Jago what she was looking for, and he wondered if she was just meticulously destroying every trace of Gisler. Eventually she slumped into the leather chair by the bathroom door and put her head in her hands and began to cry. Jago went from the window seat that overlooked the beach and the promenade and put his arms around her.

'What is it?' he asked, his heart torn.

'I thought there would be something other than the photograph. There has to be a connection.'

'Why should Gisler have the name of the Vampyre who took your blood?' he asked knowing as soon as he spoke that it would make matters worse.

'I had to know why,' she sobbed. 'We have always been so close. A family beyond time. He went on a trip to America on board a ship called the *Titanic*. An iceberg struck it and we thought he was dead. All the while he was living in Zurich.'

'Could it be someone of the same name?' Jago asked.

'It is him. I have looked at his face for hundreds of years.

He vanished when the boat sank and I never saw him again. But Mina has been with him and there is another child. They have the same eyes. It is his child, his,' she said, her voice filled with panic. 'What was he doing, Jago? Why didn't Mina tell me he was alive?'

Jago picked up the photograph again. He looked at the face of Ezra Morgan. He was smiling at Mina, holding her hand. Gisler looked comfortable in his open-necked shirt and dark glasses. There was a reflection in the glass that looked like someone he knew but he could not be sure. He studied the face of Leonhardt. It was thin, with high cheekbones and a shock of blond hair that spiked above his forehead. In the middle of his chin was a distinct dimple. Even in the sepia of the picture, he understood what she meant by his eyes. They were dark and piercing; the left eye had an iris much larger than the right, as if it had been damaged. The child appeared to have the same features and even though it looked only five or six years old it was obvious that Leonhardt was its father.

'Did you know that Mina had gone to Zurich before the war?' Jago asked.

'We had a time when we were far apart. I didn't see her for the whole of that year. I own a café, I spent my time there,' Lana answered in a way that suggested there was more to tell but she wanted to keep it secret. 'Can you see what I mean about the child?'

'He could be ten years old by now,' Jago said as Lana took the picture from him and held it to the light of the window. 'And Leonhardt, was he in the Maleficarum?'

'When he went missing on the *Titanic*, that was when Noel Kinross was made Master. Leonhardt was Master be-

214

fore him and was also the Keeper of the Oracle,' Lana said, holding back the anger of her betrayal. She went back to the chair and sank into the seat and looked out of the window at the two small islands out to sea. A large motor yacht steamed across the bay and in the street below an accordion was being played with rough hands.

'Is this to do with the Oracle diamond?' he asked, as if it were an answer to all he had been searching for.

Lana Karlstein looked at him and smiled. 'If I leave you alone, will you be here when I return?' she asked. She dropped the photograph to the floor as if she needed it no more.

'Where else can I go?' he replied as he sat on the silk sheets of the bed and smiled at her. 'I don't want to run away – what would be the point?'

'You could go back to England, hide away until we all forget about you, and live your life with your pretty girl,' she said in a tone that hinted of hidden jealousy.

'I want to find Hugh Morgan.'

Lana drew her breath, as if she were about to cry.

'I lied to you, Jago. I tried to make out that Hugh Morgan would be at the Luna Negri. But it is a place of solitude. You would be alone.'

'I know,' Jago answered. 'I thought for a moment that I might find him there but then I realised the truth.'

'And you still would come with me?' she asked.

'To Luna Negri?' he asked, knowing that her heart was changed.

Lana got to her feet and looked out the window. It was as if she had heard a sound that she recognised.

215

'I will be back soon. Stay here and –'

'I will be here when you return,' he said.

Lana reached into her bag and took out a roll of American dollars. 'If I don't come back, take these and head for London. Hide there, do anything, but don't go back to Hawks Moor.'

'But why?' he protested.

'I will lock the door and take the key. Answer it for no one.'

Lana was soon gone and Jago was left alone. He looked out of the window, trying to see her in the street below. The first hour passed slowly, as did the second and third. Jago slept for a while, his face pressed against the window ledge as he listened to the sounds of the street and harbour. Then he heard a faint click and a stumbled footstep, and opening his eyes he saw Lana. She had several large bags that she dropped on the floor.

'I slept,' he said, not knowing what else to say and glad to see her face.

Lana leant forward. The kiss was quite unexpected. Jago held her hand, then pulled her back towards him and kissed her again. He could taste chocolate on her lips and cherry cheesecake. It was then he noticed she had been crying.

'The Café Poet. And as for these, I couldn't resist.' Lana laughed, knowing his thoughts, as she nodded to the bags. 'New clothes – more fitting than a leather coat.'

Jago had never had clothes like these before. He tried on the jacket and shirts and slipped his feet in and out of the brogue boots.

'How did you know what I would like?' he asked her as he tried the tweed jacket for the seventh time.

'I saw it and thought you would look older, and it works,'

216

she said, proud of her accomplishment. 'Makes you look like a man.'

Jago looked in the mirror by the door. He looked different, much older. His hair was wild and tangled but the jacket was neat and hand-stitched.

'There is a winter coat, everything you will need.'

'For Luna Negri?' he asked.

Lana put down her bag and looked at him. 'I am not going to take you,' she said. She looked down at the red carpet with gold flowers woven intricately into the fabric. 'I think it is best that I change my plans.'

'But the Lodge Maleficarum? The orders to take me there?'

'They don't matter, Jago. Nothing matters any more,' Lana said as she walked to the bathroom and closed the door.

He heard the sound of the tap.

'But they'll come looking for you,' he said. 'They'll want to know why you never took me.'

Standing in the harsh light of the vanity mirror, she wiped the make-up from her face with the towel and looked at him. 'I went to see Renoir, the mechanic. He had just received a telephone call from an old friend in London. It would seem that the Lodge Maleficarum is no more. Last night, when we were travelling, the whole council of the Maleficarum was assassinated. Twelve of our kind were killed. There is no one to lead us, no one to keep control. The Maleficarum is no more.'

'Why did it happen?' Jago asked.

'It is all part of the prophecy. You would be born, the Lyrid of Saturn would give you power, the Maleficarum would come to an end. Every Vampyre on Earth will be killed, leaving only one. The race will start again. That is what the prophecy said and it has started to come true.' Lana tried to smile. She looked nervous, anxious about what she had to say. 'Renoir also told me that Mina was dead. Walpurgis killed her. Lucca from the Banco Perazzi telephoned and told him that Ezra Morgan has paid Walpurgis all the money he owed and has given him the same amount to kill you and Hugh Morgan.'

'What is happening?' Jago asked as Lana's words crashed about him like falling stones.

'You are to be tracked down and taken to the Cult of the Oracle and there you are to be sacrificed. Because of who you are, a Vampyre cannot do it. There is a price on your head for a million pounds. Even Renoir was tempted until –'

'Until what?' he asked.

'Until I told him I loved you,' she said simply and without emotion. 'He has painted me many times and owes me that favour. We have until tomorrow to get out of France.'

'We?' Jago asked.

'I can't let you go alone. You would be eaten alive.' She laughed as she brushed by and opened the bag of clothes. 'I have no idea where we can go – perhaps America or even Russia.'

'He will keep searching for us until we are found. I know what Walpurgis is like,' Jago said, not wanting to run from him for the rest of his life.

'So what would you do? Stand and fight?'

'If I had to,' he answered. 'Together it could be done.'

'He killed my sister. Walpurgis said she fell from a cliff, but Lucca told Renoir he could see everything in his mind and it was murder,' Lana said. She breathed hard, hoping that Jago

218

would not see inside her mind. 'Even Ozymandias is against you. He is talking to the remnant of Vampyres about what can be done. Renoir said that the only name that is spoken is that of Jago Harker. Everyone knows of you. You are a threat to us all.'

'So will Renoir betray you?' Jago asked not knowing if the man could be trusted.

'We cannot stay here. I have bought another car. If you are sure that you want to stay with me we could go to –'

'Zurich?' Jago asked knowing that in her heart she wanted to find Leonhardt.

'Zurich,' she answered. 'There is a train at midnight.'

'But what about the car?' Jago asked seeing that she had already changed her mind.

'I bought it from Renoir. He can't be trusted to keep it a secret. We will leave it in Nice before we take the train.' Lana looked at him, a crease of worry growing across her forehead. She began to speak slowly. 'Renoir told me that Heston Walpurgis knows we are in France. Morgan told him of our route to Luna Negri. He will be here in the morning.'

[20]

Le Train Bleu

A THIN WAITER in a shabby tuxedo and tight trousers walked through the narrow passageway on the rumbling train. Every compartment in every one of the ten carriages was full. The dining car had served only the first carriage and even though it was nearly midnight there were still eight carriages of people wanting to eat. Tapping feverishly at the door to the compartment, the waiter handed a drink through the opening. A hand reached out and dark eyes looked at the waiter. Then, as if he would not leave until money had been given, the waiter held out his hand.

'I have no change and you are not pretty enough for a ten-dollar bill,' Walpurgis said as he shut the door and slid the bolt, not wanting to be disturbed again.

He could hear the waiter chunter as he walked away. Walpurgis didn't care; the man was just another waiter on another train that rattled through France in the dark of night. The dinner gong rang on the wall by the stewards room. It signalled that the dining car of *Le Train Bleu* was ready to serve them as quickly as possible and push them into the already crowded bar for more drinks.

Walpurgis fastened the laces on his polished boots. He had

taken great care with cleaning them in the last four hours since leaving Paris. It had been all there was to do. Morgan had told him the route that Lana Karlstein would take to get to Luna Negri. He had been given duplicate keys to every hotel room the Maleficarum had used. He pondered the word, finding it hard to accept that the ancient order had been destroyed overnight. He had not believed Morgan until he had returned to the Hotel Julius and gone back to his room.

Julia had been waiting for him. He had sipped more of the tonic that Ozymandias had given him for the pain of the wound and as he had opened the door he could see her. She sat on the bed, wrapped in a blanket. Her red lipstick was smeared like mascara across her face. She had cried until she could cry no more. It had not taken her long to explain about the phone calls. People cancelled their reservations as news of the cull spread around the world.

'They even found Kubrick,' she had said, quite amazed. 'No one had known where he was living for the last five years. They found him and killed him. All are dead.'

Julia bit her fingernails as she stared into the darkness of the room. Walpurgis sat on the bed and touched her leg. It was cold, like death. The woman looked as though she had given up on life.

'I knew about an hour ago,' he had answered. 'Morgan told me what was going to happen and by then it was too late.'

'Don't like it,' she had snarled. 'Don't like it at all. I am leaving in the morning. Going back home to where it all started. I'm going to tell them who I am and see what they do. Funny – there is a legend about me in the valley. But this is no legend.'

221

'They won't believe you and if they do you will be killed,' he had answered.

'What else is there? There has always been order and control and now that we are free . . .' Her words trailed off as she looked at him.

'Just stay here. Keep on just as before,' Walpurgis had said, trying to keep her calm.

'If they can find people like Kubrick then what about me? If they ever wanted me dead what would I do?'

'Morgan said he wanted control of the Maleficarum – that's all. It has nothing to do with you.'

As he left the next morning, he knew that she was not convinced. She kissed him as he walked from the room, down the stairs and into the street. Now, as the train took him further south towards the coastal mountains of France, he wondered if he would see her again.

'Mr Heston, Mr Heston!' came the voice at the door as fingers tapped on the thin wooden panel.

'I'm busy,' Walpurgis replied.

'It is dinner – it cannot be delayed, Mr Heston,' the voice of the waiter insisted.

Opening the door, he looked into the narrow passageway. The waiter had gone and the train rattled and shook. Smoke blew in through a narrow crack in the window frame. The night flashed by as the half-shut blind swung back and forth, its long cord tapping against the glass. Walpurgis reached into his pocket and took out the knife and cut the cord. He wrapped the silk threads around his fingers and slid them into his pocket.

The waiter looked around the corner of the passageway.

'Just coming,' Walpurgis said before he could speak.

'The others at your table want to eat and are waiting for you.'

'Others?' Walpurgis asked. 'What others?'

'So full – so many people – no one eats alone,' he said as he walked away, not caring for the look on the face of Walpurgis.

The dining car of *Le Train Bleu* would not have been out of place on a cruise liner. It was decorated with gold leaf and on the panels between the windows were hand-painted views of France. The chandeliers above each table rattled as the train hit the joints in the track. As Walpurgis opened the door there was a sudden silence. The waiter pointed to a space at a table near the far doors. Walpurgis smiled at the other passengers who were all waiting to eat. Taking five long strides to the table, he slid onto the chair. There were two men and a woman. The men both wore dinner suits and looked like brothers. Both had Swiss beards and narrow, pinched eyes set in moon-shaped faces.

'The waiter said you were cleaning your boots,' the fatter bearded man opposite said, hoping to start a conversation.

'Yes,' Walpurgis answered as the svelte woman next to him in the tight black dress ruffled on her seat.

'We three are travelling together,' the other man said. 'We are going to Monaco to play in the casino.'

Walpurgis nodded as the man introduced himself and his friends. He didn't listen to the names; tomorrow he would leave the train and never see them again. The woman seemed interesting. She had a narrow face and long nose like an elegant horse. Her eyes were wide and deep brown. He could tell that her blond hair was dyed; the roots were just beginning to show.

'And you are?' the woman asked as she sipped the soup without getting her lips wet.

'Heston,' he answered.

'Heston? Is that all?'

'Just Heston,' he answered as she pushed the bowl away from her.

The dinner dragged slowly. Soup led to mutton and then crème brûlée. Conversation came and went and as the dining car emptied, Walpurgis stood to leave.

'You will drink with us?' the bearded man asked. 'Shame to spend the night on such a beautiful train as this and be asleep.'

'Sleep is just what I need,' Walpurgis replied. 'It has been a long war.'

'Is that where you got the wound to your leg?' the woman asked. 'I noticed you had a limp.'

'As I said, it has been a long war,' he replied. 'I wish you well at the casino and hope they don't take all your money.'

The woman laughed and the two men looked at him uncomfortably.

'That is to be seen,' the fatter of the two replied as he picked the remnants of the mutton from the fibres of his greasy black beard. 'We have enough to lose. The war was good for us.'

'I have never heard of a war being good,' Walpurgis said as he stepped away from them.

'People will always want to borrow money and someone has to provide,' the man answered.

'And with significant interest applied,' his brother said,

laughing contentedly.

'They own a bank,' the woman said. 'They are money-lenders to the rich and famous.'

'I am neither,' Walpurgis replied.

'That is a surprise,' the woman said as she held out her hand to him in a gesture of goodbye. 'I thought you were an actor on your way to the festival in Cannes. I am most disappointed.'

'I always disappoint a woman eventually,' he replied as he walked away.

A nagging doubt made him look back to the table, where he saw them in heated conversation. The face of the older bearded man was rage-red, as if their argument would make his heart explode.

Walpurgis carried on to his compartment. The steward looked out from his cupboard-like room and brushed back his long locks of gelatinous hair. 'Goodnight, Mr Heston,' he said, reading the name from the room list at the side of his door.

Walpurgis went inside and locked the door. He lay on the bed as the train rocked back and forth. At one point in the night he felt the steam engine slow down and he heard the sound of a busy platform outside. The lights of the station blinked in through the sides of the shutters as the door to the carriage opened and closed quickly.

When he woke, the compartment was in complete darkness. The train had stopped. Walpurgis sat up on the couchette. It was impossible, but he thought that there was someone near to him. He reached out his hand towards the switch for the light.

'I wouldn't do that,' a woman said in a whisper. 'They will

know you are awake.'

'What do you want?' he asked looking to where the voice had come from.

'Couldn't sleep – but then again, I never could,' she answered as he felt her hand touch the back of his arm. 'You are Heston Walpurgis, aren't you?'

'Who wants to know?' he replied, slowly pulling his arm away.

'What is the point in telling you my name? It will only disappoint you.' She laughed quietly to herself. 'Anyway, you will be dead by the morning.'

'I feel in wonderful health. A little older, perhaps but nothing that would bring my demise by morning,' he answered.

'I have been asked to kill you before you get to Cannes. Ozymandias knows of your betrayal. He too is disappointed.'

'I have never disappointed a man before, but there is always a first time,' he replied, wondering how the woman was going to try and kill him. 'Why should Ozymandias think I have betrayed him?'

'He was told by Ezra Morgan when they met for breakfast. I was telephoned in Paris and we joined the train. Lucky, really – we managed to secure the last three seats.'

'Are you a Vampyre?' he asked, not sensing anything about her.

'I hope to be. That is what has been promised. I worked for the Gestapo at Belzec. One day I came across a man that intrigued me. I discovered he was a Vampyre.'

'The man with the beard?' Walpurgis asked.

'It covers the scars on his face.'

'And he sent you to kill me – how will that be done?'

226

'You will jump from the train and be found on the side of the track. I will say that you attacked me and I fought back. The police will think you are a drunken Englishman.'

As his eyes grew accustomed to the darkness of the compartment he began to make out the shape of the woman. She sat in the chair by the window. In her hand she held a gun. Walpurgis could see the long barrel of the silencer pointed towards him.

'How did you get in the room?' he asked.

'It is amazing what a man will do for a beautiful woman. The steward has been most helpful.'

'He is a witness.'

'No, Heston, he is dead,' the woman said calmly. 'My friend needed to eat and there was nothing on the menu that he wanted.'

'So – Ozymandias wants me dead and that is it.' He sighed as if resigned to his fate.

'And then we go on to find the Oracle,' she answered, confident in what she was about to do.

'Does it exist?' he asked. 'I don't believe that a diamond could have such power.'

'It is more than just the diamond. There is an old monastery in the hills near to here. There is a rumour that the Oracle has been hiding there since before the war,' she said, Walpurgis sensing that she wanted to tell him more. He had met her kind before. A couple of kills and the confidence began to rise. They wanted the applause, the limelight, the adulation. He knew she would tell him more than he would ever need to know.

'It is a shame I will not be alive to see the Oracle. Is it near to here?' he asked.

'The Cave of Magdalene. Two of the monks were recently found dead. The legend is that they were killed by a wolf, but we know different,' she said boastfully.

'A Vampyre?' he replied tempting her to answer.

'Of course – the Vampyre is the Oracle.'

'Are you sure? I could always help you find it. I am an archaeologist.'

The woman laughed louder than she should have. 'Orders, my dear Heston, orders . . . It would have been nice, but I have been a companion for too long. I am promised that once you are dead I will become like they are.'

'What? Fat and with a beard?' He laughed.

'You are a cruel man, Heston Walpurgis,' the woman said, her voice soft and expectant.

'You could never imagine exactly how cruel I really am,' he answered.

Before the woman could speak she slumped forward and dropped the gun. Walpurgis slid his silenced Walther pistol back under the side of the bed. He lifted the woman from the floor and swathed her head in a towel from the small bathroom to stop the blood going on the sheets. Then he wrapped her in the bedclothes, opened the carriage window and slipped her to the track. She fell roughly. Walpurgis looked out just as the train began to move. The blanket caught in the wheels and dragged her beneath. He closed the window and picked her gun from the floor.

It was then he noticed the small bag by the chair. Walpurgis clicked the switch and opened the catch. He looked through the purse, taking the wad of francs and putting them in his pocket. In a small flap was a sepia photo of a man with a woman by his side holding a child. It was easy to tell they were a family. The child was the image of its father. He flicked it around in his fingers, looking for a name. On the back some words were scrawled in thick pencil: *To my beloved wife, eternally yours, Erik Von Leonhardt.*

Walpurgis didn't know the name. He slipped the photograph into the pocket of his coat and began to tidy the room. Then came a gentle knock at the door.

'Valissa! Valissa!' the man said as he turned a key on the outside.

Quickly pulling the door open Walpurgis dragged the man into the room by the scruff of his jacket. The bearded fat man fell in, stumbling across the low bed and falling against the wall.

'Have me killed, would you?' Walpurgis asked in anger as he grabbed the man, lifted him up and pushed him out of the door.

'Valissa!' the man screamed, as if she might appear like a summonsed spirit.

The man stumbled in the corridor as the train emerged from a tunnel and shook. Walpurgis dived for him. The man got to his feet and ran towards the empty dining car. He slammed the glass door and held it shut as Walpurgis pushed at it. The man let go and ran hoping to escape. Walpurgis chased on, the pain throbbing in his leg.

Through one door and then another the man ran until he pushed through the last door and and into the guard's van. It was dark and stacked with bags, cases and crates of old wine. The window on the door was open. A cold mountain wind blew around the van. Walpurgis could see no one but knew that the man was hiding.

'If you come out, I will allow you to live,' Walpurgis shouted above the roar of the wind, sensing the man was hiding behind a large mail sack stacked in the corner.

There was a sudden movement. The man looked out from his hiding place.

'Why should I trust you?' he asked.

'Don't tell me – this is your first time?' Walpurgis asked.

'Valissa – it was her idea. I was just told to keep her safe,' the man argued, his voice fearful.

Walpurgis rubbed his hands together and then cracked the knuckles on each finger of his right hand.

'I need information,' he said as he grabbed the man and pulled him to the door of the van. 'Information about who you are and who sent you.'

'I can't – please,' the man protested. He tried to drop to his knees as Walpurgis pushed him to the open window.

'Who sent you?' Walpurgis insisted as he forced the head of the man out of the window.

'Please, no,' the man shouted as the steam train billowed and thundered and he saw a distant tunnel screaming towards him. The steam engine shook. Walpurgis tightened his grip on the man as he begged for his life.

'I need to know – you haven't long,' Walpurgis shouted. 'Tell me!'

'I can't!' the man answered belligerently. He began to fight for his life as the tunnel in the mountain grew closer by the second.

'A name – was it Von Leonhardt?' he screamed as the train

rattled faster and the tunnel got closer and closer. Walpurgis pushed the man further out of the window so his back was arched away from the door and he had no way of escape.

'No – it was Ozymandias!' he screamed. 'Please, my –'

There was a look of horror on the face of the man and then a sudden crash. Blood splattered the walls of the carriage. The man was pulled violently from Walpurgis's grasp and then fell forward. Walpurgis grabbed him again, his hands smeared with blood as he held the headless corpse.

21

Gare de Mort

JAGO HARKER felt uncomfortable in the tweed suit, although it was finely cut and a perfect fit. He felt older. Lana had insisted that he brush the strands of long hair back across his forehead, and she had brushed his cheeks, which had been sallow and white, with a powdering of blusher. Jago was hungry. As they walked the concourse of the railway station, he looked at the passengers waiting for the train, feeling quite wicked inside as he eyed each one as if they were a potential meal.

One woman in particular caught his eye. She was in her thirties and obviously alone. She carried a small case made of battered leather. It dangled from her long and ringless fingers as if it were half empty. It was obvious that she was nervous. She kept looking up to the display on the notice board above her at the end of the platform. Lana smiled at Jago, knowing what he was thinking.

'There would be time,' she whispered. 'The train is delayed. The announcement says it is due to unforeseen circumstances.'

Lana pointed to the board. Jago could not read the words. He smiled at her.

'How would we do it?' he asked as he watched a covered stretcher being taken from the train and slipped into the back of a mortuary van.

'Just watch,' Lana said as she walked towards the woman and smiled at her. 'What is wrong with the train?' she asked in French, Jago unable to understand her words.

'I heard the gendarme say it was a murder. They found a body in the guard's van,' the woman answered with a shrug of the shoulders.

'My brother and I are travelling with you – do you know of a place we could have coffee?' Lana asked.

The woman hesitated as she looked at Jago. He smiled instinctively and touched the brim of the hat that Lana had forced him to wear. It was a gesture of welcome that was received with a slight move of the head.

'There is a café outside the station across the street,' the woman said as she leant back against the ornate stone pillar that supported a large glass chandelier high above them.

Lana hesitated and looked at Jago as if she was unsure about something.

'We are not from here – where did you say?'

The woman took her by the arm and laughed to herself. 'I will take you. The Police said it would be at least another hour before the train can go. I could do with a coffee.'

'My brother doesn't speak French,' Lana said as they walked towards Jago. 'I have had to translate everything.'

'You have a perfect accent,' the woman replied in English. 'I thought you were French. Your brother is cute,' she whispered.

'And he knows it,' Lana answered as they locked arms and

233

walked together as if they had known each other for a lifetime. 'I am Lana and this is Jago, and you?'

'Marie,' the woman said. 'The coffee is this way.'

Together they walked through the grand entrance of the station. The street outside was empty but for three taxi cabs. The drivers looked expectant and then, when they realised they could be of no service, grouped back together in conversation.

Crossing the avenue they walked into the alley that led to the Rue d'Alsace. Jago could see the lights of an all-night café. The tables outside were empty. The woman spoke quickly to Lana, swapping from French to English with ease. Jago walked behind. He felt sick and could feel the blood pulse through him as the excitement made him shiver. He watched Lana to see what she would do.

'Are you going far, Marie?' she asked the woman.

'To Paris. My mother is sick and I need to go and see her. I know she will be well when I get there. She calls me her forgetful daughter.' Marie giggled. It seemed out of place.

Lana stumbled on the heels of her shoes and fell against the wall of an alleyway beside a small hotel with blacked-out windows.

'My ankle,' she whispered.

Marie dropped her case and turned to help. In an instant, Lana had taken her by the arms and pulled her silently into the darkness. Jago breathed hard, looking back and forth, hoping they had not been seen. He grabbed the case as he heard a gentle whimper come from the darkness.

'Lana?' he asked.

'Quickly, Jago – she is still alive,' Lana answered.

Jago stepped into the alleyway. He could see the woman on the floor. Lana cowered over her like a lioness. The neck of the woman was smeared with blood. She looked up, her eyes frozen as if she were unconscious. Jago could sense her dying thoughts as she screamed inside. No one needed to tell him what was to be done. Jago pushed Lana out of the way and bit on the neck of the woman, feeling the heartbeat grower fainter and fainter until it stopped. He slumped back from the body.

'What shall we do with her?' he asked, his stomach sated.

'The dumpster,' Lana said as she pointed across the yard. 'If it belongs to the hotel, no one will find her until tomorrow.' Lana looked at him and pulled a white handkerchief from her pocket. 'You are a messy eater, Jago . . .'

Leaving the alley, Lana carried the small suitcase as if it had been with her every day of her life. She crossed the Avenue Thiers and walked towards the station. As the mortuary truck crossed in front of them, the driver slowed down and looked at Lana. It was a long, hard glance, as if he wanted to take in as much as he could of her face. Jago saw Lana smile at the man, then she took Jago by the hand and led him across the street as if he were a small child.

They waited together in silence. With a a mixture of fear and exhilaration, Jago could not stop thinking of what he had done. He could feel the blood fill his stomach but felt nothing for the woman.

Lana stood by the gate, tapping the heels of her shoes against the cold stone. A small group of people gathered around them, waiting for the train. Jago knew they were talking about the murder on the *Train Bleu*. An old man spoke with his hands, his fingers curling around every word he said as if he were a painter.

'What now?' he asked Lana.

She turned and pulled him close. 'If only I could tell you, Jago – but this is far too public a place.'

'Are we still going to Zurich?'

Lana sighed as she smelt the blood on his breath. 'We have our tickets. But things are changing so quickly.'

'But will we ever get away from them? If they want me that badly, surely they will keep looking for me?'

Lana thought for a moment as she bit her lip and looked around the station. 'We could take the war to them. There is only a handful left. I know people who would fight with us,' she said in a reluctant breath.

'Fight who?' he asked.

'Ezra Morgan, Ozymandias, Walpurgis . . .' Lana said as if the words were a kind of prayer at a funeral mass. 'They want you dead – if they were no more . . .'

The sound of the steam engine stopped the conversation. The gate to the platform opened and the crowd filed through.

The old man ranted at the gendarme. 'Vichy, Vichy . . .' he said again and again. 'Peutagne . . .'

The gendarme looked at the old man and laughed as he pushed him through the gate and then, as if the words had moved him, he walked away.

Jago and Lana followed the crowd and boarded the train. They sat in an empty First Class carriage. The lights from the station chandeliers reflected on the windows.

Lana snuggled closer to Jago and buried her head in his shoulder. 'We should go to London, find Ezra Morgan and kill him,' Lana said in a whisper, as the door to the compartment was slammed shut from the outside and the engine rumbled.

For the next hour they didn't speak. Jago could not get the picture of the woman in the alleyway from his mind. He could see her eyes staring up at him as she held on to life. It was as if the bite from Lana had paralysed her like the toxic venom of a spider.

The express rattled through the remains of the night, following the line along the coast. It was the way they had driven from Cannes before dumping the car. Lana had feared that the old Vampyre Renoir would have told those back in London where they were. As they drove to Nice she had said that they would leave the car by the harbour; when discovered, it would be presumed that they had taken the night ferry to Sardinia.

As Jago sat and stared at the approaching dawn through the window of the train, he felt hopeless. He was like a rat in a pipe, guided to the entrance and knowing that someone was waiting to kill him. He had played this game at school in London. They would linger by the drain and lure the creature from the sewer with the smell of cheese. Someone would wait with a bludgeon and as the rat peeked out, consumed by hunger, it would be struck dead. He tried to think what could be ahead of him. Biatra and Hugh were but a distant memory. Jago had trouble remembering what they looked like; he could see the outline of Biatra's face in his mind but the details were vague and elusive.

Lana held him close to her. He knew she wasn't asleep. She had been a Vampyre far too long to be in need of reminding what human life was like. As each day went by he desired less and less of his old life. The need for food was now all but gone. He still liked to drink coffee and could taste the burnt cinnamon clinging to the back of his throat, but even that gave him no pleasure. One by one, the habits of his old life dropped away.

As the train approached St Raphael Lana stirred from her rest. She sat up quickly, as if she had heard someone call her name. At the same time, the engine whistled and steamed as it went slowly into a long tunnel. The lights in the carriage dimmed to darkness.

Lana gripped Jago's hand.

'I feel something near. I have not sensed this for a long time, Jago. We have to get away from here.'

'It's just the tunnel – that's all,' Jago insisted as the train slowed and the wheels screeched on the track.

'I can sense it. They are here – we have to go.' Lana was panicking. Her words were short and quick.

'But –'

Lana stood up in the darkness as if she was waiting for the carriage door to open. The tunnel slowly filled with smoke from the engine.

'Quickly, Jago, we have to get off the train. They are here.'

'Who?' Jago asked as Lana walked blindly along the carriage, trying to find her way out.

'It's her. I know she is here, I am her twin. But she is supposed to be dead.'

'Mina?' Jago said, the word sticking in his throat.

'And Medea – they are calling my name, I can hear them. They have come for you, Jago. They will kill us both . . .'

'But she is your sister,' Jago said as he tried to find her in

238

the complete blackness that now swirled around him like an impenetrable tomb.

'It matters not,' she answered, her voice in a faraway whisper. 'I have betrayed her. I fell in love with you and that is enough.'

Jago heard the door of a carriage slam shut, and footsteps clattered from the carriage behind him. He stepped forward as he heard the screams of the passengers.

'Lana?' he shouted as he stumbled against the door. Finding the lock, he turned it quickly.

'Here,' she answered as the lights flickered.

Jago turned. Lana was hiding in the far doorway. 'We have to leave, now.'

'Open the door, Jago Harker. What have you done to my sister?' Mina screamed from the other side. 'Don't make me come for you, Jago . . . Lana, what has he done to you?'

'I was taking him to Luna Negri – just as you asked,' Lana shouted back.

'This train is going the wrong way for the Black Cave and you bought tickets for Zurich,' Mina shouted as she rattled the handle of the door and banged on the glass.

'Jago, we have to get away from them,' Lana insisted, holding out her hand to him as the carriage lights burnt brighter.

'Lana! Lana!' Mina Karlstein screamed, her face pressed against the frosted glass.

'It has to stop, Mina, it has to stop . . .' Lana answered as Jago ran towards her.

'Open the door, sister,' Mina growled, her teeth bared as she stepped back from the glass.

There was a sudden crash and the glass from the door exploded towards them. The old man from the platform burst through the door headfirst and slumped over two rows of embroidered leather seats. His throat had been torn open. Death had come quickly, as there was only a slight issue of blood.

'Run, Jago!' Lana shouted as Mina gripped the inside handle and twisted the lock.

'Don't you dare run from me,' Mina screamed at her sister. She kicked the door open and gave chase, smashing the chandeliers dangling from the roof with her clenched fist.

As they ran through the carriage, Jago locked the door behind him, though he knew it would not keep Mina Karlstein back for long.

'Is she alone?' he asked.

'No – I could hear Medea calling my name. She has been with my sister for many years.'

'How do we stop them?' Jago asked. He slammed yet another door as they ran through the dining car and into the guard's van.

'You won't – she loves to kill, far more than any Vampyre I have ever known. And when they are together they are like dogs.'

Jago locked the door behind them. On the floor by the window was a large stain of blood. It had been crudely mopped but the red tarnish was still visible.

'We can go no further,' Jago said. He began to build a barricade against the door with cumbersome wooden boxes of Menton lemons.

'Mina will kill us. We have to get from the train.'

No sooner had she spoken than the engine pulling the carriages from the tunnel began rapidly to gain speed, as if it were running out of control. Without warning there came the first of three sudden thuds against the compartment door.

'Lana – let me in. I have to speak to you.' Mina Karlstein spoke in a snickering voice that sounded as if she was drunk.

'You are dead. I heard that Walpurgis killed you. He has boasted of it across Europe,' Lana shouted as she stepped back away from the door.

'He only thinks I am dead. The fool watched me fall to the sea at Hawks Moor but I swam away – swam away, dear sister.' Mina laughed. 'How are you going to swim away from this?' she asked.

'How did you find us?' Lana asked.

'We asked Renoir, the artist in Cannes. He didn't resist, but he will never paint again,' Mina answered slowly. 'Then we found the woman in the dumpster. We had heard that Walpurgis was coming to Nice and we were waiting for him when Medea saw you get on the train. Then we followed and waited for the tunnel.'

'Walpurgis is here?' Jago shouted.

'He has come for you. Yet his own fate awaits him. Are you frightened, Jago Harker?'

'Of you or Walpurgis?' Jago asked as he piled more boxes against the door.

'It is a trick. She is keeping us talking – Medea is near, I can feel her,' Lana whispered.

'However did you guess, Lana? I can hear what you are saying – do you forget that we are the same creature?'

'Then if you are the same you will let her live,' Jago shouted as the train rattled.

'I don't love her that much. I always wanted a brother,'

Mina answered as Jago slowly opened the door and looked outside as the engine slowed for a corner. 'Don't think of jumping – not at this speed.'

'We will take our chances, Mina. This has to end.'

'Don't let her kill me,' Lana pleaded.

Jago grabbed Lana and before she could resist he pushed her from the train. The door burst open and Mina Karlstein stood with Medea amongst the scattered boxes. He looked back and then leapt to the door. Medea grabbed him by the leg and with all of her strength pulled him back. He hung half out of the train as the ground sped beneath him. Jago looked back to see if Lana had survived the fall. He could see nothing but the mist rising from the ditch that hugged the track.

22

Renoir

IN THE STREET behind the Café Poet, Heston Walpurgis drank five more drops of the linctus that numbed the pain of the wound to his leg. He looked at the tall green door next to the garage and counted the flakes of paint that clung to the wood like dead spiders. Putting the small bottle back in his pocket, he reached out and turned the handle of the door and stepped inside.

Walpurgis could smell blood. It was fresh and somewhere close by. He turned in the small passageway to the door on his right and pushed hard. It gave way easily. Flicking the switch, he went into the garage. A white Porsche was covered with a cotton throw that let just the fender be seen. He could tell from the shape what it was – no one but Porsche made cars like that.

'Renoir!' he shouted out hoping the man was somewhere near.

'Here . . .' came the voice in reply. It was the weak and frail voice of a man who was about to die.

Walpurgis felt the handle of the pistol in his pocket. He clicked back the hammer as he walked slowly around the parked cars to where the voice had come from. Turning the corner, he could see the long workbench covered in tools all neatly placed.

'Renoir . . .' he whispered.

It was then that he saw the pool of blood on the floor by the wall. Looking up and following the drops of blood, he saw Renoir. The crucified man hung from the wall just below the ceiling. His hands were nailed to the wooden beam that supported the floor above.

'You have come to kill me?' Renoir gasped.

Walpurgis didn't answer. He got hold of a long ladder and gathered a rope, wrench and engine winch from the workbench. In ten minutes Renoir was lying on the sofa in the tidy back office of the garage. Walpurgis boiled hot water on the stove and tore towels into strips.

'So who did this to you?' he asked as he cleaned and bandaged the wounds.

'Why should you want to know – haven't you come here to kill me?' Renoir asked. 'You are Heston Walpurgis. I was told you were coming.'

'Who should want to talk about me?' Walpurgis asked.

'My banker in London. He said that you visited him. All that is ever talked about is Heston Walpurgis and Jago Harker. Both of you are English and both of you will bring our downfall.'

'Did Harker do this to you?' Walpurgis asked as he finished wrapping the wounds.

'I'm surprised you don't already know. She mentioned your name. Told me that if I ever met you I was to say she would enjoy killing you,' Renoir replied. He laughed with a shallow breath.

'Was Harker with her?' Walpurgis asked.

'Mina Karlstein was with Medea. They did this to me – they wanted information. It was a warning to anyone who thought that they could go against them.'

'Did you tell them what they wanted to know?'

'Everything. It was either that or they would cut off my head. Mina wanted to know where Harker and her sister were staying.'

'Where was that?' Walpurgis asked calmly as he tried to smile at the Vampyre.

'They were at the Carlton Hotel. I had them followed and then they went to Nice. My companion was not as lucky as I. Medea left him in the incinerator. He didn't deserve what she did to him.'

Walpurgis thought for a moment, his eyes looking over the old calendars that hung on the wall. By the desk was a set of keys hanging from a brass hook.

'Is it right that you Vampyres like to keep the key to every house you ever lived in?' Walpurgis asked.

'You are not to be fooled, Heston. We keep the keys so that we can go back at night and take blood from those who live there now – that has always been a myth,' Renoir gasped. 'There is no truth in that at all. They are just a keepsake, a memory of what once was.'

'And the Maleficarum, is that now a memory?'

'It has all gone and is no more. There has been a revolution. Power always destroys itself in the end. We had become arrogant and thought we would rule the world. Now things have changed. You are an epitaph to that – you and Jago Harker.'

'Well, he won't be around for much longer,' Walpurgis replied as he got to his feet.

'Ozymandias and Ezra Morgan have both asked you to kill him?' Renoir asked as he tried to sit up.

'You know that?'

'Have you not realised that it is you they seek to do away with? Can't you see that this is a glorious game that they are playing with you? My banker told me that they had even wagered vast amounts of money to see who would be the one to outwit you. When you have all eternity to live it is amazing what people will do to fill their time.'

'So are you saying this is all a game?' Walpurgis asked.

'A game in which you are a pawn,' Renoir replied as he slumped back in the sofa. 'They will kill Jago Harker – but they will also kill you. What you don't understand, Heston, is that a Vampyre likes drama. Murder is an art. It is not just for the taking of blood. It has to be done with style, planned to the last moment. You are just a puppet.' Renoir sighed. 'You may think that you are searching out the next victim, but in truth they are leading a path to their door. It is all a trap . . . Beware, Heston Walpurgis.'

Renoir closed his eyes and said no more. Walpurgis thought of what to do and fought the urge to take the gun from his pocket and shoot him there and then.

'So I am already a dead man?' he asked as he walked from the room.

'As good as, my companion,' Renoir muttered under his breath.

Walpurgis stood at the door and looked around the garage. He felt a sudden pang of sadness, as if he lamented all that

Renoir had lost. 'You were once a famous man and gave up everything for this?'

'Happiness is far more important than the notoriety of success,' he answered. 'Besides, the motor car will be the art of the future. I am happy with what I do.'

Walpurgis didn't look back. He walked to the incinerator and looked inside. It was just as Renoir had said.

The door creaked shut. Renoir shouted: 'It shall all end at the Cave of Solitude – Magdalene will show you the way – the way of the true blood.'

Walpurgis locked the garage door behind him and slipped the key through the letterbox. He walked down the street to the Café Poet and sat outside as the sky grew brighter. The streets of Cannes were still empty. The long-haired girl behind the counter took his order and soon brought him bread and hot chocolate. Nearby he could hear the sounds of the open market and the churning of car engines as the town awoke. He looked out across the promenade to the distant islands in the bay. The sky was layered with every shade of blue, rising up from a white horizon.

On the wall by the harbour a man was waiting. His face was covered by a newspaper held with gloved hands. Walpurgis sipped at his drink and wiped the chocolate from his lips. He looked towards the old town. Another man, dressed just like the first, was standing inside the silver phone booth by the bus station. He held the receiver to his ear but didn't speak. The man looked towards Walpurgis and smiled.

Slipping a ten-franc note from his pocket and onto the table, Walpurgis walked away. As he looked back he saw the man on the promenade throw down his paper and walk towards him. At the same time the door of the phone booth opened. Both men were now coming towards him, their hands in the pockets of their short leather coats.

'Companions,' Walpurgis whispered to himself as he walked beyond the Hotel de Ville and turned into the narrow alley that led to the old town.

Looking back, he saw the men breathing hard, trying to gain on him. Walpurgis began to run, the pain in his leg becoming even more intense as he climbed into the old town with its narrow streets and high houses. As he reached the walls of the castle the men still followed at a distance, knowing he would soon be out of breath.

There was an open door to a small garden. Walpurgis went in and sat on the step of the house and waited; his hand in his pocket gripped the pistol, which was already fitted with the long silencer.

'Ran out of courage?' one of the companions asked as he pushed up the brim of his hat and looked at Walpurgis. 'I heard you were wounded and would be easy to catch – all a matter of time.'

'Who sent you?' he asked.

'All we know is that we have to take you to a place not far away from here,' the second man said as he too stepped into the garden, pushing back the branches of a fig tree.

'And you expect me to come with you?' Walpurgis asked, his finger on the trigger. 'I at least expect to know where I am going and who invited me.'

'It's not far. She said we were to bring you there unharmed. Please don't make us hurt you,' the smaller man said in perfect English.

'Mina Karlstein?' Walpurgis asked as he eyed the men warily and waited until they were standing next to each other.

The older man smiled. Walpurgis could see his dirty and broken teeth.

'You would be wise to take the gun from your pocket and place it on the ground,' he said as he aimed his own gun at Walpurgis. 'Yet I know that you will come with us. Mina said that you would not be able to resist.'

'And what if I don't want to go?'

'Then we will be forced to kill you here and now.'

'You'll wake the people sleeping above us and they will see you,' he answered.

The man aimed the gun at his head.

'Okay, I'll come with you – there is no need to shoot.'

Walpurgis slowly drew the gun from his pocket and lowered it to the ground. Then suddenly he stumbled, rolled forward and, before the men could get out of the way, he fired the gun. The bullet shot the first man in the leg. He fell to the floor. The second man looked startled as his friend screamed in pain. He pushed against the gate, stumbling over his colleague as he tried to get out of the way.

Walpurgis took aim again. He fired, the bullet smashing into the wall and breaking a branch of the fig tree. The first man rolled on the floor screaming, trying to reach his own gun that lay just out of reach. In the house above, a woman came to the window and banged against the glass. Walpurgis pulled up the collar of his coat and kicked the gun out of the way as he gave chase.

The second man ran down the street towards the entrance of the castle. He was too far away to shoot. Running as fast as he could, Walpurgis cut through a side alley and along the top of a low wall that stretched out like a snake's back. The man ran on, looking over his shoulder every few yards. Then, when he thought Walpurgis was out of sight, he hid under an old portico of the castle wall.

'Got you,' Walpurgis whispered as he stepped from the shadows and put his arm around the man's throat and the gun to his head. 'Explain how you found me and where Mina Karlstein wants to take me.'

'We don't know the place – never been there before – we just have the co-ordinates. It is in the mountains – I have it marked on a map.'

The man tried to reach into his pockets. Walpurgis had heard enough. He hit out, and the man fell to the floor. Taking the jacket from his back, he left the man in the dark recess of the portico.

He searched the pocket as he walked down the empty streets to the harbour. Finding the small folded map, he looked at the range of mountains to the north-west of a large coastal town. His bloodied finger followed the route from Cannes marked in black ink. Marked against the side of a steep cliff was a small ink cross, and next to it was inscribed the word MAGDALENE.

Taking off his coat, he emptied his pockets and slipped on the leather jacket. It fitted well, even though the man was smaller than him. When he got to the harbour, Walpurgis put his coat in a dustbin, making sure it could not be seen. He looked across the harbour as a steamboat sailed in and he counted the money in his wallet. 'Train from Toulon – car from there. Should be at the cave by nightfall,' he said to himself as he walked along the harbourside towards the centre of the town.

Walpurgis didn't see the long black sedan driving slowly along the promenade. Watching his every step, the driver pulled in to the side of the road and waited. Still trying to read the map, Walpurgis stepped from the pavement to cross the street. The black sedan leapt from its parking place and veered towards him. He could do nothing as the car struck his side.

Walpurgis rolled across the bonnet of the car and onto the road. The door of the car opened. A tall man got out and, lifting him with incredible strength, dragged him into the back of the car.

'They always say that if you want a job doing then it is best to do it oneself,' Ozymandias said as he leant forward and slapped Walpurgis across the face. 'I see from the jacket that you are wearing that the companions are no more.'

'Ozymandias . . . But how –?' he asked.

'You had become too much of a threat to us. When Ezra and I decided to put an end to the Lodge Maleficarum once and for all, you became expendable.'

'So why did you have to track me down?'

'What is left of our community are all coming to this place. It would have been too conspicuous to have you kidnapped and brought here so we had to think of a plan to get you to come to France. Ezra and I knew you would obey. The bait was Jago Harker, but we had him all the time. We could have done away with him at a moment's notice.'

'Where is he now?'

'That is the problem,' Ozymandias answered as the car

sped off through the empty streets. 'It would appear from recent correspondence that Mina Karlstein and the woman she is with have decided to hold him for ransom.'

'Why don't you just go and get him?' Walpurgis asked as the man in the back of the car gripped him firmly so he couldn't move.

'We don't know where they have taken him,' Ozymandias answered in a strained voice. 'And I can't risk letting you go to find him. I take it you know what our plans are for your life.'

'You should have left me to rot in that Polish jail,' Walpurgis answered, wondering how he would free himself from this.

'It was sad that the war ended when it did. I was quite surprised. We had every confidence in the mad corporal winning – then again, he was a Bavarian.'

'So Mina is not with you in this?' Walpurgis asked.

'We had such confidence in her and yet she has decided that she needs insurance. When Ezra came up with the idea of killing off the Maleficarum and its followers I thought she would be on our side. Now she feels she has to be reassured that she will not be culled with the rest of them.'

'I take it we are going to the Cave of Magdalene?'

'I am always amazed at how you manage to discover everything for yourself. It has been decided that you are to become one of us. A man as psychotic as you is too good to remain human.' Ozymandias took a small glass vial from his pocket. 'I know how you want to live and how you fear death. Madame Arantez told me all about your conversations.'

'I think I have changed my mind since then.'

It is a shame really. The linctus I gave you to take away the pain is a very slow poison. The only way to stay alive is to keep drinking it. If you stop your body will feel as if it is on fire and you will slowly burn from the inside as every nerve disintegrates. Not even a man like you could stand the pain. You will beg me to kill you.'

'Not if I have killed you first,' Walpurgis snapped as he struggled to be free.

'That will not happen,' Ozymandias answered. 'If you want to live, then you will have to become one with us. We have a very special ritual planned in three nights' time. A sacrifice that will bring about the dawn of a new age.'

'Witchcraft,' Walpurgis snarled as the car lurched through the narrow streets of the old town and headed towards Mougin and the hills near Grasse.

'Not quite – more of a ceremony of deliverance. You will be there and that is when your *wife* will take what is rightfully hers . . .'

'Vibica is alive? I thought –'

'Your wife is alive and well. She was protected from the rigours of the war and brought to France. She is quite safe and looking forward to meeting you.'

'And what of Toran Blaine?' Walpurgis asked.

'Your rival in love is dead – or so I believe. We will soon know for sure. In return for my help, Ezra Morgan has promised that I can use the Oracle. Everything is prepared. The blood of Jago Harker will be used to ignite the stone. Then we shall all see the future.'

23

The Convent of Magdalene

JAGO SAT IN THE BACK of the taxi between Medea and Mina Karlstein. They pressed uncomfortably against him so that he couldn't move. Neither of them spoke. Since capturing him on the train they had both been silent. Mina Karlstein had pushed him from the carriage when it had arrived at Toulon and marched him from the station through the crowds to the small taxi rank. Then she had opened the door of a battered old taxi, sliding across the back seat as Medea forced Jago to follow.

The driver stared ahead as he drove through the narrow streets. Jago stared at the reflection of his bearded face in the mirror on the windshield. He tried to catch his eye and show him that something was wrong, but the driver refused to even glance at the boy.

Soon they had left the town behind. The car struggled with the winding mountain roads, creeping around the tight corners as it climbed higher and higher. Jago wiped the sweat from his brow as the driver finally caught his eye.

'Convent?' he asked Mina Karlstein. 'Are you sure you want the Convent?'

His English wasn't perfect. The man sounded Italian and

looked Turkish. His hair was greased back and his double chin made him appear older than he was.

'The Convent Hotel – do you know it?' Medea asked sweetly as she reached out and rubbed the back of his neck.

'Shall we stop before we get there? It is a long way beyond Riboux. I have some wine in the car and bread. I could take you for a walk,' the driver answered as he rubbed the back of his neck against the tips of her fingers.

Jago saw Medea look to Mina Karlstein. He dug deep into his pocket to find the Vampyre compass. It was gone. 'Mina,' he thought to himself knowing she had taken it from his pocket whilst he had slept.

'I suppose that might be nice,' Mina answered. 'Find somewhere an hour before we arrive. The sun should be quite warm then.'

'I know a perfect place. It has a fantastic view. You can see all of France.'

'That would be good,' Medea answered as she continued to rub the back of his neck with her long fingernails.

For the next hour, the driver explained the route. At every corner he gave details of less than interesting facts. Jago tried to cloud his mind and numb himself from the journey. He thought of Lana and wondered if she was alive. And then a sudden dark thought crept into his mind: he was taken back to the day when he had been alone in the library at the house of Crispin Draigorian. It had been the day when the poltergeist had made itself known. Jago could feel again every drop of fear that had surged through his veins. He shuddered visibly as the hair stood up on the back of his neck. Medea looked at him as if she had felt the same.

The taxi stopped suddenly, the brakes squealing as it turned off the road into a dusty lay-by.

'This is the place,' the driver said proudly, as if making a great discovery. 'I will get the picnic and call you when it is ready.'

He got out of the car and opened the trunk. Jago stared through the window. The scarp fell away below them. Blocks of white stone were piled one on the other at the edge of a cliff, and gnarled bushes grew out of the rocks surrounded by patches of small flowers.

'I will kill you, Jago, if you try to escape,' Mina said coldly. 'It would give me great pleasure.'

Jago sensed doubt in her words. The driver set out the rug and a large reed basket and wine and then opened the door for Medea.

'All is ready,' he said excitedly. 'I always take the opportunity to eat well.'

Medea laughed. Jago saw her eye the man and then look to Mina.

'Why don't we take our food over to the rocks and look to the sea?' Medea asked. 'These two want to talk and I need to get to know you.'

The man slipped his fingers into his belt and nodded in agreement. A broad smile spread across his unshaven face. He picked up an open bottle of cheap wine and carried it across to a pile of rocks by the side of the cliff.

Mina took hold of Jago by the hand.

'It won't be long,' she whispered. 'Stay in the car.'

Medea put her long, slender arm around the man and then took hold of his hand.

'Let's go further, so they can't see us,' she whispered as he swigged from the bottle. 'You have something that I need.'

The driver followed. At one point he looked back. Jago smiled at him as he disappeared over the edge of the ridge to a path that led down the side of the scarp. He took a last look at Medea. She stopped on the ridge of large rocks and smiled at Mina.

'He has a minute to live,' Mina whispered, an obvious look of intense glee on her face. 'I do hope she remembers the keys to the car.'

Her throwaway comment made Jago shudder. Just like the woman at the railway station, the taxi driver had been chosen at random to die. Had he not spoken, Jago wondered if they would have decided to kill him.

'Do you need to eat?' he asked Mina.

'Why – does it bother you?' she asked begrudgingly. 'Since you cosied up to my sister, I didn't think you would have been concerned at all.'

'He's just a taxi driver,' he answered.

'She was just a woman at a station,' Mina replied with a snarl of her lip.

There was no scream. In fact there was nothing to say that the man was dead. Medea walked slowly back to the car, the keys draped on her longest finger and held like a prize.

'He tasted like vomit,' she said as she got near. 'I made sure it looked as though he had fallen – got drunk and jumped to his death.'

'You drive and I will look after Jago,' Mina answered as Medea slinked into the front seat, pulled up her tight skirt and turned on the engine.

257

By later that afternoon, as they drove along the narrow roads near La Coutronne, the car was nearly out of petrol. The engine juddered and stopped, and Medea pulled in to the side of the road.

'If they find the car they can trace it to you,' Jago said as Mina pushed him out.

'Thought of that,' Medea answered. 'It's not far to where we are going and they will never find the car.'

'Give us an hour, we don't want to arrive together,' Mina said as she kissed Medea on the lips.

'An hour will be too long to be without you,' she answered as she touched the tip of Mina's nose.

'I will make up for every lost minute,' Mina replied softly.

'And every second?' Medea asked.

Taking a path across country, Mina kept looking back to the car at the side of the road. Soon it was just a small speck in the distance. Jago wondered if he could run away. He eyed her warily to see if he could kill her. She was more of a man than a woman; her features had grown harsh with time. Jago thought how different she was to her sister. Lana had a heart, she was beautiful, and now as he walked across the desolate highlands of the plateau, Jago realised that he loved her.

'Where are you taking me?' he asked Mina as they walked side by side.

'You will soon see,' she answered coldly.

'Walpurgis will come for us,' he answered.

'I hope so – it would be good to see him again.'

'And Biatra, Hugh and Jack Henson – what have you done with them?' Jago asked.

'It matters not. They are of no consequence any more.'

Mina looked at him as they stopped on an outcrop of rock. She thought before speaking. 'She can't help it . . . Lana can't help falling in love. I have seen it so many times and this is no different. You are just one of a thousand men who have come and gone. Don't get all sentimental.'

'She is beautiful,' he answered.

'But she is a monster just like you and me. A monster that would have grown bored of you and in the end killed you.' Mina tugged on the sleeve of his tweed jacket. 'Perhaps it is best that she is dead – do you know what happens to Vampyres when we die, Jago?'

'The same as what happens to everyone else – nothing,' he replied not wanting to speak of death.

Mina walked on and kicked stones from the path. With every step she looked back to him and then to the horizon, as if she was waiting for him to escape.

'When I heard you had been born my heart leapt with joy,' she said as they followed the path down a long slope towards a patch of trees. 'The whole world awaited you like a saviour. There is a day coming when that expectation will be fulfilled.'

'The Oracle and the prophecy?' he answered.

'The Cult of the Oracle believe in a life beyond death. Living in this world becomes tiresome. Even Vampyres look upon death as a rest from the world. To live beyond the grave is something I desire.'

'Then for your sake I hope it is true. If it had not been for your faith my life would have been different,' he said as the path fell more steeply and mist came over the hills towards them.

'If it had not been for the Cult of the Oracle then you would not have been born,' she snapped as a low rumble of thunder broke from the distant clouds and echoed around the hills. 'The sole purpose of your birth was to bring peace and life. Strackan needed you – it was his wish that we should follow the Oracle. When the diamond was lost, the Oracle lost her power. Now it has been found all is well.'

'But the Maleficarum have been killed – Ezra Morgan had them all murdered.'

'It was necessary. There were too many people with ideas of their own. Our success has been our loyalty to one another. When the faction came two hundred years ago life began to change.'

Mina stopped as the first drops of rain began to pound the dry earth and form pools in amongst the rocks. They took cover in the patch of trees and listened to the rain beat against the ground.

'I hate the rain,' Jago muttered. 'It reminds me of London.'

'Julius Cresco?' she asked, as if she knew all about the man who had secretly guarded him all his life.

'He would sit on the balcony of his flat and watch the rain. He didn't care,' Jago answered as he caught the occasional drops that fell through the branches of the trees. 'Will he live for ever, now that he is dead?'

'Julius did not believe, so his fate is unknown. I heard you killed him,' she said, her words more of a question.

'He killed himself . . .' Jago left the words hanging and walked away.

Mina followed him, always keeping a yard behind, knowing that if he decided to run, she could catch him.

Within a mile a solitary stone building came into view. It looked out of place on the vast plateau beneath the high ridge. At each corner was a spire like an English church. Beneath the spires were small arched windows.

'That is the Convent of Magdalene. It is where we will be staying,' Mina said as she walked faster.

'A convent?' Jago asked, his voice surprised.

'They follow Magdalene. If only they knew the truth,' she answered, her words harsh and cutting.

When they arrived at the large oak door, the rain had stopped. Water dripped from Jago, and his tweed coat was sodden with rain. Mina Karlstein rattled the metal knocker. Footsteps echoed along the corridor and then five bolts were slipped from their holders as the door opened.

'Mina?' a voice from the darkness chirped. A small face appeared. 'You haven't changed in all this time.'

'The usual room?' she asked.

'Everything is as you required,' the woman answered. Her eyes peered from behind a net veil that covered her face and formed a peculiar hat on the top of her head.

Jago could not take his eyes from her hands. They were small and knotted, as if the fingers had been woven together. They stuck out from the sleeves of the long brown shroud in which she was wrapped, the only part of her body that could be seen.

The woman welcomed them in with an elfin bow.

'Are the other people here?' Mina asked the woman in a hushed voice, so as not to be overheard.

'Tomorrow,' the woman answered.

She walked ahead of them, leaving Jago to close the

261

immense door and slide the bolts. At the bottom of a long staircase made of ebony tiles, the woman stopped and flicked back the sides of her veil. Her face remained covered but Jago could see the outline clearly. It was as if her lips were two thick scars. Her eyes were deep and sullen and encased in folds of crusted scales like the bark of a tree. Jago had seen this before.

'Along the landing to the tower and take the second corridor and the third door,' the woman said, before turning and disappearing into the darkness of the hallway.

'You've been here before?' Jago asked Mina as she walked up the stairs.

'Often,' she answered, the heels of her boots clattering against the wood.

'Why do they wear the veils?' Jago asked.

'The Convent is a secret order. No one, not even their companions, know what they look like. They keep complete silence other than to speak to guests.'

'Why are we here?' he asked.

'It cannot be told – well, not yet,' she answered as they walked the passageway to the room. 'This is the door,' Mina said as she turned the brass handle on the old door and pushed against it.

Jago peered in. The room was large, with five mullioned windows lined with lead. The light scattered across the polished oak floor. Mina gestured for him to enter. There was no bed, only a long sofa and two leather chairs. A fire was set in the far wall. It crackled, freshly lit, the flames just catching to the wood. By the window, on a small table, was a glass decanter filled with a deep red wine and four silver mugs. Next to the decanter was a small folded piece of paper sealed with red wax.

Jago took the paper and read the inscription.

'It is for you,' he said offering the letter to Mina.

She looked perplexed as she reached out and took it from him. Jago watched the expression change on her face as she read the note.

'They already know we are here,' she snarled as she tore the paper and threw the fragments in the fire. 'How did they know?'

'Who?' Jago asked standing back from her rage.

'Ozymandias and Ezra Morgan. They know you are here.'

'Aren't you with them?' he asked. 'Didn't they send you for me?'

Mina looked about the room and poured herself a glass of wine and then drank it quickly.

'You had become a tool for which Medea and I would bargain for our lives. Just like you, we too have been double-crossed. Ozymandias and Morgan want us both dead. In fact, they will not be happy until we are out of the way. Taking you was our guarantee of life. Now they know we are here, the trap is set.'

'What will you do?' he asked as she poured another glass of wine and drank it quickly.

Mina savoured the linctus and sniffed the glass. Jago could sense it had been mixed with blood. Her cheeks reddened as she looked at him.

'They will have what they want. The letter is quite clear. If we leave you here and go from this place they will give us seven days to get out of Europe. We are being banished

. . . The world has gone mad. Before you were born, everything in life had order. We drank blood, lived a good life. Even when the faction came things remained the same. The Maleficarum saw to that. Now, Jago Harker, you have changed everything.' Mina slurred her words. 'If you look up to that ridge you can just see the outline of a monastery built into the cliff. Within those doors is the Oracle of Magdalene. That is the place where they took your friends.'

'Why are they there?' he asked as she slumped in the sofa and dropped the empty chalice to the floor.

Mina Karlstein began to laugh. 'They need you, Jago – the whole world needs Jago Harker and his precious blood. The Oracle proclaimed your name to the world before she was entombed in her alabaster coffin. They need you to bring her back to life. The boy and the diamond . . .'

'But I have done nothing,' he shouted.

'Would you love me? Would you love me like you do Lana?' Mina asked as she tried to stand. 'Am I not just like her? An identical image? If you can love her then you can love me.'

Mina gripped Jago by the collar of his soaked jacket and tried to pull herself towards him.

'It's not like that,' Jago protested as he stepped away from her.

Her hands slipped from his coat and she fell to the couch. 'Just look at you,' she barked as her eyes closed and she slumped against the leather. 'You think you are so special. Everyone wants Jago Harker . . . All they want is to rip out your throat and drink your blood – even if it tastes of poison.'

He watched as she tried to speak. She lay on the couch,

her head pressed against the thick cushions, unable to move.

Jago sniffed the decanter. 'You have been poisoned,' he said.

Mina Karlstein didn't speak. She arched her back and rolled from side to side as the spasms shuddered her arms and legs – like the crushed cat that Jago had once watched on Brick Lane on the first night of the bombings.

'Torafugu,' she whispered feebly, like the prayer of a dying child.

24

Dead Lavender

THE DOOR OPENED, taking him by surprise.

'She is dying,' Jago said as the veiled, cowl-clad figure of the woman came into the room.

'I know,' the woman answered calmly. 'It was I who poisoned her.' As Jago looked at the woman, her breath beat against the veil excitedly. 'Why didn't you drink?' she asked him. 'It is just a powerful sedative, it wasn't meant to kill her – perhaps she has drunk too much. Luna Negri . . . Luna Negri . . .'

He ran to the door. The woman took hold of his arm and pulled him back with incredible strength. Jago was smashed against the wall and the breath burst from his lungs.

'What are you?' he asked as he felt in his pocket for the knife he had hidden in the lining.

'We are here to guard Magdalene. She is not to be disturbed by the likes of you,' the woman hissed as she stepped back to stop him running towards the door. 'Just drink the wine like a good boy,' she whined.

Jago took hold of the decanter. 'How much will kill me?' he asked as he stared at the face that was pressed against the veil.

'Just one mouthful and you will be fast asleep.'

'I am not here to do any harm to Magdalene – whoever she is.'

'Magdalene has been in the cave for two thousand years. She was the first of our kind and took the kiss of our Master,' the woman said as she took a long brass key from within her garment.

'I have no argument with you – please allow me to leave,' Jago pleaded.

The woman laughed.

'Drink the wine – take two gulps and pray you live,' she demanded.

Jago raised the decanter to his lips. The woman leant towards him as if to see if he took a drink. He held the bottle by the silver neck and raised it further to his lips.

'Drink it, drink it . . .'

Seeing his chance, Jago twisted the bottle quickly in his hand and as the woman lurched back he smashed the decanter across her face. The veil fell to the floor and revealed, staring at him, a gargoyle. Her eyes were slits in thick, bark-like skin. Her lips were swollen and criss-crossed with deep cuts. The woman fell back against the door.

'See how it tastes for yourself,' Jago shouted as he pushed her out of the way.

The woman grabbed him by the arm, her knotted and gnarled hands stronger than he could ever imagine.

'Stay here,' she snarled as she bit at his fingers.

Jago hit her with a clenched fist that cracked the thick wooden skin. The hag fell to her knees and grabbed his feet. Jago jumped out of the way, kicking her as he lunged for the door. On the sofa, Mina Karlstein stirred as she fought the poison.

Taking his chance, Jago ran from the room and back down the stairs towards the door. The woman screamed: 'Magdala Cantata!' The words echoed around the cold halls and corridors of the convent.

Before Jago could take another step, every door in the convent slammed shut. Bolts dug into their keepers and the sound of strange voices began to echo out. As he ran along the long passageway towards the stairs he could hear a faint moaning. Then, second by second it grew louder and louder until the building began to shake with the sound. It juddered in his head as the rumbling moans of every woman locked in their tiny cells cried out.

'Magdala Morte . . . Magdala Morte' came the words again and again until they reached a shrill crescendo.

As they sang, the walls shook. Jago could no longer stand. He dropped to his knees and crawled along the cold tiles towards the door. The words grew louder and louder until his ears were bleeding and he could think of nothing else. No longer could he see, as the words inhabited his mind.

'Magdala Morte,' he began to say as he lay on the floor and shivered. 'Leave me, leave me alone . . .'

His hands were numb. His lips stiffened, his eyes blurred. The music was both within and without. There was nothing of the world but the rhythmical chanting of the hidden women.

It was then that he made out the shape of the woman from the room. She walked towards him, her veil in place, her hands clasped around the handle of a knife.

'If Jago Harker refuses to take the wine, then he shall have to know death,' she said, her words piercing through all other sounds.

He could not move. Propping himself on one elbow, he held out his hand as if it would stop her.

'Please, stop the music,' he pleaded.

The light from the moon streamed in through the coloured glass of the window on the stairs. Jago looked up as the sky darkened. A shadow crossed the window. The woman stood before him and raised the knife to strike.

There came a smashing of glass and the sound of the strips of lead falling to the floor. The woman looked up, giving Jago a chance to escape. He tried to move but his limbs were frozen solid like icy branches of winter trees.

Like a dark bird that had flown across the moon, Medea fell to a high landing and got to her feet. The voices subsided to a murmur.

'*You?*' the woman said, turning from Jago.

'What have you done with Mina?' asked Medea as she stalked the woman.

'Sleeping,' she answered. 'Sleeping like a child in the womb.'

'Poisoned!' Jago managed to shout as the numbness went from his arms. 'Wine and aconite.'

As he crawled from the woman he saw the look on the face of Medea. She stared at the woman through the bright rimless eyes of a starved hound.

'Why did you do this?' she demanded loudly as her hair fell about her neck like the ringlets of a medusa.

'For her own good – we cannot have the tomb of Magdalene

disturbed again. You should all go away – far away and leave us be . . .'

'Then you should have let us alone, you meddling witch.' Medea screamed as she leapt from the landing high above them and fell through the air.

The woman lashed out with the knife. Medea landed upon her, knocking the woman out of the way. Without warning the woman stabbed at her, striking a blow across her rain-soaked blouse. Jago saw a faint issue of blood.

'Silver blade – bone handle – blessed by Borgia himself,' the woman sneered. 'Not one of your kind could escape that kind of blade.'

Medea cupped her breast, holding her wound as she realised what would happen.

'Magdala Cantate!' the woman screamed through her veil stained with wine and blood. 'Magdala Cantate!'

The singing suddenly began again, louder than before and rattling the iron fetters of the long avenue of lamps that dimly lit the hallway and staircase.

'You will die with me,' Medea cried as she lunged forward, pulling the cowl from the woman with one hand.

Dropping the knife, the woman screamed. Small and frail, she stood before them. Her wrinkled flesh hung like that of a shelled turtle. Medea punched out, breaking through her ribs with an open hand. Grabbing the heart, she pulled it from within. The woman gasped and her eyes widened, bulging as they gorged with blood.

'Hail, queen of heaven!' the woman cried. It was her last breath as she dropped from the hand that grasped her pumping heart.

Medea held it in her palm as the beats grew faint and then stopped.

'I no longer have the desire for all of this, Jago,' Medea said. She slumped to a tread of the stair and held the wound beneath her breast. 'Now I will know if all that I have believed all of these years is true.'

'I can't stop it,' Jago answered. 'The blade is silver and has cut through to the bone.'

Medea laughed mockingly as she gasped for breath.

'Such a small wound and yet quite fatal,' she mused over the long open cut to her skin. 'I was the daughter of Aetes, King of Colchis. Memeros and Pheres were my children. Once, I even poisoned a dragon. It was Theseus who brought me into the world of the Vampyre. Would you believe it, Jago? That was a long time ago. I killed the whole of the Ninth Legion. I took them one by one, night by night, as they stumbled through Northumbria. It was on the site of their temple that I met a young boy who would change my life. The moment I bit into his soft white skin, I knew I was dead. Do you remember that night, Jago Harker?'

'How could I ever forget?' he answered as he picked up the knife from the floor. 'I thought it was a dream.'

'I wished it could have all been different for us both. You are a curse to my kind, Jago. A curse from which none of us can escape. There is a power, a force that surrounds you and keeps you from harm. Look at us – Mina is poisoned, and I, I am dying . . .'

Medea began to sob, holding her face in her hands as the tears trickled through her fingers, her heart filled with remorse.

271

With her tear-stained hands she reached out and pulled him closer to her. 'I am no one. It is you who have meddled with my life, you who have brought all this about.'

Jago closed his eyes and kissed her. Medea smiled, a cough spilling from her throat as her lungs filled with blood.

'I am glad you didn't understand,' she whispered. 'That is a far better way to die. Kiss me again, Jago.'

As their lips met, Medea sighed. Blood dripped from her lips. Jago tore her white shirt and wiped her face, then placed the soaked rag in his pocket.

Laying her against the stairs, he could see the wound. It was much deeper than he had thought. He held the blade in his hand then tore more of her bloodied shirt to wrap around it.

The Convent fell silent.

And then Jago heard the doors on the landing above begin to open one by one. Footsteps marched along the tiled floors, and flashing through the smashed window on the landing were the lights of a car. They lit the upper corridor. Jago heard brakes squeal and doors slam.

'Open up! Ozymandias is here!' a man shouted as he pounded his fist against the bolted portal.

Jago ran up the two flights of stairs to the broken window. In the courtyard below he could see Ozymandias. He was sitting in the back of a long sedan with Walpurgis at his side. Another car was parked just out of sight – Jago could see the pattern of its headlights shining across the wet gravel. The man at the door continued to shout. On the corridor above him, the footsteps drew closer . . . Jago was trapped.

As the first cowled woman appeared on the landing above

him, Jago crawled through the broken window and onto a thick stone ledge. He saw at once how Medea had got into the Convent – the terracotta roof of a small adjacent building was just a step away. This fell gently to the side of the courtyard and a cluster of ancient olive trees near where the car was parked. Their leaves jangled in the high branches that towered above the roof.

Jago held his breath as he walked dangerously close to the edge. He hoped no one would look up. Stepping from the ledge, he stooped down and hid behind the stack of a tall chimney. The stones were red hot, heated by the sun and the fire below.

Echoing from the house, Jago heard a door slam. Another man shouted out. 'Medea is dead . . . the boy has escaped!'

Ozymandias got out of the car and crossed the gravel towards the house. Walpurgis remained seated, his arms folded as if he was resigned to his fate. A guard in a long leather coat held a gun in his hand, pointed to the floor.

Screaming came from the house, followed by gunshots. Jago slipped quickly from his hiding place, across the roof and into the trees. He climbed through the branches until he was above the man. Ozymandias and all the others were in the house.

'What are you going to do with me?' Walpurgis said to the guard.

'Keep you here, and if you try to run I will kill you,' he answered.

Jago looked to the house. The door was shut. Several more gunshots sounded from within.

'What are you doing to them?' Walpurgis asked.

'They are of no use. Ozymandias does not want any witnesses to what will happen,' he answered.

'But Jago Harker has escaped and Medea is dead,' Walpurgis laughed. 'What will Ozymandias do without them?'

'Harker won't get far away, his life is over . . .'

Like a dull lead, Jago dropped to the ground. He kicked at the man as he fell. Walpurgis jumped from the car and before the man had hit the ground he had snatched the gun from his hand. With a sudden blow he struck the guard over the back of the head.

'I thought it was you,' Walpurgis said as he dragged the man to the cover of the shadows around the house. 'Why aren't you running from me?'

'I heard what the man said. He would have shot you if you had tried to escape. You were the prisoner of Ozymandias.'

'So that makes me a friend?' Walpurgis asked sarcastically. 'I haven't forgotten what you did to me.'

'People change,' Jago said as he helped Walpurgis hide the body, dragging the man by his legs deeper into the darkness. 'There is a cave near here. I have to go there. I am trying to find my friends.'

'Taking on the Oracle by yourself?' Walpurgis whispered as they hid by the wall.

'What other way is there?' Jago replied as he edged along the wall.

'Ozymandias has poisoned me. I am a dead man walking. There is nothing for me to lose,' he answered like a condemned man before the gallows. 'What he gave me to heal the wound is in fact killing me. If I stop taking the linctus I will be ravaged by death.'

'Then stay with him,' Jago said.

'I have enough for one more day. Perhaps there is another way of escaping death,' Walpurgis replied. 'I will come with you to the cave – both our futures may be found within the tomb of Magdalene.' Walpurgis took Jago by the hand. 'They all want you dead, Jago Harker. They want to kill you to bring the Oracle to life.'

Jago didn't answer. He looked out across the plateau to the the hills beyond. He could make out a crest of rock that ran across the horizon like a row of dragon's teeth. Far below, in the midst of the scarp, he could see the window lights of the monastery carved out of the solid rock. They had shone through wars and famine to beckon pilgrims from far away. As the sky cleared and the light from the moon transformed the world in a shroud of cerulean, more shots rang out from the Convent.

'What is Ozymandias doing?' Jago asked as they picked their way through the long dry grass that surrounded the house.

'One by one he is getting rid of his enemies,' Walpurgis answered. 'He had set a trap for both of us. And like you I was fooled.'

'I have to kill Ozymandias and Ezra Morgan – this is all I can think about. It's what I have to do.'

'And that they know. It will come as no surprise to them.' Walpurgis laughed. 'Between us we have a gun and a knife.'

'Then we have an advantage,' Jago replied as they walked quickly towards the scarp, leaving the Convent far behind.

[25]

Notarius

THE LONG WALK to the scarp took three hours. Neither of them noticed the flickering of the light that reflected from the lens of the binoculars trained on them from the roof of the Convent. Along the way Jago told Walpurgis of London, Julius Cresco and the time at Hawks Moor. They followed the line of the ridge and walked through the outer edges of the deepening yew forest that covered the hillside. Within the cover of the trees Jago slowed his pace. He wished that Vampyres could fly. He had once seen a film about vampires at the Bethnal Green picture palace. Julius Cresco had taken him along and told him not to tell his mother.

'Sometimes it is best to be frightened without your mother knowing,' Cresco had said as they had walked the busy street to the crowded picture palace. 'You will like the film *Dracula*. I once met the star, Béla Lugosi – a nice man, if slightly short for a vampire.'

Jago could now see the joke – going to watch a film about vampires and being taken along by a Vampyre. He wondered if Cresco had laughed on the inside, thinking to himself how funny it really was. Lugosi had turned into a bat and flown through the air. How far from the truth, Jago muttered under his breath. He was not affected by sunlight, nor did he have to sleep in a coffin. He laughed to himself.

'Happy?' Walpurgis asked as he stopped under an ancient tree and leant against the thick trunk to gather his breath.

'Béla Lugosi,' Jago said. 'Julius Cresco took me to see him years ago.'

'*Dracula*?' he asked, a smile suddenly broadening on his face.

'He knew every word, as if he had seen it time and again,' Jago answered.

'And you never suspected?' Walpurgis replied.

'I just thought he was the weird old man downstairs. Now I can see the truth. He was my protector. They paid my mother like a brood mare,' Jago said, his voice tinged with anger.

'They would have blackmailed her, cheated her and never told the truth. That is their way.'

Jago could see the hate in his face. 'And you?' he asked.

'I married a Vampyre. Didn't know until it was too late. Fell in love and married her,' Walpurgis said as he looked to the branches above him.

'Do I know her?' Jago asked.

'Vibica de Zoete,' he replied in a quiet voice. There was a long and awkward silence. 'I take it you knew her,' he said eventually.

'I saw her die in the train crash after she had come from the house of Ozymandias.'

'Vibica isn't dead. She is alive and she is here and she is intending to do what she wanted all those years ago. Ozymandias told me that I too am to become a Vampyre and my

277

wife will be the one to take me.'

'Then why are you coming with me?' Jago asked, not knowing what could be in his heart.

'I have to see her again. No matter what I have to see her for the last time,' he answered.

'But she will take you and you –'

'It is a chance I want to take. I need to know more.'

'Why?' Jago asked.

'She left me for another man. I need to know why,' Walpurgis said, his voice hushed.

'Toran Blaine?' Jago asked.

'You know him?'

Jago looked to the ground before he answered. 'He reminds me of you in so many ways,' he said. 'You could be brothers.'

'I want to kill him and I have been cheated of that. Ozymandias said he is dead. He took my wife from me and that can never be forgiven.'

'Then you will ask her why?' Jago answered.

'And once I know I will be ready to die. What is the point in living with a broken heart? I have voices in my head. They come and go, tormenting me every day. They speak to me about every catastrophe in my life. One voice in particular taunts me about Toran Blaine. When I know *why*, then I can silence them for good. See these marks?' Walpurgis went on as he rolled up his sleeve. 'I punish the voices by cutting these. The pain keeps them far away.'

Walpurgis walked on, faster than before. They cut through the undergrowth to a path of crushed stones littered with leaves. It stretched ahead of them higher and higher as it cut through the dense forest.

'This way,' Jago said as they walked above the tree line. 'I can see the entrance.'

He pointed to a building that looked as though it grew from the rock. The slanted stone roof was etched from the cliff that towered above; the neatly chipped stones were knitted together so that they looked like solid rock. The only sign of human habitation were the mortared walls and the carved steps, which twisted and turned from the forest to the door of the grotto. Stretching to each side were high cliffs that carried on to the horizon like the back of a leviathan gripping to the earth.

'Mount Lazari – the Mountain of Lazarus and the Cave of Magdalene,' Walpurgis said. 'Vibica told me of this place. I never thought she would ever come here. She said there was a legend of a woman who had lived for thousands of years, an Oracle who could see the future. The Maleficarum had her placed in an alabaster coffin so she could not escape. I thought it was just another of her stories.'

'When did you discover she was a Vampyre?' Jago asked.

'I found her eating one of my friends. I worked for a university in America at the time, as a collector of ancient artifacts. One evening I came home and found that Vibica had hung my colleague by his ankles from the meat hook in the pantry and drunk his blood. I understood then that she was different from most women I had met before.'

They walked on the exposed path towards the house that stuck from the scarp face.

'Do we just knock on the door?' Jago asked.

'I will tell them we are pilgrims visiting the shrine. They

are sure to let us in and from there we will have to see.'
Walpurgis laughed. 'I have a gun and you have a knife and
they have a monster locked in a glass case.'

The steps seemed to cling to their feet, dragging them
back with weariness. Jago could hear Walpurgis draw a tight
breath as he held the wound on his leg and tried to stem the
seeping of blood through his trousers.

Taking the small vial, Walpurgis sipped the linctus and
then looked to see what was left.

'Is there no way of overcoming the poison?' Jago asked.

'Vampyres are experts with poison – they have had eternity to work out what will kill their enemies.'

They were soon at the door to the monastery. Walpurgis
banged the bronze hammer against the wood and the door
opened slowly. A bald-headed old man in a white robe peered
suspiciously at them.

'Yes?' he said, looking at Walpurgis through eyes that hung
in wrinkled flesh. 'What is it you want?'

'We are pilgrims. We have come to see the shrine,' Walpurgis answered easily.

'The shrine is closed – has been for all the war. It was the
only way to keep it safe,' he answered.

'My friend and I have come from London. I need help – an
injury from the journey. At least would you tend my wound?'

The man thought for a moment and then looked beyond
them to the forest and then to the sky.

'I suppose . . .' He paused. 'I suppose you could rest for an
hour.'

Walpurgis slipped the gun from his pocket and placed it
against the brow of the man.

'What I need will take more than an hour. Are you the only one here?'

'Only I . . . Brother Notarius, alone – a hermit of hermits.'

Walpurgis pushed him inside the stone building and when Jago had followed he closed the door.

'It would not be wise for you to lie,' Walpurgis said as he clicked the hammer of the gun and smiled.

'There are two people who are sick, in the infirmary. I tend to them every day. They are asleep and will be for some time.'

'Why?' Jago asked. He looked around the candlelit room stacked with boxes, cobwebbed books and crates of tinned fruit.

'They have been poisoned. Brought here so that the mountain air will be good for them. Their protector has paid me in fruit. Canned and preserved but still as fresh as the day it was picked.' Notarius pointed to a can of peaches that stood proudly on the fireplace cut from solid rock.

Walpurgis looked at Jago and then around the room. In a blackened, cauldron-like pan on the fire a thick stew bubbled.

'I think we should see them. Lock the door, Jago, and then we shall go with Brother Notarius and see his guests.'

'It would not be advisable. They are greatly disturbed; the poison has frozen their features into dark grimaces. I wait for its effect to diminish and then they shall be well,' Notarius said in a gruff voice.

'How long will that take?' Jago asked.

'Perhaps a year – maybe longer,' he said as if Jago should know the answer.

'What poison would do that?'

'Torafugu,' Walpurgis said before the man could speak. 'It is Vampyre poison. It brings on the symptoms of death.'

'Not quite,' answered Notarius excitedly. 'You cannot speak or move a finger – but you can hear everything. Their eyes are open but they see the world as if it is a dream and yes – you were right – it is Vampyre poison, made from the liver of a fish and served in a stew.'

'Who gave it to them?' Walpurgis asked as he pushed the man towards a small door in the side of the wall.

'About that I do not know. They came to me that way. Cold – as if dead. Hardly a breath has left their bodies in all this time,' Notarius answered. 'Why such an interest?'

'I have not seen a case of Torafugu for many years. I would be interested to know who they are.'

Brother Notarius looked at him suspiciously. His face changed as his lips broke in a smile that showed his wine-stained teeth.

'Are you sure you have time, Mr Walpurgis?' he asked to their surprise. 'Ozymandias knows that you are on your way to this place and has asked me to telephone him when you arrive. If I have not called within the hour he will send the companions.'

'Walpurgis?' Jago asked.

'He and Cardinal Theodore are great friends. This time has all been arranged. Especially for you – Jago Harker?' The man looked at him with enquiring eyes that peered out from under his thick brow. 'I am right, am I not?'

'I am Jago Harker,' he said.

'How long do we have?' Walpurgis asked.

'An hour at the most, probably much less. I would insist

that we all stay together, Jago.'

Walpurgis looked at the man as if he knew why he should be so adamant. 'Take us to them,' he insisted.

'Harker should go first. Just follow the passageway to the chamber.' Brother Notarius pointed to the corridor cut from stone and lit by tall red candles. 'It is quite safe.'

Jago walked quickly along the passageway, aware that Walpurgis and the monk followed on close behind. The tunnel narrowed, its walls chipped and chiselled where ancient hands had cut it from the stone. He walked on, gathering his pace. A small doorway was just ahead. Jago stepped through as he stooped into the chamber.

He stopped suddenly as he looked at two stone plinths made of a darker rock. On each was a body covered in purple velvet. The arms of each figure were placed neatly to the side; their wide-open eyes stared at the low ceiling above them. Tallow lanterns filled the room with an aromatic smoke. Despite the half-light, Jago didn't need to guess who they were.

'It's Biatra and Hugh,' he said in a sharp and shocked breath. He held his hand to his face to cover his words.

'How long have they been here?' Walpurgis asked the man calmly.

'A few days,' he answered. 'The man came some time before the girl. Both had been medicated before they arrived. It is my job to keep them asleep and not kill them,' he said proudly. 'One morsel more than they need and both would die,' he said.

'Will they live?' Jago asked.

'As long as they are cared for,' Brother Notarius answered.

'How long does the poison last?' Jago said, his voice

cracked with pain.

'A year, perhaps more. They will not wake for some time. They are deep within Luna Negri . . .'

'But that is a place in the Carpathian mountains,' Jago snapped angrily at the man. 'I was told –'

'Luna Negri – the black moon – is a place within the mind. It is a prison for Vampyres, a punishment for a crime that doesn't warrant death. The poison entombs them within themselves. They are in hibernation until the allotted time. There is nothing that you can do. It is a prison without walls, a safe place where they are held captive without manacles or iron gates. They are trapped in the darkness of their imaginations. It is not a place I would choose to dwell.'

'Walpurgis, we have to set them free,' Jago declared.

'It cannot be done. Their fate is sealed. Forget them, Jago.' Walpurgis looked at Jago and saw tears trickling across his cheeks; he wished he hadn't spoken. He turned to Notarius. 'Whatever happens this night, make sure they survive. Care for them, or else I will come and kill you.'

'It is my redemption, a task I will never give up,' Notarius answered. 'I promise I will care for them, whatever else is asked of me.'

'Be sure of your words, for I have a knife so sharp it can cut the soul from the flesh,' Jago screamed as he stood by Biatra and stroked her cold face and looked into the lifeless eyes. 'I will come back for you. Whatever it takes. In a year or ten thousand years I will not forget you,' Jago whispered to her before he kissed her face. 'I promise I will be back.'

Biatra made no sign in reply. Even though she could hear his words, she was trapped like a mute within her body. Jago smoothed her hair from her brow and looked at the fading mark on the side of her face. As he traced the scar of the cleft lip with his finger a single tear dropped from his cheek. It landed on her lips and slipped within quite silently. Jago did not see the tear of love that welled from her eye and was soon lost in the folds of red hair. Inside she screamed his name, but the posion had made her mute and numb.

'We hold you to your promise,' Walpurgis urged the man. 'Whatever happens . . .'

'The rules of Luna Negri cannot be broken. They are in a safe place. No one is allowed to take their lives – that is what was written long ago and shall always be obeyed.'

Without warning, the door of the outer room opened. A sudden draught trembled the flames of the candles so they darted and danced, lengthening the shadows that scurried across the low roof of the tomb.

'Silence,' Walpurgis said as he pressed himself against the wall. 'Which way can we escape?'

Notarius pointed to a small dark gap in the far wall that they had not seen.

'The cavern runs deep into the mountain. It is the place of the Oracle and her servants.'

'Jago, go quickly. I will stop them until you get far away. Go to London – hide there.'

'No,' he answered, 'We shall fight.'

'Do as I say, boy,' Walpurgis commanded. 'Don't you forget I too have been paid a high price to kill you.'

Five Hundred Faces

WALPURGIS DID NOT scream for long. His cries chased Jago as he ran down the long tunnel lit only by small candles in hollows cut from the rock. Jago could hear him trying to fight. The other voice that echoed through the cavern was that of Ozymandias. He laughed as Walpurgis was thrown around the room like a rag doll.

'It is no use running, Jago Harker. There is no escape from this place,' Ozymandias screamed and cackled like a madman.

Jago did not look back. He ran deeper into the cavern, following the twisting and turning of the stone-hewn corridor. There was no sound of pursuit and he slowed his pace, walking carefully over the broken rocks that littered the floor. To each side were other tunnels, foreboding and unlit. Each was cut from the rock, carved to the same height and sculpted with elaborate faces. He followed the lights of the tiny, well-tended candles.

No sound came from the steps he took. As he touched the walls of the cave he could feel them becoming warmer, as if the rocks were starting to roast from within. The air was thick with incense that scented the air from somewhere deeper in the cavern. Strands of smoke threaded their way towards him like the twisting backs of snakes. In the corner of a small culvert were the bones of a man. The long-dead fingers gripped the handle of an axe. The man lay where he had been killed, the back of his skull cracked and split by a single blow. Empty eye sockets stared at Jago from the broken skull and the jaw hung limply from its hinge.

He pressed on, climbing a flight of thin steps that spiralled upwards through the white rock.

There was a sudden opening. The tunnel became a gallery above another cave. He looked down, knowing he was not alone. It was then he saw her. Vibica de Zoete stood by a stone slab covered in red velvet. She stroked the head of a man wrapped in white linen and in a deep sleep.

'Toran Blaine,' Jago thought.

'You are right,' Vibica whispered. 'It is my dear Toran. How long will you hide, Jago?' she asked, her whispered words clear in his mind.

Jago stepped from the shadows and looked down.

'I thought you were dead,' he said as she looked up at him.

'I was lucky to escape the train. Just like you, Toran and I were thrown from the wreckage. Sadly he has never recovered and has slept since that night.'

'Is he going to die?' Jago asked.

'Toran is in Luna Negri. He will remain this way until he can be healed. That will not happen until the Oracle has been resurrected,' Vibica said as she gestured for Jago to come to her. 'There is no way out of these caves. Ozymandias will soon be here. You could run around for a few days, but eventually you would be caught. Help me cure Toran and I will help you escape,' she said.

'How can I do that?' he asked.

'Give me some of your blood. Give it to me before Ozymandias sacrifices you. It suits him for Toran to stay this way so I will remain with him. He sickens me. Ozymandias is a revolting ogre.'

'But you are married to Heston Walpurgis,' Jago asked.

Vibica laughed, throwing back her head as the sound cascaded around them.

'So he told you . . . Ozymandias assured me that Heston would be kept out of the way chasing a wild goose. He asked him to kill you so that he would never discover what we had in mind for him.'

'And what is that?'

'He is to become one of us. The founding of a new generation of Vampyres. If Ozymandias has his way then you will be dead. But the Oracle will be alive and he will be king.' Vibica looked at him as he walked towards her. 'Just three drops of your blood and then Toran will live.'

'Medea said it was like poison,' he answered as she stroked Toran on the cheek.

'It will wake him from sleep. Your blood is an elixir. That is why they want to kill you. It is the only thing that will bring the Oracle back to life.'

'What good will it do him?' Jago asked.

Vibica stepped away from the stone slab and walked towards Jago. He looked her in the face. Running down her left cheek was a crinkled scar. She saw him stare and instinctively put her hand to her face.

'It was from the explosion and I took many months to

recover,' she said, knowing his unasked question. 'The Oracle has been in this place for two thousand years. Once she was human and knew secrets that some in the world would want to be hidden forever. She came to these caves to hide from the Church. The Pope wanted her dead so that no one would ever know her secret.'

'What does she know that is so important?' Jago asked, stepping back from her and listening to the dripping water that fell from the roof above.

'The Oracle knows the future of the world and can answer any question. We need never fear an uncertain future again. Ozymandias has promised that now the Maleficarum has gone, we will be ruled in peace. The Oracle will tell us all we need to know.'

'Don't you need a diamond?' Jago answered.

'It has been here all along. Ezra Morgan brought it to this place just before the war. I was smuggled from England and have kept the diamond safe all this time.'

'And my blood?' he asked.

'They will cut out your heart and squeeze the blood from it on to the diamond. Then the Oracle will come to life,' Vibica answered.

'And if I die before they can do that?'

The voice of Ozymandias answered: 'Then I will cut off the head of Biatra and Hugh Morgan and you will know that they are dead as well.' He stepped from the shadows of the tunnel. 'It is something I promise I will do, even though it goes against our code. If they die whilst entombed in Luna Negri they will never know any peace.'

Jago turned. Ozymandias stood behind him flanked by

two companions. Walpurgis was cuffed with a steel bracelet on each wrist. His face was bloodied and bruised with marks that matched the thick knuckle-guard on the hand of the man holding him.

'Don't believe him, Jago,' Walpurgis slathered as his mouth filled with blood. 'They could never break the code.'

'That is a chance you may have to take, Jago. This is all about your willingness to give your life for someone else. It is what you were born to do. Like the master of Magdalene, you too are a saviour.' Ozymandias laughed and then looked at Vibica. 'Is everything ready?'

'They are all here,' she answered.

'Have they been waiting for a long time?'

'They have fasted for three days – just as is required. All the Cult of the Oracle are here.' She stopped for a moment and looked at Walpurgis. 'All except for Mina Karlstein and Medea.'

'They will not be coming,' Ozymandias said sharply. 'There was an accident at the Convent. Medea is dead – isn't she, Jago?'

Jago nodded in agreement.

'Did you kill them, Jago?' Vibica asked as their eyes met.

'It was Ozymandias – he killed them,' Walpurgis shouted. The man holding his arm twisted him to the ground.

Vibica looked at Ozymandias. He shrugged his shoulders.

'Medea was already dead when we entered the Convent and Mina –'

'She was poisoned – she drank poisoned wine,' Jago answered before he could say another word.

'On whose instructions?' Vibica asked. Ozymandias tried

to look away. 'Was it you?'

'They were loose ends. Both of them had tried to bargain for their lives. Mina sleeps and will do so for a year and a day. The boy is correct – Medea is dead.'

Vibica de Zoete turned from them and stroked the forehead of Toran Blaine. She looked back just for the briefest moment to savour the glare on the face of Heston Walpurgis.

'Then we should wait no longer,' she said suddenly. 'All is ready. Take Walpurgis to the chamber. The casket of Magdalene is already open. The Cult of the Oracle are awaiting.' The taller of the guards grabbed Jago by the arm as if to drag him away. 'Ozymandias – tell them to leave Jago. He has to be prepared.'

'What if he tries to escape?' the man asked.

'I will stay with her,' Jago said. 'It is finished.'

'Don't be a fool, Harker. Fight them until you can fight no more,' Walpurgis insisted.

'They have won – can't you see that?' Jago shouted back. His words echoed in the dark cavern.

'Jago . . . Please, Jago,' Walpurgis begged.

'When you become like us then you will see that Jago is right,' Ozymandias answered. He turned to Jago. 'I am so glad you do not want to make a fuss. What you are doing will be remembered for ever.'

The man dragged Walpurgis from the cavern. Ozymandias and the other guard followed down a small passageway lit by red candles. Vibica waited until they were far away and their footsteps could be heard no more.

'Do as I say and you will live.'

'Why should you help me?' he asked.

'I remember that day at Hawks Moor. I couldn't help but think how beautiful you were. I have not forgotten that thought all these years. If only things had been different,' Vibica reached forward, cupped his face in her hands and kissed him on the lips. 'I sense you are in love.'

'I was in love – she is dead.'

'Biatra? Medea?' Vibica asked.

'Lana Karlstein,' he answered softly.

It was some time later that Vibica de Zoete led Jago away from the chamber where Toran Blaine rested peacefully, along the passageway and into a vast darkness.

Although the blackness went on and on, Jago knew that he was in the presence of many people. Vibica carried a dim candle that lit the ground about her feet. She stopped on a small stone step.

'I bring you Jago Harker – Son of Strackan – True Blood of True Blood – begotten not made – of one with Magdalene,' she shouted in the darkness.

A flutter of applause danced about the cavern. Then, one by one, small lights appeared as more candles were lit. The darkness unfurled and faces came into sight, some nearby, others far away. Jago saw Walpurgis. He was tied to a wooden cross, his shirt torn from his bloodied body and leather straps bound around each wrist. Before him was a long open coffin that looked as if it was made of thick glass. Inside was the body of a woman wrapped in a shroud. As the candles banished the blackness, Jago could see more and more people. Standing a few feet away by a stone altar was Ezra Morgan.

On a small, black satin pillow was a large cut diamond.

Morgan reached out his arms and with outstretched hands

begged for silence.

'*Five hundred faces and all so strange. I feel like a waif before the wind – tossed in an ocean of shock and change,*' Morgan sang with all his heart. 'Those are my favourite words. Stolen from a school high on a hill – but quite fitting for this time,' he said to Vibica. 'Taken from the Temple of Constantine – hidden in the eaves of the Great Window – the Oracle diamond, the life of Magdalene,' Morgan shouted as he held the diamond in his hand.

'It is time – is all ready?' Vibica asked him.

'True blood for true blood,' Ezra answered as he slipped back the hood of his robe.

'And my husband?' she said as she looked across the marble cavern to the cross.

'He is willing,' Ozymandias said from behind the mask of a goat.

'Now is the time,' Morgan declared as five hundred faces looked on.

Vibica walked silently toward Walpurgis.

'You don't have to do this,' he screamed. 'Vibica – no!'

Vibica ignored his words. She dropped the hood of the cowl and let the cloak slip to the floor. Grabbing his face with her long fingers, she held him fast. Then, pushing his head back against the cross, she exposed his neck. For a long, long moment, she looked at the vein that beat ever faster, dancing under his skin.

'Just do it,' Walpurgis muttered, knowing there would be no other end. 'It is a stupid clemency that spares the conquered foe.'

Vibica looked him in the eyes and smiled. 'If only you

'would have done this all those years ago,' she whispered.

'Did I have a choice?' he answered so only she could hear.

Vibica leant forward. She kissed him on the neck and then bit as hard as she could. His skin trembled, cracked and punctured. Blood oozed down his neck and across his chest. Ozymandias shook excitedly.

All those gathered began to scream and growl in delight. The cavern echoed with hundreds of voices as they shouted for the blood of Jago Harker.

Vibica slumped to the ground. Her mouth drooled blood. Walpurgis shuddered as the venom burnt through him.

'NO!' he screamed as he fought against the poison that seared through his veins. Then his head slumped and his body hung limply from the cross.

'Now the boy, now the boy,' Ozymandias insisted as he helped Vibica to her feet.

'Stand where I told you,' she said to Jago, and then to Ozymandias: 'Give him the diamond in his right hand.'

Morgan forced the diamond into his palm and pushed him towards the glass coffin. All those gathered began to shout and scream. The noise grew louder and louder. Jago did as she had said. He held the diamond in his hand and stood by the coffin.

'The dagger, the true blood,' Ezra Morgan intoned.

Vibica slipped a long dagger from the folds of her dress.

'He must do it to himself – we cannot take his blood,' she said as she handed Jago the dagger. 'The hand that holds the diamond must be the hand that gives the blood.'

Jago took the dagger and, with a short stab, cut his wrist. The cavern was silenced as they waited for the blood to trickle from the skin. He looked at the hundreds of people staring at him through the shimmering candlelight. Long dark shadows danced across the roof of the cave as a shrill breeze whistled through the rocks.

'Is this what you wanted?' he shouted at them. 'To see me die?'

Ozymandias looked at him. 'Again, again . . . more blood,' he wheezed nervously, anxious that Jago should do as he said.

'It is time,' Ezra Morgan said to Jago.

'Help me, father,' Jago asked him.

Ezra Morgan stepped forward and took hold of the hand that clasped the diamond.

'I was there when you were born. I saw you when you were moments old. It was meant to be that I would be a shepherd of your life and of your death . . . Do this for me, Jago – do this for me . . .'

Something about the look in the eye of Ezra Morgan made Jago stop for a moment. He seemed to be pleading to be set free, demanding with each glance.

Jago took the long blade and slipped it into the pocket of his coat. Then his fingers searched for the small silver knife within.

'What is it?' Jago asked.

'I am too old and have had enough of life,' Morgan whispered as he pushed some crumpled papers into the pocket of Jago's jacket.

'Are you sure that Strackan is my father?' Jago asked.

'It is true,' Morgan answered.

'No!' screamed Ozymandias as he saw the silver knife dart from the pocket and glance through the air. It stuck Morgan in the heart. Ezra gasped and then fell back.

The crowd gasped as a single drop of blood fell from Jago's wrist. It dropped into the glass coffin, landing on the parched skin of the woman.

'Stop him!'

Jago threw the other dagger to Vibica.

Vibica took hold of Ozymandias and, with one blow, severed his head with the long knife in her hand.

'Run, Jago! Do what I told you!'

As Jago ran, the crowd of Vampyres fell upon Vibica like a pack of dogs. He could hear her scream as they tore at her flesh. Jago did not look back. As he ran back the way he had come, he counted his steps, just as Vibica had told him. Turning left and then right, he ran on in complete darkness. In his hand was the diamond. He clutched it within his fingers as if it were his life.

'Take it to the Temple of Constantine and leave it in the wall beneath the Great East Window,' Vibica had said. 'If you do that – then they will never find it. Then hide, Jago – find a new life and forget this place.'

Her words went over and over through his mind as he ran. Taking the next turn to the right, after one hundred paces, he opened his eyes.

'Notarius, what are you doing?' Jago asked, seeing the monk cowering over a pile of wooden boxes in the corner of the small room where he now stood.

'You are a good man,' the monk said with a sense of insight. 'This will stop them following you. It was meant for the Gestapo if they ever came to the shrine. If I turn this handle every door and passageway will be blown, and this will become their tomb.'

'But what of Biatra and Hugh?'

'I have enough food for the year and I am used to my own company. When they wake from Luna Negri I will set them free. I know a way from this place. Go through the door and down the stairs and keep running, Jago Harker – run for your life . . .'

As Jago ran from the monastery and along the forest track through the ancient avenue of yew trees, the ground beneath him shook. On the high scarp rocks trembled and slowly began to fall. One by one they rolled down the hill until the avalanche took hold.

Fragments of stone blew out from the cliff face as the bomb exploded. A blanket of rock fell suddenly, covering the door to the monastery in a cloud of white dust and blocking every window from sight. Where once was the entrance to the Grotto of Magdalene was now a jagged pile of rubble and broken rock. A veil of dust shaded the monastery from sight. As he looked back Jago thought of Vibica and Heston Walpurgis, Biatra and Hugh.

'Forgive me, forgive me,' he shouted.

'Who is there to forgive you?'

The Cardinal stepped from the shade of a tall tree. 'I take it you are Jago Harker?'

'And you are the Cardinal?' he asked the man.

'Wherever you go is mayhem and strife. You leave Vampyres dead in your wake. You are a monster.'

'Monster?' Jago asked as his hand shook. 'I was created for your purpose. The son of Strackan, and you call me a monster?'

'I have waited two thousand years for this day and you have destroyed it. They called me Judas the Fool. Now they are all dead and I am still alive. I betrayed my closest friend so that I could live for ever.'

Jago did not speak. Lunging at the Cardinal, he stabbed him in the heart and held him until he fell from the knife.

'Don't get in my way,' Jago snarled as he kicked the corpse from the path and watched it roll down the slope into the darkness of the forest.

[27]

The Vampyre Quartet

JAGO HARKER stood on the corner of Ludgate Hill as the rain beat down around him. Water spouted from the overflowing gutters of the Banco Perazzi and washed against the taut skin of the bat-wing umbrella he gripped in his hand. For a moment he hesitated, hardly daring to knock on the door.

Without warning, the viewing slat opened suddenly and two piercing eyes stared out into the half-light of the early morning.

'It is true, you really are alive,' Fredrico Lucca said in surprise. 'I had heard rumours that Ozymandias was dead and that you had murdered Ezra Morgan, but Vampyres gossip worse than women. Then last week I had all the proof I needed.'

'I am alive,' Jago said, 'and there is business that I have to attend to.'

Reluctantly, Lucca opened the door to the bank. Jago stepped inside and shook the water from the umbrella.

'I never thought I would see you again. The Maleficarum has gone and there is no one to tell me what to do. I took it upon myself to try and make things as they were. When

I heard the rumours that you had survived I decided to . . .' Lucca stopped talking and looked at Jago. He studied him intently.

'Who told you that I lived?' Jago asked as he leant against the counter.

'The Sinan – the Vampyre compass was returned to the bank. The note was anonymous and asked that it be placed in your deposit box. I had to be sure that you were alive and sure enough, it pointed to the east and your name was still on the scroll.'

'And Lana Karlstein?' he asked.

'I never looked that far. All I could see was that three hundred and fifty Vampyres were missing from the scroll. Their names were smudged black as if they had never lived.' Lucca sighed, knowing he had lost many friends. 'It is easier to ask who is still alive. I will let you see for yourself.'

'Ezra Morgan gave me this – he asked me to kill him.'

'Asked you?' Lucca said as he took the parchment letters from Jago and examined them closely. He read what was written carefully, muttering the words as his eyes scanned the pages. 'Goodness – goodness indeed. It was all planned for some time. Everything is given to you and Hugh Morgan, and there is even enough for the girl.'

Lucca then began to read from the parchment. 'I Ezra Morgan being of sound mind can no longer bear the life that I have been cursed to live. It is now time for me to move on to a world where I can make right all that I have done. I go there with an open heart . . .'

As Lucca read on tears trickled slowly down his cheeks. 'He found all that he had been looking for in a dark cave on a French mountain. Ezra Morgan wanted to die and he knew that you would help him.'

'I saw the look in his face, his eyes pleaded with me – there was nothing else that I could do.'

'And Ozymandias?' Lucca asked.

'Vibica de Zoete killed him,' Jago said coldly. 'Cut off his head.'

'Interesting,' he answered. 'There was one new name on the Sinan – that of Heston Walpurgis.'

'He is still alive?' Jago asked in disbelief.

'See for yourself,' Lucca rasped as he lifted an old box from beneath the counter and opened it in front of Jago. 'I have kept this with me all the time. I cannot believe what it says,' he said as he opened the box and brought out the Sinan. 'Vibica is dead, but Walpurgis a Vampyre – how?'

Jago told him all that had gone on. Lucca listened intently with eyes that wished they could have seen the occasion for themselves.

'Then they fell on Vibica and killed her. I could hear her screams,' Jago concluded.

'They all died just as the prophecy said they would. You bring trouble to our world, Jago, and it is still not over,' Lucca answered.

'What do you mean?' Jago replied.

'A quartet of death. That is what it said. The flood – the fire – the earth . . .'

'That is just three,' Jago said.

'And the whirlwind,' Lucca whispered, as if his words could conjure such a thing. 'The final death of us all and possibly the world. The flood was the great wave at the labyrinth. The fire was the explosion at the house of Ozymandias. And the earth was what has just happened.'

'Then what is to come?' Jago asked.

'There was a time, Jago, when the life of a Vampyre was going to the opera, eating at a fine restaurant and taking the train to Rome for the winter. Some of us drank the blood of our companions and others chose to hunt for their prey. Everything was done with great sophistication. Strackan lived in the north and was just a legend and the Lodge Maleficarum kept order. Then you were born. The rumours of your birth soon spread. Where you lived was kept secret but we all knew that trouble was just a few years away. It was your birth that divided the Maleficarum. There were no angels, no shepherds – just the knowledge that destruction would come to us all.'

'So there is more to come?' Jago asked.

'I think you know well that once you had killed all of the Vampyre Quartet then Strackan would be the only one left to be destroyed?' Lucca asked.

'That is what was said,' he answered.

'The gate of death is open,' Lucca said softly.

'He is my father,' Jago answered.

'Then best do it quickly before he comes for you. Strackan will know that you are alive and already those of our kind that are left here will begin to conspire,' Lucca said as he handed Jago the Vampyre compass. 'Track him down and kill him and then we will all be safe. He is the whirlwind, the destroyer of lands and the bringer of war. I have money for you here and took the liberty of putting right everything at Hawks Moor. I fancied living there myself.'

'I would have to go alone, Hugh and Bia are . . .'

'Luna Negri?' Lucca asked, his voice filled with disillusion. 'I have been there myself for a crime I did not commit. They will feel well rested when they wake.' The man rolled the scroll in his fingers. 'But they are still alive – their names are on the scroll.'

'It is a list of the damned that would be better burnt,' Jago said as he took the parchment from Lucca. Looking at the names that were left on the scroll, he counted them one by one. Jago searched for the name of Lana Karlstein. 'It's not there . . .' he said as he searched again.

'Who is it you are looking for?' Lucca asked.

'Lana . . . Lana Karlstein,' Jago answered.

'She will not be found. That was never her real name. Karl-stein was the man who took their lives. He too changed his name. To find her you will have to find the name she was given at birth.' Jago looked at the paper as his hand trembled. Lucca saw his distress. 'Perhaps she will come looking for you – if your bond is strong, she will find you.'

Five hours later Jago stood on Platform 9 at King's Cross station and listened to the train hiss and heave as coal and water were loaded onto the engine.

The platform was empty. Jago clutched the bag that Lucca had given to him. In it was a bundle of five-pound notes wrapped in newspaper, the Sinan and a sealed envelope. Lucca had told him that within would be everything he needed to start a new life at Hawks Moor. In his hand was the key that Lucca had handed him for the house. It was new and polished and without a turning mark. It warmed in his hand

303

as the first few passengers walked towards the open doors of the carriages.

His mind was cast back to the day his mother had died and he followed the line of children on to the train. Now there were no soldiers or guards. The barrage balloon that had hovered over the station was gone. The platform was swept and the smell of coffee and bacon filled the air.

Jago followed a tall man in a long black coat. The man seemed familiar, and he smiled as he passed by and doffed the peek of his hat with a gloved hand. His face was thin, with cheek bones that looked as though the skin was pulled tight across them, and his chin was dimpled.

Jago pulled up the collar of his coat and then felt for the diamond in his pocket. It filled the palm of his hand. For a moment he felt like throwing it down on the line so that no one would find it. Then he quickly changed his mind, as if the stone itself begged to be kept.

The man in the black coat stepped onto the train and then looked back. Jago thought nothing of it. He had travelled through France and into Denmark before he had taken the ferry back to England. He had been on many trains, often doubling back on his journey to make sure he wasn't being followed, and by now he didn't care. The Maleficarum was no more. Ozymandias and Ezra Morgan were dead. Jago felt free – and more than that, he felt safe. As he walked to the train he planned that within the year he would return to France and wait for Hugh and Bia to wake from Luna Negri. He would hire a car and a driver and take them back with him to Hawks Moor. In that time he would find Lana Karlstein and they would be together.

All these thoughts jumped through his brain faster than he could remember them. They danced and dived back and forth, swirling like the fog that now rolled in under the cavernous steel arches of the station.

'All stations to the north,' the guard shouted as he raised his green flag and then blew three short blasts on his whistle. Last call passengers for York and Edinburgh.'

Those places seemed far away. Jago shuddered as he stepped on to the train. As he thought of returning to Hawks Moor alone, his heart missed a beat and then pounded in his chest. He thought it was the blood he had drunk with Lucca before he had left. It had been warm and thick, and had tasted of chocolate. Jago had mixed his with some cream and sprinkled cinnamon seeds on the top. He disliked drinking alone and was glad that Lucca had offered him food before his journey.

As he stepped into the long carriage, Jago found a seat by the window. He held the First Class ticket in his hand, feeling like he didn't belong. He remembered the sheep he had shared the journey with long before.

A fat guard scurried towards him as the wheels on the train began to roll and glide faster and faster.

'This is First Class – can't be having you in here,' the man said until he noticed the colour of his ticket. 'Ah, Whitby . . . Change at York and then at Scarborough – enjoy the journey.' He tried to smile at him as he spoke, his raised eyebrow the only sign that he was puzzled as to how Jago had been able to buy the ticket.

The steam train hauled the carriages through the outskirts of London. Alone in his compartment, Jago looked at the remains of the bombed-out houses and derelict streets until they broke into scattered fields and then unbroken country-side. The sky was bright blue and not marred by a single cloud. Except for the billows of steam that occasionally blotted out the morning sun, it stretched clear from horizon to horizon.

As the train sped through the dark and sooty station of Doncaster, the door to the carriage opened and the man in the long black coat walked through. He carried a small bag in his hand and counted the seats as he walked along. Seeing Jago, the man smiled. Jago tried to look away.

'Travelling alone?' the man asked. 'Do you know how long it will take to get to York?'

Jago looked at his watch, not wanting to speak and wondering why the man had chosen to take the seat opposite.

'Twenty minutes,' he answered.

'Darius Malmquist,' the man said, holding out his hand. 'I never like to speak to strangers.' He laughed.

'Jago – Jago Harker,' he replied.

The man held his hand for an uncomfortable amount of time. 'Nice to share this part of the journey,' he said, finally letting go of Jago's hand and moving to sit next to him. 'I always get nervous that I will miss my stop and be taken far to the north.'

Jago looked at him closely. He seemed to be human – there was the usual rattle of trivial thoughts that Jago could feel. His face was lined but not to the extent that Jago would say the man was old. There was a glint on the short tufts of thick hair that stuck out from under the black fedora. They looked as if they had been dyed black. But it was the skin of the man that made Jago more concerned. The flesh on his face was mottled; it was as if he had been burnt and then new skin had re-grown to cover the scars.

'Are you changing at York?' Jago asked, trying to break the uncomfortable silence. He knew that he had seen the man before but could not remember where. It was as if he were a living dream.

'I am staying there for a few days. I am a publisher of books and I am visiting a woman who owns a tea room. She has written a cookery book that she wants me to publish.' The man spoke excitedly, as if the book would change the world. He opened his case and pulled out a tattered manuscript and pointed to the title. '*A Year of Family Recipes*,' he said. 'Do you know of Betty's Tea Room? I have never been to York before but hear it is in St Helen's Square and looks like the interior of an ocean liner.'

'I don't live there,' Jago replied, wanting the man to leave him.

'I have a ration voucher for coffee,' the man said, pressing a crumpled ticket into his hand. 'Perhaps if you ever visit you could have a drink on me. Tell Betty you met me on the train. I am sure she will make you most welcome.'

The bag that Jago had been carrying suddenly dropped to the floor. The man picked it up, quickly putting it back on the seat. Darius Malmquist then got to his feet and nodded to Jago. 'I will have to make ready for the arrival at York.'

'But there is plenty of time,' Jago answered.

'That may be so, but I cannot wait . . .'

'Ten minutes?'

'I must be by the door ready to step from the train. It is

something that has always bothered me. I would hate to get left behind.'

Jago looked at the stitching on the cuff of the black coat. It was perfect in every detail. Everything about the man was incredibly precise. The cuffs of a white linen shirt could just be seen, pinned together by glinting diamond cufflinks.

'Perhaps I will see you at Betty's Tea Room,' Jago said as Malmquist turned to walk away.

'Perhaps . . .' the man replied without looking back.

It seemed to take an age for the train to arrive in York. But eventually the engine slowed, rattling the compartment, and slid alongside the platform like a slowly docking ship. Jago stepped onto the stone flags and watched Darius Malmquist as he walked briskly towards the stone arch and the taxi rank outside the station. It was then that he saw the man stop, look back and then wave at him.

Jago instinctively lifted his hand and gestured as the man opened the door of a waiting cab and quickly disappeared inside. Crossing the platform to find his connection, Jago held the coffee voucher in his hand and looked at the lettering. There, in the corner of the ticket, was the familiar wolf's-head sign of the Banco Perazzi.

'Vampyre,' he said to himself with a smirk as he crossed the bridge and found the small train about to depart from Platform 3.

The afternoon went quickly as the train made its way to the coast. Clouds gathered and a blustery wind blew old newspapers along the platform at Scarborough Station. Jago changed trains again and watched the coast come nearer as the steam engine crawled towards Ravenscar. It was a one-class carriage.

Farmers were packed in next to women in service returning to Whitby from their day off. Jago stood for the journey and looked down across the horseshoe bay towards Hawks Moor. When the engine stopped to take on water, Jago slipped from the crowded compartment and walked across the track. Taking the cart road, he trudged towards Baytown. In an hour, he stood outside the doors of Hawks Moor.

The house had changed. All of the ivy was stripped from the walls. Fresh gravel filled the driveway and the windows had been re-glassed and painted.

Taking the key from his pocket, he slipped it into the lock and turned it slowly. The door opened with a wheeze of air. The house didn't smell the same as the last time he could remember. Now it had the fragrance of toffee and roses. As he walked in everything seemed different.

In the hallway, three leather sofas now hemmed in the stone fireplace. A Byzantine rug covered the stone floor and on the wall above the mantelpiece was the painting of the Vampyre Quartet. Each face was in place – even Ezra Morgan stared down with lifeless eyes. The painting was now complete and as bright as the first day that Julius Cresco had put the paint on the dry canvas. He looked around the room. The staircase wall was hung with old swords and shields. Looking down from the landing was the stuffed head of a wild boar.

Jago felt something deeply fulfilling. It was as if a job had been done and a purpose achieved. He was home, Hawks Moor now belonged to him, and in a year Hugh and Bia would wake from Luna Negri.

'Mr Lucca telephoned,' a voice said as the kitchen door opened.

'Henson?' Jago shouted in excitement as his old friend walked towards him with a tray of tea.

'It is good to see you again, Jago,' Henson said, as tears rolled across his cheeks.

[28]

Slugwert

THE AFTERNOON FADED into long cups of tea and cosy conversation by the fire. Henson explained that after he and Biatra had been taken from Hawks Moor they had let him go in Whitby. It was Biatra they wanted; he himself was superfluous, irrelevant, and Jago thought that Jack Henson looked far older than he could have ever imagined. His hands were wrinkled and the lines around his eyes were deep and grooved. Even the strands of long hair were now thinning. He was ageing like an ancient tree nearing the end of its life.

There came the unwelcome thought that Henson was old and one day soon would die – Jago tried to rid the idea from his mind but something must have given it away.

'I am not as young as I once was,' Henson said as he smiled at Jago. 'And yet you have changed very little.'

'I feel older, and . . .' He sighed, not finishing what he wanted to say.

'So becoming a Vampyre was not as you expected?' Henson asked.

'Do you ever wish you could go back in time?' he replied abruptly, reaching out his hands towards the fire.

'Often. There is so much in my life that has gone wrong, so much that I have done that I regret. I long to revisit the past and perhaps I could have saved my wife and child.'

'I would never have come to Whitby if I had known what was to happen. This has been a fateful place.'

'The Vampyre Quartet had your life controlled. Now they are dead,' Henson answered hesitantly. 'But there is one still alive.'

Jago looked up from the sofa at the portrait of the Vampyre Quartet. He stared at each face. Cresco, Trevellas, Morgan and Draigorian all looked down at him with benign smiles, as if they could tell what weight pressed on his heart.

'Strackan?' he asked.

'After the entire Quartet has been killed, then his life can be taken. He is defenceless,' Henson said as he stacked three more logs on the fire and watched the flames engulf each one. 'It is what has to be done.'

'He is my father,' Jago replied reluctantly.

'He is a monster who tricked your mother and controlled your life. If he had his way you would be dead. Strackan would show no remorse in killing you. Remember that, Jago. He is a killer – that is all.'

'When I saw him last he was almost dead and could only do his work through a Lestrigon,' Jago said.

'Blood zombies and skin-reapers, that's all they are. Half dead and never alive – puppets.' Henson spat the words angrily. 'Strackan is a coward who should be hunted down and killed just like you once said you would do.'

Jago looked at the flames in the large stone fireplace. Outside Hawks Moor a gust of wind rattled the eaves of the houses. Far away he could hear the waves crashing against the rocks. The sounds were comfortably familiar and yet they chilled his bones.

'I never thought I would ever get to this time,' he said as he listened to the moaning of the oak beams above his head. 'When I was in France, I thought I was going to die. If it hadn't been for Ezra Morgan I think I would.'

He stopped, suddenly aware of his surroundings. This house knew too much. It had been a witness to much death and destruction. Hawks Moor was more than stone and lime mortar; it had memories and thoughts of its own, it harboured centuries of greed and malice.

Jack Henson smiled. 'It has to be done. I will help you in any way I can. Whatever you think, Strackan has to die. That is what you have to do. Kill him like you killed the others.' He ran his long fingers through his hair like the spines of a comb.

Jago thought for a while.

'I have the stone that Ezra Morgan cheated from Walpurgis. It is supposed to be an oracle that can tell the future. I have to find the Temple of Constantine and hide it by the east window.'

Henson laughed. His shoulders hunched up and down and his face went red. His mouth burst open with mirth as he wheezed his breath. 'Temple of Constantine?' he asked as he laughed again. 'Who told you of that place?'

'It was Vibica de Zoete. She told me on the night I escaped from the cave. Do you know where it is?' Jago asked.

'They are always so dramatic, the damn Vampyres. They can never tell a straight truth.' Henson laughed again.

'Constantine was Roman. In 306 he was proclaimed Emperor in the Principia of Eboracum. Many years later, on that site was built the Church of St Peter. That is where you have to leave the Oracle diamond.'

'Eboracum?' Jago asked.

'York.' Henson laughed. 'It has been under your nose all this time. Some say that Constantine was a Vampyre and that he even faked his death so that he could live on without being recognised. Some even say that he is Strackan and that there is a tomb in the crypt beneath the church that belongs to him. It is covered by a Doomstone carved with images of those being thrown into hell.' Henson shuddered. 'He had to return to the dirt that spawned him. Vampyres are all the same – can't escape the place where their blood was taken.'

Jago ran his tongue over his teeth and looked at him. 'How do you know these things?' he asked his friend suspiciously.

'When my wife was killed I had to find out who did it. I had heard of the beast Strackan and all the legends of the Vampyre Quartet, but I had to know the truth. I went to the Church of St Peter and broke into the crypt. I found an ancient carving of a monster and then I knew that a Vampyre had taken her. I have dug graves in Whitby all of my life and been privy to some things that most minds could never understand. On the night before my wife disappeared, I was visited in the graveyard by a young man who offered me a job. I had to work for him as his companion. The man told me he was a Vampyre and needed me to protect him from what was to come. When I refused, he said he would make sure I lost something very close to me. The next night they took my wife and child.'

'Who was it?' Jago asked.

'He said his name was Darius Malmquist.'

'*Malmquist?*' Jago exclaimed. 'I met him on the train from London. He told me he was a publisher of books.'

'He is many things but he is not a publisher of books. Where was he going? Did he say?' Henson looked excited; his hands fidgeted with the cuffs of his coat.

'He said that he was going to meet a woman in York and publish her book. He told me the name of a coffee house and gave me a voucher to buy coffee.' Jago rummaged in his pocket and showed Henson the crumpled ticket. 'Betty's Tea Room . . . And it carries the mark of the Bank of Perazzi.'

'They must know you are here,' Henson answered. 'I heard that there were still some Vampyres loyal to Strackan.'

'There can't be that many left. I looked on the Sinan. Many are now dead and even those still alive appear to be fading.' Jago looked in his bag to find the Sinan and the compass, but though his hand searched every compartment he could find nothing. He lifted the bag to the chair and peered inside. 'It's gone. I had it with me and it has gone.'

Jago thought where it could be and then he remembered. 'Malmquist – it was Malmquist on the train . . . He knocked my bag to the floor and then picked it up. He took it, he took the Sinan from me –'

'He has the Sinan?' Henson asked.

'He must have taken it.'

'Then he will know all of your movements,' Henson said as he got to his feet. 'It is not yet finished, Jago. I have a bad feeling about all this. Malmquist would not just appear and make himself known to you. He would know that you would tell me and that I would know who he was. They want you to know you are not alone. I took the liberty of moving in to Hawks Moor because I thought you would need me around. Now I am glad I have.'

'And now –?'

'Tallow is the gravedigger. He can talk to the whisperers just as well as I could, and he is near to Mrs Macarty. Do you have the diamond?'

Jago searched the pocket of his coat and pulled out the diamond and held it for Henson to see. It sparkled in the flames of the fire, each fine cut of the gemstone burning brightly as it reflected the blaze. The stone sent out shimmers of light that illuminated the dark shadows of their faces. As Jago stared deep within the diamond misted until it was like a dark cloud and then swirled and ebbed like a running tide.

'I can see something,' he said in a whisper as Henson looked over his shoulder.

'That is the temptation of the Oracle. It was never made for us to look at. The stone seduces the heart and the mind.'

'I could keep it – no one would know,' Jago answered. His eyes were being pulled deeper into the heart of the stone.

'And it would fill your head with nonsense and gobbledygook,' Henson snapped.

Not hearing what Henson had said, Jago stared into the stone. He could feel a gentle heat on his hand, as if the stone were melting into his palm.

'I can see the world,' he muttered, his tongue stumbling over the words as he looked at the changing scene that was unfurling before him.

Henson looked at the diamond, but to him it was just as

before. It reflected the light from the fire and cast a sparkling light across his face.

'What can you see?' he asked as Jago lifted the stone closer to his face.

'A town . . . with a river . . . a tall church and swirls of doves circling the spires.' He spoke slowly, as if he were looking down on the world.

'And?' Henson asked eagerly, forgetting the seduction of the stone.

'It takes me closer,' Jago said as the scene changed and the roof of the cathedral opened up and he seemed to fall within. 'There is a statue, a man holding out his hand, the bones of his fingers crumbling to sand.'

'What else?'

Jago put down the diamond and looked at Henson. 'I saw myself,' he said slowly, as if he didn't want to say any more.

'What were you doing?' Henson asked, seeing the fear on his face.

'It was a dark room. I was alone. I could see . . .' Jago stuttered. 'I think I was dead.'

'See, I told you it would trick you. That sort of thing always does. I knew a woman in Whitby who spent all her time looking into a crystal ball. She even forgot to eat and died of starvation. It had her caught so fast she could not get away. Rubbish, that's what I say, total rubbish . . .' Henson snatched the diamond from his hand. 'Take it to the Church of St Peter. Hide it in the vault just as you were told. We can take the train tomorrow. I will come with you.'

Jago didn't speak. He looked at the stone, wanting to snatch it back. He thought of Biatra and Hugh caught in

Luna Negri. But more than all the images flashing through his head, the face of Darius Malmquist burnt in his mind's eye.

Henson took the stone, placed it on the mantelpiece and stepped back. 'Best keep it there – you can't be looking at it. Vampyre eyes see funny things at the best of times,' he said gruffly as if to chastise him. 'All you need is to rest. We'll get rid of that stone and it will do no one any harm. Then we'll start to lead a normal life.'

'Normal?' Jago asked sarcastically. 'I have brought about chaos with every step. My friends are captured in a prison of the soul and buried beneath a mountain. I have a monster wanting me dead and that monster is my father.'

Henson looked at the floor and bit his lip. 'Wrong word, Jago. Didn't mean it that way.' He spluttered. 'I meant to say that we could live at peace. In a year we can go and find them, bring them back to Hawks Moor, but before that there are things to be done.'

Jago knew what he meant. It was as if Henson had only one thought on his mind.

'Could you kill your father?' Jago asked.

'If I had to,' Henson answered.

'How would I find him?' he asked.

'I think he will find you. If Strackan still lives, then he or one of his companions will track you down.'

'Malmquist?' Jago asked.

'Perhaps. Perhaps he already waits for you. That's why I will go with you to York when you take the Oracle,' he said insistently.

'I will go alone,' Jago answered. 'If I am to do it I have to be alone.'

'But they could be waiting,' Henson answered.

'A chance I have to take.'

'At least let me come with you on the train,' Henson insisted.

Jago thought for a moment before he spoke. 'Are you frightened of dying?' he asked Henson, who looked surprised by the question.

'It is inevitable that we die,' he answered, avoiding the truth.

'What do you think is beyond?'

'I don't know. I have often thought about this as I dug the graves. You Vampyres aren't eternal; you are just putting off what will one day happen to us all. Why do you ask?'

'The Cult of the Oracle believes in a world after death. A place where their souls will be cleansed of all the blood they have taken. When I was in Nice, I killed a woman for her blood. I often wonder if I will have to repay that debt,' Jago said sullenly.

'That's just what Darius Malmquist said to me,' Henson answered. 'When he asked me to become his companion he said that he felt that every life he took was a debt he had to repay. He told me he could never escape their faces and that they haunted him.'

Jago sat closer to the fire as if the chill in the air was penetrating his coat. He gave a shudder and looked at the flames.

'I have never told a soul, but when I killed Crispin Draigorian he told me something. As I slipped the knife into his heart he looked at me and told me that I would bring an end to the curse of the Vampyres and to their world. As he died he told me that I would kill the king.'

'Does that frighten you?' Henson asked.

'I feel as if I am being hunted and they need to be stopped. If I have to kill every Vampyre until I am the only one left then it has to be done.'

Henson looked up to the painting of the Vampyre Quartet above him. The face of Ezra Morgan stared down. He looked at peace, as if in another world. Henson gazed at the painting, his eyes going from face to face, then he stopped and pointed to the picture with his long bony finger. Within the painting was something he had never seen before. Crispin Draigorian was holding the diamond in his hand. Henson was sure that it had appeared only now.

'Do you remember ever seeing that in the painting before?' he asked Jago as he pointed to the diamond. 'It's the Oracle, I am sure of it.'

Jago looked at the painting and saw the glimmering of the crystal in the hand of the Vampyre.

'It changes with each death,' Jago answered as he took the crystal from the mantelpiece and held it towards the painting. 'It's like it wants to tell us something of what will be.'

'We should take it from the wall and burn it,' Henson said as the light from the fire danced on the canvas. Slowly, before their eyes, the dark background of the painting began to lighten. In the far distance was the brightening image of a church tower. It broke from the cracked paint as if it were being painted in front of them. 'It can't be – the Temple of Solomon . . .'

The Temple of Solomon

THE NINE-O'-CLOCK TRAIN from Scarborough edged its way slowly into York station. It was an hour late and had crawled along the banks of the fog-bound river like a wounded dog. The carriage was empty, apart from several boxes of chickens and the overweight ticket collector who had stared at Jago throughout the journey of the single-carriage train.

Stepping onto the platform, Jago looked behind him, making sure he wasn't being followed. There was no one to be seen. Pigeons filled the iron girders above his head and looked down on him as he walked quickly towards the large mahogany doors that led into the street.

Above the clouds, the sun attempted to penetrate the thick fog that filled the street, hemmed in by the old town walls. An old bus shuddered by, spewing out acrid black smoke as passengers jumped on without waiting for it to stop.

Jago looked at the hastily scribbled map that Henson had drawn on the back of a torn cigarette box. He read the instructions: *Over the bridge – straight on – keep to the right – turn into Blake Street – left on Stonegate – be careful – make sure you are not followed.*

Jago was soon over the bridge. He could see small ferry-boats steaming beneath, cutting through the dark fog and vanishing almost silently away. He turned right and pulled up his collar as he walked along Blake Street. Far ahead he could see the welcoming lights of a coffee shop on the corner. There was already a long queue outside, mainly women in winter coats and woollen hats with heavy bags. Jago was soon in Stonegate. As he looked up he glimpsed a brief view of the high church tower as it momentarily broke through the mist. He gripped the diamond in his left hand and pushed it deeper into the pocket of his coat.

Jago stopped at the end of the street and waited. He leant against the wall of a toyshop and looked back, while pretending to look into the window. Even though it was mid morning, the lights in the window glistened on the aluminium aircraft and chubby dolls that hung from wires to attract the children. After checking again he walked across the road to the small door at the side of the church. Just as Henson had told him, it was unlocked. Jago scurried inside, closing the door behind him and making his way along a narrow corridor. Henson had told him that if he was found all he had to do was say he was a pilgrim who was lost. It would be an easy lie, as it was just how he felt.

With ten paces, Jago found a passageway on his left and, just as he had been told, there was an even smaller door. He turned the iron-ring handle and disappeared within. A stone staircase led down and down. Jago followed it in complete darkness, trusting his feet to find each step as he slid his hand along the wall and counted the paces.

'Thirty-seven, thirty-eight . . .' Jago reached out. His hand touched the rough-hewn wood of the door in front of him. 'Henson was right.'

He found the handle and, slipping his hand through the opening, flicked the switch. A dim glow ebbed around the door and lit the stairwell behind him.

Pushing the door fully open, Jago stepped inside the room. It stretched out before him, the stone walls growing from the earth. A smell of damp ground hung in the air in swirls of dust blown by the breeze from the door. Stretching towards the gloom was a row of stone piers etched with chevrons cut by hand. The arches held up a crumbling plaster roof that sagged between the stone columns. Jago looked at the old electric light that swung slowly back and forth like a dowsing stick. Before him were row upon row of neatly stacked coffins. The oldest were made from hollowed rock; others were carved from hewn trunks. Those nearest to him were made of wooden planks nailed together with ill-fitting lids.

The lamp cast its eerie light into the dark corners of the side vaults. He shuddered as an icy chill tingled his spine. Reaching into his coat, he took out the small flashlight given to him by Jack Henson and shone it into the darkness of the vault. It was littered with boxes; some were broken open, their contents strewn across the floor. Like the forgotten artifacts of an old museum, axes, swords and armour were piled in the corner. As he moved the flashlight around the vault, its thick beam of light shone on a carved face.

Jago stood for a moment, the glazed eyes of the statue staring back at him. He shuddered like a dog and then smiled to himself and walked towards the statue.

Long cobwebs trailed down from the ceiling in that part

of the vault. They were thick with plaster dust and swung slowly back and forth. As Jago walked, he brushed them aside with the back of his hand. The statue that continued to stare at him had the face of a woman with a long, elegant nose. The stone was painted, and as there had been no light to fade the colours they looked as bright as the day they had been created. The woman's face was smooth as marble, her hands gentle and reaching out in welcome.

A voice spoke from behind him: 'That was my wife. Well, one of them . . .'

Jago turned slowly. He recognised the voice.

'Darius Malmquist,' he said reluctantly as he faced the man standing by the door. 'How did you know that I was here?'

'The Vampyre compass. I took it from your bag. Lucca told me that he had given it to you. It was the final thing that he said to me.'

'The final thing?' Jago asked.

'I killed him. He was no longer any use to me,' Malmquist answered.

'So you are not a publisher of books?' Jago asked.

'Books are for librarians . . . Though I did once meet a librarian who was a Vampyre – she intrigued me greatly.' Malmquist laughed. 'I take it that you have the diamond with you?'

'And you want it?' Jago answered.

'What else?' Malmquist snapped arrogantly.

'What will you do with it?'

'Take it back to the cave and complete what should have been done before Ozymandias decided he would be king,'

Malmquist said. He slipped his long coat from his shoulders, draped it over a pile of boxes by the door and then brushed the sleeve of his velvet jacket.

'Henson told me that you wanted him for a companion,' Jago said, wondering if he could escape from the crypt.

'That old dog. Lucky still to be alive – but then again . . .' Malmquist stopped as if he knew more but didn't want to say.

'You murdered his wife,' Jago answered him. He wondered if he should strike first.

'Not I. A very dear friend – as you well know.' Malmquist turned and began to walk away from him. 'I have much to tell you and it is best that we are not disturbed.'

Jago followed. He could feel his heart pounding in his chest.

'I remember being like you. It was three thousand years ago.' Malmquist paused for a moment as if to remember something from the past. 'In the name of Hades, has it been that long?' He sighed.

'You sound as if it is a curse,' Jago said as he walked behind him.

'More than that, Jago. We are meant to be born and then die. In death we are changed into something else. Becoming a Vampyre is an anomaly and an enigma – it is not what is meant to be. I have been a coward and dare not face death. It is as simple as that. In life I have been many things and many people. I have a thousand names and have lived throughout the world.'

'You seem familiar,' Jago said.

'More familiar than you would ever know,' he answered.

Intrigued, Jago racked his brains to disturb the memory of the man.

'Erik Von Leonhardt?' Jago asked, remembering the photograph as the face came to mind.

'You have heard of me?' the man asked with a laugh. 'Not one of my better disguises. My eyes always give me away.'

'I knew Lana Karlstein before –'

'Lana is alive. I had heard that you had an attraction for her. I have known Lana for many, many years and you would have made a good companion for her. She is no more than a mile from where we are – but you will never see her.'

Jago felt his heart leap. It twisted in his chest with excitement.

'So what do you want from me?' Jago asked.

'The diamond and just to talk. I have heard so much about you and after all, we are brothers.' Malmquist spoke solemnly as he turned to Jago. 'That's why you are here. Vibica de Zoete promised me that she would tell you to come to this place. You were not bringing the diamond to be hidden for ever – you were bringing it to me.'

'Brothers?' Jago asked slowly, hating to say the word.

'Strackan is my father as he is yours. It was all a very long time ago, but that is the truth.'

'Truth?' Jago asked. 'What is truth when spoken by a Vampyre?'

'The first hundred years are always the hardest. It is as if all that is human clings to your soul. Eating and drinking are the first things that are shaken free and then sleep is done away with. Only then will you know what it is like to be a Vampyre.'

326

'I think you are lying to me,' Jago said, determined to find the truth as Malmquist led him deeper into the crypt.

'Sadly it is the truth. I am the Vampyre child of the oldest Vampyre ever. It was our father who created the Sinan and gave it to the world. In the beginning it was him alone.' Malmquist smiled as he waved with his hand for Jago to follow. 'Now he is nearly dead, and not even your blood can revive him.'

'Is he here?' Jago asked as Malmquist led him towards a large stone sarcophagus in the far corner.

'That is the place of the king,' Malmquist said. He pointed to the stone tomb. 'He does not have much breath left for us. But perhaps he will know you are here. When he is dead, I will take his place and you will bow to me.'

Jago laughed. 'I don't think so,' he said softly under his breath.

Malmquist slid the cantilevered lid from the sarcophagus.

'Son – behold your father. Father – behold your son . . .'

Jago stood next to the tomb and looked inside. There, wrapped in a silk robe with only his face exposed, was a young man. He looked just like Malmquist – the eyes, the face, were just the same.

'He is different from the last time I saw him,' Jago said.

'The disease has almost left him. When he is dead he will look just like the day he entered our world.' Malmquist reached in and stroked the face of Strackan. 'I brought him here. It was a special place. I remember the day he was made Emperor of Rome. It was in this very chamber. I had pretended to be his father and he my son. We had done that for generations and in many lands. The Romans were easily fooled. We would fake our deaths and then appear fifty years later and start again. Ridiculous, really, and it became quite tiresome.'

'You have lived all those years and find life tiresome?' Jago asked.

'I speak seventy languages, have kissed the most beautiful women in the world, have ruled nations and amassed great wealth. And yet life can become boring and tedious,' Malmquist snapped, growing tired of his brother.

'If he was the first Vampyre, what came before him?' Jago asked as he sensed a change in Malmquist.

'Before him there was only the demon. It was cast down from the highest place after it had battled with angels. It came to this world and found our father. At that time he was a King in Babylon. The demon offered him wealth and he took all that he could. That was at the dawn of time, and now look at him.' Malmquist poked Strackan in the chest. 'He isn't even strong enough to live his life through a Lystrigon, and all thanks to Jago Harker.'

'I didn't ask for this life,' Jago answered.

Malmquist laughed.

'It was here where you were brought to life. I watched from the shadows. He brought your mother here. She thought it was her lover Hugh Morgan when all along it was my father.' Malmquist sniggered as he watched Jago bristle with anger. 'I need the diamond. Are you going to give it to me – or shall I prise it from your cold, dead fingers?'

'Cold? Dead?' Jago asked, his voice sarcastic. 'Which comes first?'

'Don't make me kill you, Jago. This is no place to spill Vampyre blood.'

Suddenly, Jago lashed out with the torch, smashing Malmquist across the face. Then as the man staggered, blood spurting from his lip, Jago snatched the key to the door from his hand and ran.

'Don't think I won't kill you,' Malmquist shouted as several drops of blood fell into the sarcophagus.

In thirty quick strides, Jago was at the door. He fumbled with the key in the lock. His hand trembled as he tried to slip the iron rod from its keeper. A hand grabbed his wrist and pulled him from the door just as he turned the key.

'Get away from me,' Jago screamed as Malmquist tore at his clothes like a mad animal.

'Give me the diamond!' Malmquist shouted, tearing the sleeve from Jago's coat.

Turning quickly, Jago reached inside his pocket and pulled out the silver knife that Henson had insisted he take with him. Seeing the blade, Malmquist jumped back.

'Stay away from me, Malmquist,' Jago ordered as he flashed the blade back and forth.

Then a kick in the chest knocked Jago against the wall. He dropped the knife and gasped for breath.

'This isn't a game,' Malmquist insisted. He kicked him again and Jago slumped to the ground.

Malmquist stepped forward and rummaged in the pockets of Jago's coat. His hand gripped the diamond.

'It is not yours to have,' Jago said wearily as he tried to find the energy to breathe.

'If only you had been different, I had much that I wanted to tell you,' Malmquist shouted, blood pouring from his face. 'But you are a fool, Harker, a stupid fool . . .'

Malmquist grabbed Jago by the throat and lifted him from the ground with one hand as he held the diamond to his face. Jago was held against a column of the crypt, his feet dangling in the air.

'Leave me, take the diamond,' he croaked as he tried to wrench the hand from him.

'Too late, Harker. I have the diamond and now I will have your life.' The vault echoed with Malmquist's voice. He tightened the grip of his hand. Jago gulped a last gasp of air as the world clouded and he slipped away.

'NO!' shouted a voice from the darkness.

Malmquist dropped Jago to the floor and turned in horror. There, staggering towards him through the murk, was Strackan. The man could barely walk. He held out his hand towards them.

'Strackan!' Jago muttered as he gulped the air in mouthfuls.

'Your father – both of you. Stop what you are doing,' Strackan commanded, his voice frail and weak.

'It can't be – you were dying,' Malmquist raged. 'When will it be my time?'

He bent and picked up the knife from the floor and walked towards Strackan, holding out his arms as if to embrace him. Jago looked on.

'It was your blood. I could taste it,' Strackan said. 'I knew you were both near to me – I could hear you.'

Malmquist came nearer his father with his arms outstretched.

'The last time we were here . . .' Malmquist said as he embraced Strackan. 'The last time . . .'

330

Without warning, he plunged the dagger into his back. Strackan screamed and fell to his knees.

'Why?' he asked, palms outstretched.

'You thought you were the power when all along it was me. You played games with four fools for hundreds of years whilst others plotted to destroy you. And then – and then you were no longer satisfied with me and had another son.' Malmquist pointed to Jago. 'Look at that snivelling, weak, pathetic boy. That is what you created. Could he have done all that we did? Could he have changed the world? Could he have started wars, changed nations, discovered new lands?'

'At least he wasn't born from the belly of a pig.' Strackan laughed as he fell back to the floor. His hand reached out towards Malmquist.

'You are not fit to live,' Malmquist said as he put the heel of his boot to Strackan's throat and pushed as hard as he could. 'I told Ozymandias to start the war and at the same time fed Morgan with lies. It was me all along, and you thought your subjects were just restless.'

'Come with me . . . Come with me now . . . Do it, Jago, just do it!' Strackan roared.

Malmquist saw the reflection in the eyes of Strackan. In an instant, the axe had come down as fast as Jago could swing the stock. It sliced through the velvet jacket. Malmquist shuddered as the blade broke through his ribs. Jago pulled it from his flesh. He raised it high above him and then crashed it down again.

Malmquist dropped to his knees. His head rolled across the dirt-stained floor and stopped at the wall. The diamond fell from his dead hand and landed near to Strackan.

Jago stood with the axe in his hands and looked at his father.

'Is this what you wanted?' he asked the dying Vampyre. 'Do you want me to kill every Vampyre that I meet?'

'You are not one with us, Jago Harker,' Strackan wheezed as he drank his own blood that oozed from his mouth. 'You will never be like us, never in all the years that you shall live. I remember when I first saw you in Whitby. I thought things would be different. I would drink your blood and you would follow me. Instead you tried to kill me.'

'You kept my mother as a brood mare, you had us watched every hour of the day,' Jago answered as he watched the life ebb from his father.

'That was Trevellas. I bade them leave you to grow on your own. They felt you had to be protected,' Strackan said slowly.

'You killed Mary Barnes . . .'

'She is not dead – merely a prisoner,' he answered.

'Where? Where is she?' Jago demanded, wanting to know for the sake of Biatra.

'Closer than you would ever imagine and yet far enough away for her never to be found. Your mother was very sweet, she tasted of summer fruits – did you know that, Jago?' Strackan tormented him as he tried to crawl back to the sarcophagus, floundering for breath.

'Where is she?' Jago demanded.

'You will never know. I will die and it will not be by your hand. Everything will remain the same. The curse will not be broken.'

Jago closed his eyes and swung the axe. He felt it drive home and then strike the stone beneath. It sparked against the ground. Strackan cried out and writhed on the stone floor. He reached back, trying to take hold of the axe blade and pull it from him. Jago twisted the handle turning the blade deep within. The Vampyre screamed again. Jago struck him again and again until he screamed no more.

Strackan was dead. The Oracle diamond was at his finger-tips.

[30]

Betty's Café

JAGO WALKED BACK to the train station the way he had come. He had waited for three hours before leaving the crypt. He had placed the bodies of Strackan and Malmquist in the stone sarcophagus and slid back the lid over them. Then, locking the door and going back up the stairs, Jago had thrown the key into the gardens, hoping it would not be found.

His own coat had been torn and covered in blood so he had taken the long hunting jacket that Malmquist had discarded. It fitted well. In the pocket he had slipped the diamond, which he cupped in his hand as he walked along Stonegate.

It was late in the afternoon. The streets were empty, the fog had long gone and the sun cast cold shadows down to the street. He walked briskly. His thoughts danced like his footsteps on the cobbles. All he wanted was to return to Hawks Moor and tell Henson what had happened. It would be hard to recount, but the urge in his heart was to tell someone what he had done. Toying with the idea of just shouting out that he had killed his father, he felt joy and excitement mixed together, fizzing in his stomach and making him feel sick.

Jago looked in the shop windows and all he could see

was the reflection of Strackan. He was being haunted by the memory of this father, which burnt into his mind with all the terror of a dark night. He could see the eyes of the Vampyre within his own. They were so much alike, and now he was dead there was a growing sense of regret.

Stopping on the corner of the road, he looked across the square at the brightly lit café that stood on the opposite side. The sun was fading and cast a long shadow from the Mansion House with its walls painted burgundy and white and its black railings. The long shadow of the chimney pointed to the door of the café. Jago felt the banknotes in his pocket. It was two hours until his train and he wanted to do something vaguely human again. If what Malmquist had said was true, then that would soon fade. He had no idea what to expect in the days to come. Something within him wanted to give himself in to the first policeman he saw and confess to the murders – but what would the officer say when he told him he was a Vampyre and had just killed a man who was once the Emperor Constantine?

He dismissed the thought quickly and walked across the street. There was no queue like the one he had seen that morning. Most of those shoppers had long gone; now the street was an avenue for workers leaving their offices to get the double-decker buses that would take them home.

As he crossed the square he looked through the large plate-glass windows and picked out a seat inside. He wanted the one by the window with its back against the stone pillar. Malmquist was right: the inside of the café looked just like that of an ocean-going liner. A waitress in a black skirt, a striped blouse and a pinafore looked at him as he walked towards the door. Jago checked his reflection in the glass for some sign of what had happened, but all looked well.

The waitress continued to stare at him as he got closer. She was pretty and reminded Jago of Biatra – or what he could remember of her. It was as if being in Luna Negri took away the person from the memory of those that had known them. He tried to think of something particular about her, something he could remember.

As he pushed open the door of the café he was surrounded by sudden warmth. Jago looked around as the girl walked towards him. There was a mirror on the wall with hundreds of names etched into the glass.

'Table?' she asked politely. She looked him up and down. 'By the window?' Jago nodded. 'A nice coat,' she said as she smiled. 'Madame Betty had a friend with a coat just like it.'

'It must be quite popular,' he answered, not wanting to sound rude. He looked at the pulse of the veins in her neck. 'The names etched into the mirror – what do they mean?'

'In the war we had a lot of American airmen use the café. Before they went on a mission they would scratch their names on the glass with a diamond pen.'

Jago looked surprised. 'The war,' he muttered knowing it was still recent.

'Hungry?' she asked as she pulled out a chair from the table by the window, the one that he had thought of sitting at when outside.

'Who is Madame Betty?' Jago asked as he sat down and slipped the coat off his shoulders and rested it on the back of the chair. It was then he saw the girl look at the cut on the side of his face.

'The owner of the café. She is not here. She's visiting Harrogate, where we make our own brand of tea.' The girl spoke as if this were information that Jago would want to know.

'All the people have gone,' Jago said as he looked to the street.

'They don't stay long. They still think there is a war. Do you want a drink? We close in an hour,' she said, wondering if he was just wanting to sit down and stare like so many young men coming back from fighting. 'Don't mind if you just want to sit there. I'll bring you an empty cup and you can pretend – just in case Madame Betty comes back and thinks I'm slacking.'

'I would like coffee. I have a voucher,' Jago said as he pulled the crumpled voucher from the roll of banknotes in his pocket and handed it to her.

The girl stood still. Jago saw her hand shudder as her smile changed to a slight frown.

'Not seen one of those before. Madame Betty told me about them. You can have whatever you want for free,' she said. She tried to calm her breathing and slow her pulsing heart. 'Coffee? Cake? Sandwich?' she said quickly, but she left the table without giving him time to reply.

'Yes . . .' he said forlornly as she walked to the kitchen.

Jago saw the girl look back as she got to the door. It was as if she could not be sure of something and wanted to take a second look.

Outside, an old man swept the street with a brush. He pushed the litter towards a handcart and then scooped it up with his gloved hands. He worked on until every scrap of rubbish was picked from the cobbles. Every now and then he looked at Jago and smiled. Jago gazed into the darkening street and lost track of time. The waitress came back and tapped him on the shoulder as if to remind him where he was.

'Here are cakes and sandwiches, if you want to eat them. I don't mind if you don't,' she smiled. 'You been at the war?' she asked.

'You could say that,' Jago answered. He looked at the neatly cut triangles of bread that oozed cream cheese and cucumber.

'Well, enjoy,' she said as she turned to go.

'I haven't seen cucumber in years – where did you get it?' he asked.

'Madame Betty grows it at her house. I am only allowed to give it to special guests,' the girl said innocently. 'If you don't like it I could always –'

The girl stopped speaking as the door opened and a woman stepped into the café. She was wrapped in a fur coat that draped to the floor as if she were shedding her skin. A small velvet hat clung to the side of her head and rippled with glistening diamonds. The woman was fresh-faced with red cheeks and a long, thin neck. Jago looked up, unable to believe his eyes.

'You look as though you have seen a ghost,' the woman said. 'I am Madame Betty, the owner of the café – and you are?' she enquired, as if she had never seen Jago before.

Jago stared into the face of Lana Karlstein. He trembled as she pulled her fingers from a long silk glove and held out her hand. He was sure it was her; there was no doubt. As she smiled at him his heart raced.

'It is a pleasure to meet you,' he said, his voice shaking as he looked at the waitress. 'Have we met before?'

Lana Karlstein smiled at him as she squeezed his fingers.

'I wish we had met so long ago,' she said as she sat at the table and nodded for the waitress to leave them. 'I wish I had spent every night in your presence since the beginning of time.'

'I thought you were dead,' Jago whispered, half under his breath.

'Lana Karlstein died when she fell from that train. It was time for a change. I had been Madame Betty before and just being near to Hawks Moor reminded me of you. I knew you would come back,' she answered. 'I take it that Leonhardt and Strackan are dead?'

Jago nodded and looked at the table.

'Leonhardt was always a strange man. He could never decide if he loved or hated the world. He told me that he had met you on the train and given you the ticket. I prayed that you would come here'

'I had no choice,' Jago answered, not letting go of her hand.

'And what of you, Jago Harker – what do you believe?' she asked as she moved closer to him.

'I know that I had thought I had lost something quite precious and now it has been found,' he said as he leant towards her and they kissed.

'Paradise was lost and now it is found,' Lana whispered. 'I hope we can be together.'

'Why didn't you tell me you were here?' he asked.

'I told Lucca and took him the Sinan. Did he not say?'

Jago looked at her as if it didn't matter. 'It is all finished.

The Oracle said it would end this way and it did,' he answered.

'We are both alive, and that is all that matters.'

Neither of them saw the man in the shadow of the doorway. He pulled down his hat and lifted the collar of his leather coat to keep out the growing gloom of evening. He looked out from the alleyway next to the picture house and slipped a gloved hand into his pocket. Taking the revolver from within, he loaded six silver-tipped bullets. Then, slamming the chamber, he pulled back the firing hammer and cocked the trigger. As the fog rolled along the street, fresh from the river, the man left the darkness behind. He stepped from the alley and walked towards Betty's Café.